W9-CQU-326

Thorn-Field

Thank you!
I hope you
enjoy the read.
James

Thorn-Field

JAMES TRETTWER

thistledown press

©James Trettwer, 2018
All rights reserved

No part of this publication may be reproduced or transmitted in any form or by any means, graphic, electronic or mechanical, including photocopying, recording, or any information storage and retrieval system, without permission in writing from the publisher or a licence from The Canadian Copyright Licensing Agency (Access Copyright). For an Access Copyright licence, visit www.accesscopyright.ca or call toll free to 1-800-893-5777.

Thistledown Press Ltd.
410 2nd Avenue North
Saskatoon, Saskatchewan, S7K 2C3
www.thistledownpress.com

Library and Archives Canada Cataloguing in Publication
Trettwer, James, author
Thorn-field / James Trettwer.
Short stories.
Issued in print and electronic formats.
ISBN 978-1-77187-170-9 (softcover).—ISBN 978-1-77187-171-6 (HTML).—
ISBN 978-1-77187-172-3 (PDF)
I. Title.
PS8639.R4785T56 2018   C813'.6   C2018-904559-0
C2018-904560-4

Cover and book design by Jackie Forrie
Printed and bound in Canada

An earlier version of "Godsend" was originally published in *TRANSITION* magazine. "Leaving With Lena" was previously published in *Wanderlust: Stories on the Move*, by Thistledown Press. The poem "Heavy Water" is a portion of "The Depths" previously published in *Arborealis: A Canadian Anthology of Poetry*, by The Ontario Poetry Society.

 Canada Council for the Arts   Conseil des Arts du Canada   Canadä   SASKATCHEWAN ARTS BOARD | cultivating the arts

Thistledown Press gratefully acknowledges the financial assistance of the Canada Council for the Arts, the Saskatchewan Arts Board, and the Government of Canada for its publishing program.

ACKNOWLEDGEMENTS

"Bring It On" was a winner in the SWG Short Manuscript Awards for fiction. The *Thorn-Field* collection was a winner in the SWG John V. Hick's Long Manuscript Award. Thank you to the Guild for these opportunities.

Many hugs to Byrna Barclay — mentor and motivator by boot — without you, this collection would never have been. Supportive feedback on early versions of the stories by present and past members of the Bees writers group is much appreciated. To gillian harding-russell and Connie Gault, your generous feedback and support is also much appreciated. Linda Biasotto, you were with me in English 252 and during all these intervening years, your ongoing support is incalculable. Duff Marshall, many thanks for that initial encouragement all those years ago — ou kept me going. Michael Kenyon, couldn't have done it without you. Thank you to Thistledown Press for taking all this on.

To my family, Coree and Krista, the first to hear these stories, your early feedback was invaluable. Sherry, I wouldn't have been able to pull any of this off if you weren't there for me. I am most grateful to you all.

Author's Note: A valuable source in the writing of some of the stories in this book is John Burton's *Potash: An Inside Account of Saskatchewan's Pink Gold*, Regina: University of Regina Press, 2014. For the sake of storytelling, I have taken liberties with some historical facts. At the time of writing, there are no crown owned or operated potash mines in Saskatchewan. There are also inaccuracies in potash mining operations in this collection because I have taken narrative license with some details for the sake of story. Any errors or omissions are entirely on me.

for Byrna

CONTENTS

Threading Through Thorn-Fields

LOURDES FLOATS. SHE DRIFTS OVER the Liverwood Potash Corporation mine. The mine's plume is bright-white, reflecting a waning gibbous moon in a starless sky. Drifting with the plume on its lazy, south-easterly course, she veers toward the town of Liverwood. Descending, she passes over Liverwood Creek. She knows what is about to happen.

She tries to steer toward a treed hollow nestled in an oxbow of the creek near the Motel 6. She catches a glimpse of moon reflecting on water. Birch and Laurel Leaf Willow enclose the hollow. The creek's shore is thick with Canadian thistle. The creekbed is exposed and dry while the hollow morphs into a flat, endless plain of thistles, the thick stocks six feet high, their purple flowers open and turned toward the plume — their surrogate sunshine. The lush growth suddenly shrivels and turns tinder brown as if poisoned by a toxic rain.

Through the middle of that brown field, Lourdes runs. The thorns on the shrivelled and spiky leaves and stalks shred her pajamas and ravage her exposed flesh and bare feet. She doesn't feel any pain. Only a tingling on her hot, sweating skin.

The thorny stalks writhe. They entwine her legs and she falls on her face. She is naked from the waist down, prone on her stomach, and also watching from the ether. In the surrounding light — neither dark nor sunlit but brown as the dead field — a thistle's lone flower, purple and vibrant, lifts from the thorns, then it too fades to brown and shrivels into a hard, spear-shaped seedpod. Thorns seize Lourdes' ankles, biting to the bone, and force her legs apart. The seedpod thrusts between her inner thighs. Thrusts inside her.

A newborn baby cries once. She feels her womb explode.

Lourdes opens her eyes. Drenched in sweat, she thinks of Mary Bliss — then her father. She retreats to the hollow in the oxbow of the creek not far from the motel. Her hollow.

∽∾∽∾

She sits high in a birch tree near the shore.

Looking down, Lourdes sees her eleven-year-old self enter the hollow.

Her father died in a mine accident two weeks ago. She is staying with the Treadwells who own the Motel 6 while her mother, Edna, is off — somewhere. The Treadwells let her stay by herself in the hollow as long as she promises that she will stay away from the creek.

A crow perches on a lower branch of the birch. It's head cocked, the bird stares at its dead mate lying on the ground. Lourdes leans against the lone picnic table and studies both birds. It is her *birch-hollow pair* and it is the male that is still alive; he has the iridescent purple sheen across his plumage. Lourdes approaches the dead bird. She picks it up, cupping it in both palms. The female crow has been shot through her upper shoulder.

The male croaks a single, throaty caw. He does not fly away when Lourdes carries his mate to the creek's shore. He lets out another plaintive croak, hops to the other side of branch and watches, head again cocked to one side.

With her bare hands, Lourdes digs a hole in the muck. She buries the female beside a single thick-stemmed Canadian thistle. The thistle, with its many purple flowers drooping in this dappled morning light, will be the grave marker.

For the next few days, any time Lourdes goes to the hollow, the male flies up from the grave to the birch and perches on that same branch. He watches her until she leaves. She does not know what the male does when she is not in the hollow.

Lourdes sits at the picnic table and leafs through the Scholastic book, *Anne Frank — Beyond the Diary*. Mr. Treadwell gave her the book to read and said she should think about Anne, "who was young just like you." She doesn't understand what Mr. Treadwell wants her to think and she can't relate to the story. But she does wonder how so many families could get along all crammed into an attic together.

The male croaks his single, throaty caw. This gets her attention. The bird flies down and lands on the very spot beside the thistle where his mate is buried. He lets out a crow's typical and raucous *caw-caw-caw* and zooms up, buzzing her. A wingtip brushes her hair and he is gone. *See*, she tells herself, holding the book against her chest, *I'm not the only one suffering.*

ɷɷ

Damp with sweat from another dream of the Thorn-Field, Lourdes is calm. She is so calm, she is not bothered by the fact that her sixteenth birthday was forgotten the previous Saturday. She did not expect a party anyway, or even acknowledgement of the occasion.

After stretching, she rolls on her side. Her rickety twin bed creaks. She stares at the faded beige walls of her bedroom. It is the smaller of two bedrooms of a mobile home where she lives with Edna and whatever boyfriend her mother might have staying with her.

The carpets in the place are worn down to the underside mesh in heavy traffic areas. The kitchen and bathroom linoleum is worse, with the bare wood of the trailer's floor exposed. The windows leak and water has stained the frames brown. Black, flaky mould blooms from the corners of the outside walls. The front door has a lock but a hard push will open it. Snow piles inside the door in winter and the furnace roars constantly. All taps drip and the toilet flushes itself every half hour.

Then there are the other noises — Edna, yelling, moaning, screaming, the blare of the portable television her mother constantly watches: snowy afternoon soap operas and dramas on the two available non-cable stations. The TV occasionally disappears to the pawnshop near month's end, when money is short. Some months,

12

the TV is returned by Herb, the owner of Liverwood Pawn and Surplus. Herb then stays the next few nights with Edna. He is the current boyfriend and Lourdes can hear him snoring in her mother's bedroom right now.

The noises from Edna's bedroom are always intolerable. They are harsh, with severe thumping, sometimes slapping sounds, and swearing. Herb, especially, likes to talk. Lourdes can only cover her head with her pillow and turn up the MP3 player her father gave her before he died.

But the worst sound of all is silence. When the furnace isn't running, when Edna isn't moaning, or rambling in some kind of drug- or alcohol-induced stupor — at least letting Lourdes know she is still alive — the silence smothers her. Suffocates her. On these occasions she snaps awake. She lies in bed, panic building, thinking she can escape if Edna would only die of an overdose. Guilt immediately knots her stomach. Then, no matter how hard she tries, she can't go back to sleep until she checks to see if Edna is alive. She has to get up to check on her mother. Then she can't sleep afterward anyway with Edna's raspy breathing, which may cease at any time, echoing in her ears. Lourdes wants out but not at the expense of another person's life. At the same time she doesn't know how she can stay much longer.

She rolls on her back and stretches again. Her skin feels crusty now that the sweat has dried. She hears Herb still snoring and decides to shower.

Letting a cool flow wash away the crust first, she turns the water off to lather her thick, wavy, copper-red locks that hang down past her shoulder blades. Then she lathers her lightly freckled body.

The bathroom door slams open. Like the front door, the bathroom lock works only occasionally. Herb pulls the shower curtain back. His shirt is off, exposing thick black chest hair. He is scrawny, with ribs showing under his droopy man-boobs. He has a potbelly from too much beer and sitting behind his pawnshop counter or lounging on Edna's bed or couch.

He sees Lourdes and gawks, open-mouthed. She instinctively covers her breasts with one arm and reaches the other down, covering her genitals.

Herb, still gawking, scratches his mass of thick black hair, combed straight up, on his oversized head. Then he scratches one of his long sideburns. The other hand kneads his checked, lumberjack shirt. He scans her body up and down.

Lourdes stares hard at him. She feels her face burn. Her stomach burn. The burn turns into a hateful rage that bursts up and out. She does not scream or yell but speaks in a low voice through clenched teeth. "What the fuck are you doing?"

"I, I didn't hear the water running." Herb's voice is half an octave higher than its normal rat-like squeak. He shifts his body, cocks his head and grins. "They say you should save water and shower with a friend, you know. And now that you're sixteen, Edna says, it'd be all legal. And just so's you know, I like 'em chunky."

This time Lourdes does scream. "Get the fuck out of here before I gut you like the fucking pig you are." She takes one step out of the tub, fists raised.

Herb steps back. His eyes bulge like those of a terrified mouse caught in a live trap. From somewhere, Edna calls, "Herb?" Face returning to its normal shifty sneer, he lifts his chin and says, "Maybe next time, punkin. I hear a real woman calling." Shoulders hunched, he shuffles out of the bathroom.

She stumbles back into the tub and flings the shower curtain closed. She turns the water to hot. Shaking, she slides down and sits in the tub. Squeezing her stomach flab in both hands until it hurts, she is afraid the skeleton image of Herb is now permanently etched in her mind. The shakes turn to a quiver while the water continues to flow over her.

She does not cry.

☙☙☙

The next morning, a sunshiny Sunday, Lourdes is at the stove. It has only three working burners and the white enamel is chipped and blackened all across the stove top. No matter how hard she tries, she can't get the stove clean. She also cannot repair the broken hinge on the oven door. She doesn't have the tools or a replacement hinge, both of which Edna refuses to buy. So the door hangs askew and the oven never bakes properly.

Eggs and rye bread, the day-old bread she always buys on her way home from school, fry in their battered skillet. The skillet's plastic handle has been long broken. She has jury-rigged a replacement handle with a cut-down, wooden mop pole fastened with a nut and bolt. When the skillet handle first broke, Edna tried to fry with a pot.

Edna manages to shuffle into the kitchen just when Lourdes moves the bread and eggs onto plates. She pauses and leans against the wall for support. She takes a breath and staggers toward the kitchen table. Falling forward, she grabs the back of the chrome chair with both hands and plops down with a sigh. Her whole body sags.

Edna is becoming more and more gaunt. At five foot four, she weighs barely 100 pounds. Her thighs are blackened with finger-shaped bruises. Her knees and shins are covered in red scrapes and scabs. Her stringy hair is falling out. Lourdes finds strands everywhere, including inside the bread bag after Edna has grabbed a slice and eaten it right over the bag without closing it. Her pockmarked cheeks and dowager's hump make her look like a woman in her seventies even though she is only thirty-six years old.

This morning, she wears a long-sleeved, beige turtleneck sweater that hangs down to her upper thighs. It is a hot June day so the sweater is likely meant to hide traces of whatever new experiments are tracking down her arms. Her button nose is always raw and red, with dried skin hanging on the edges of her nostrils. Her long delicate fingers, that once played their electric piano before it was pawned at Herb's, are yellow with nicotine and already gnarled with arthritis.

Lourdes bangs Edna's plate in front of her, then sits across the table, also banging her own plate in place. Edna ignores her except for a quick glance in her direction. She is fully aware of the smouldering rage in her daughter. Careful not to glance up again, she begins to eat with her fingers, sopping egg with the bread, face hanging over her plate.

Lourdes says, "I don't want that drug-pushing Herb here anymore. Same with your other creepy lovers. Do it at their place. They make me sick."

"You shouldn't provoke Herb like that," Edna says, face still over her plate.

"He barged in on me. The door was supposed to be locked. You should get it fixed."

"Locked." Edna snorts. "How was he supposed to know you were in there? You didn't have the water on."

"I don't waste water while I soap up. I keep telling you that."

"And I keep telling you, water is included in the lot fees. Who cares how much you use?"

"That's not the point."

Edna finally looks up. "Yeah, the point is, you tried to entice him, you fat little slut. He told me so. You know he likes 'em fat."

For the second time in less than twenty-four hours Lourdes is in shock. She can't respond.

"Can't think of a come back because it's the truth." Edna sneers. "I dare you to deny it. You wanted him in there so he could fuck you."

"Fuck you!" Lourdes still can't swallow. She jumps up, clenches her fists. Unclenches them. The thought of being with Herb makes her want to vomit. Bile burns her throat.

Edna staggers to her feet, using the table for support. "Deny it. You can't. You want to take him away from me. It wasn't bad enough you fucked Barton and then *you* lost the baby."

She erupts. Throws her plate at Edna. She misses only because of a hasty throw. The plate shatters against a cupboard door. Food and lethal fragments fly. The cupboard door cracks.

She races around the table. Edna tries to slap her when she lunges. She grabs Edna's wrist. Twists, hard. Something snaps when she bends Edna's arm down and behind her and forces her to her knees.

Edna screams. "You're hurting me. Stop. I didn't mean it about Mary. I'm sorry."

But the damage is done. Irrevocable. Lourdes pushes her mother to the floor, hard, with both hands. Edna quickly rolls over and scuttles under the kitchen table, whimpering, "Lourdes. Please. Stop."

Just as in her dreams, when she hears the baby's strangled cry in dead fields of shredding thorns, her arms become crow wings. She flaps hard and propels herself to the ceiling. Lightheaded from being airborne, she drifts along the ceiling and watches herself.

In the hospital — almost a year ago now — she was not allowed to even hold her baby to say goodbye.

She stomps to her bedroom and rips her cardboard suitcase from the closet. She dumps the old graded school papers worth keeping and the few books she owns onto the closet floor. She grabs her four pairs of panties, all riddled with holes and coming apart at the

18

seams, her three bras, beaded from wear, and her two pairs of jeans and six over-sized T-shirts and flings them into the suitcase. Almost as an afterthought, she takes her only pair of pyjamas from under her pillow and drops them on top of the T-shirts. Pulling the jeans drawer out of her bureau, she lifts out her spiral notebook journals — hidden where Edna and her friends would probably never find them — and tucks them inside the lid pocket of the suitcase. She grabs her MP3 player and stomps to the bathroom. She packs shampoo, toothbrush and toothpaste, and seizes all of the tampons, including Edna's supply.

Edna cowers silently under the kitchen table as Lourdes marches from the bathroom, through the kitchen and out the door, leaving it open. She leaves the trailer with no backward glances or any words from Edna. Through it all, Herb has continued to snore, undisturbed, in Edna's bedroom.

Lourdes still does not cry.

Slowly circling above herself and watching, the crow feels only grim determination while the girl marches on, toward what will hopefully be a safe place. Poplar leaves brush against each other with a soothing sigh in the morning breeze. Lourdes turns out from the poplars' cool shadows among the cluster of trailers in the mobile-home park and onto the already sun-warmed road. The park is just within Liverwood town limits, half a kilometer east of the highway that runs north from the town toward the mine. The mine's ever-present plume glares in its early morning climb skyward.

Reaching the rise in the gravel road, she can see her destination: the Treadwell's Motel 6. Harold Treadwell is a skinny, six-foot-four Englishman who hates the name Harry. He always says, "I'm not named after any snot-nosed prince. Call me Treadwell."

Lourdes secretly calls him Long-shanks.

Long-shanks and his Greek wife Helena are her pretend grandparents. Three of her four real grandparents died of various addiction-related diseases and she never knew them. Her father's mother, who is still alive and living somewhere in Florida, disowned her only son shortly after he married Edna.

Labouring underground for twenty-five years, Long-shanks worked his way up to Shift Production Manager at the Liverwood Potash Corporation Mine before he retired and bought the Motel 6 with his wife. During his mining days, he mentored and was a friend to Lourdes' father. The Treadwells were always available to babysit, usually on a moment's notice on any sort of occasion. They had no children of their own and they were close to her father.

She marches on, now and then passing the suitcase from one hand to the other. Feeling the strain in her shoulder, she thinks there should be a thunderstorm or tornado to mark this event. After all, *Wuthering Heights*, which she read in grade nine, had some sort of storm at serious, dramatic moments, didn't it?

The silence is absolute. There is no traffic and no birds sing in the tree-break between the motel and the houses on the edge of the town. She hates the way the sun shines and retreats from it. She dives down and back into herself. She crosses the deserted highway and trudges across the gravel parking lot toward the Treadwell's living quarters attached to the motel. Normally, she would pass through the lobby to report for table service and dishwashing duties in the restaurant. The Treadwells still pay her in cash because she was just fifteen when they hired her.

Lourdes knocks on the screen door of their living quarters that is shaded by the overhang of the upper floor in that quadrant of the motel. The inner door is open and she smells the Treadwell's Brazilian dark-roast coffee. Her stomach suddenly knots. This is it. The moment of truth. If the Treadwells turn her away — she doesn't know what to do next. Or where to go. There is no going back.

Her whole body sags as if the weight of the entire earth at the lowest crosscut of the mine is pressing down on her. She has that oppressed, smothered feeling like the time she went underground in the mine service elevator with her father. In that terrifying and rapid descent in a garage-sized elevator car, she needed only a single look through the wire-mesh sides at the endless strata of dirt before she clung to her father's legs. Face in his thigh and eyes squeezed shut, she refused to step off the elevator— just like the narrator in the Guy Vanderhaeghe story she read in English Lit class.

Lourdes hears Helena's accented voice. "Who could that be?"

Helena appears at the door, opens it, and scowls. Her lips are thin and her lower jaw juts out. The knot in Lourdes' stomach turns into a searing pain that rips upward and across her chest. She quivers, then shakes. Her lower lip protrudes. She can feel her eyes burning and bulging. The tears are welling up, blurring her vision.

She is lost after all.

But then the woman, still grim faced, opens her pudgy arms wide and says, "Gods and little fishes. What has that wicked witch done now?"

Lourdes drops her suitcase and collapses into Helena, who is as short as she is round, and her arms can't reach all the way around her torso. She presses her face into Helena's shoulder, body heaving with racking sobs.

Helena strokes her hair and whispers, "It's all right. Let it all out."

When she is spent, she lifts her head and says, "I'm sorry."

"You sorry for nothing. Sit down. Come." Helena leads her by the hand, stepping around Long-shanks who, she realizes now, is standing behind his wife, one hand on her shoulder, his other hand holding a wad of facial tissue. He passes her the wad.

She nods thanks and gives him a quivery smile.

He is totally bald on top. The remainder of his still-blond hair is curly and thick on the sides and back of his head and grows down into sideburns and moustache in a yellow flow of hair in the Victorian-age style. Skinny and gangly, he wears khaki pants and a comfortable casual shirt with epaulet loops on the shoulders. He is so different from Herb.

Helena wears a grey, man's dress shirt that hangs over her thick upper thighs encased in stonewashed blue jeans.

Lourdes dabs at the stain of tears, spit, and snot on Helena's shoulder. "Your shirt. I'm sorry."

"No worry about this." She takes the tissue from Lourdes and gently wipes under her nose and then under her green eyes.

"She's a tough old bird, lass," says Long-shanks, taking a towel from the chrome stove handle. "What's a little wet between mates?" He separates the two, handing Helena the towel, and gently guides Lourdes to her usual place at their kitchen table. He says, "I've got your coffee in. Black, two spoons of brown sugar, well stirred. I had to do *summat* while the sob-fest went on."

He points a bony finger at her. "Don't look at me like that. You won't have me blubberin' like a wee lass too."

Helena slaps him with the towel. "It might do you good, Old Coot, to cry once in a while."

"Shove that towel in your gob, woman. Don't tell me what to do."

Lourdes laughs out loud. She is safe here.

Helena says, "Tell us all about it."

She tells them about Herb. Tells them about the fight and Edna's response. "I threw that plate as hard as I could. I wanted to smash it in her face. What if I had hit her? The cupboard door smashed apart. How could I do something like that? What kind of a horrible daughter . . . horrible person am I?"

Helena grips her by both shoulders, leans down and looks her directly in the eyes. "You couldn't help it. Not your fault. You never think that. Never. Understand me?"

She nods.

Leaning back, hands behind his head, gangly legs crossed at the ankles and stretching out to almost the middle of the kitchen, Long-shanks says, "And don't feel guilty 'bout leaving the wicked witch either, lass. You did the right thing. And you did right coming to us. I've been thinking while all this crying's been about."

He goes on to say that now she is sixteen, she can be hired permanently. She can also live in one of the hotel's rooms for as long as she wants. The room he has in mind is the smallest in the motel with a hallway utility closet containing a furnace jutting into it. The room is usually vacant because of the noise and the fact that its size allows for only one double bed. Of course, she will have to clean rooms to pay for her room and board. However, this is all contingent on two things. Long-shanks looks at his wife. One, Lourdes has to take a server job in the restaurant weekends and evenings at busy times, and two, she has to finish highschool.

He says with a sharp edge to his voice, almost a challenge, "Anything to add to that, woman?"

"How can I add, Old Coot?" Helena replies with a frown. "You don't let me get a word in *edgeways*."

Lourdes isn't fooled by their harsh banter. She caught the momentary softening of Long-shank's expression when he barked his challenge at Helena. She sees Helena's eyes widen slightly for a split-second when she gives him an infinitesimal nod.

Even though she is exhausted, she agrees to work that lunch hour and has her first crack at serving the church crowd. She does her dishes duty afterward. She revels in the work. Focuses on it. It is better than thinking about Edna and what has happened. She has supper with the Treadwells and spends the evening with them over a small birthday cake and coffee.

Helena escorts her to her new room. She continues to force herself not to think and focuses on how short Helena is, watching her large buttocks sway, noticing how the woman walks with one foot placed in front of the other; the way a model walks.

Alone in her room, she undresses and falls into bed without brushing her teeth or putting on her thin pajamas. She won't think. She just lets fatigue wash over her. The starched motel sheets rub against her skin while she stretches spreadeagled on the double bed. How much better the motel bed feels than her rickety twin at the trailer. There, she had to endure a lumpy mattress, and a worn top sheet that offered little protection from her scratchy horsehair blanket.

For the first time since her father died, Lourdes sleeps a deep, dreamless sleep until Helena knocks on her door to wake her up for school the next day.

ⵄⵄⵄ

If only all of her sleeps could be dreamless.

The crow watches over her motel room. Edna, in a tattered, man's "wife beater" T-shirt, which exposes folds

25

of loose skin on her belly, is here to take her back to the trailer. Her mother grabs two handfuls of her hair and drags her out of bed. She seizes Edna's wrists. Her bare feet slip on the carpet.

Edna's black panties, the white of the waistband's elastic showing through the thin spots in the fabric, hang on her bony hips. The tangled mess of Edna's stringy black hair hangs down, hiding her face and brushing against Lourdes' skin like creeping vines.

Edna is a silent dynamo. She does not scream or yell. Her grip is unbreakable and energy inexhaustible.

Lourdes sweats and gasps. Her heart hammers in her chest. She lets go of Edna's wrists and chops at the inside of her elbows. Edna falls on top of her. She can smell booze on Edna's breath as she seizes her mother's face with both hands and plunges her thumbs into her eye-sockets and pushes her away by kicking straight with both legs. Edna crashes against the far wall.

Silently covering her eyes with both hands, Edna shakes her head once and then lunges, arms outstretched, hands grasping air, streaking across the room like a skeletal spectre from a B-grade horror movie.

Lourdes scrambles sideways. Jumps up and bolts through her motel room to the brown field of thorny thistles. Edna's form is silhouetted against the open motel room door in the brownish light, her arms still outstretched, open hands still grasping air.

Lourdes runs through the field. The shredding thorns trip her. The seedpod thrusts and she awakens with a start and immediately thinks of Mary. She retreats to her hollow. Deep breathing, she tells herself to calm down. She's safe in the motel with the Treadwells.

She's been here for more than a year already.

Herb was arrested for drug trafficking and Edna burned the trailer down months ago and disappeared.

Calm now, but still covered in sweat, Lourdes slides out of bed and heads for the shower, mentally preparing herself for the breakfast rush.

Cool water washes away the night sweats. Grade eleven is finished and she's proud of her straight A's. Her academic standing, if she can maintain it, should help her achieve a scholarship or two at university. However, she wants to put in as many hours as she can over the summer and the next year to save for tuition. Lathering herself with the water off, she focuses only on the day's work ahead.

After ten hours in the restaurant, acting as both greeter and server and working kitchen clean-up, Lourdes steps outside for a much needed smoke. She puts the cigarillo to her lips, fully aware that she has inherited her parents' addictive personality traits. Food being her weakness, and determined not to be an addict like them, she's taken to smoking cigarillos, without inhaling, to kill her appetite. She also smokes because she's determined to avoid obesity and all of its related diseases. She has also taken up running four to six times a week.

Taking her Bic lighter from her pocket, she wonders why a tanker truck is idling on the highway, right beside the motel property. The big rigs always park in the vacant gas station lot on the other side of the motel when the drivers come for a meal.

About to light her cigarillo, she hears someone behind her shuffle along the sidewalk from the direction of her room. She turns and bile surges. Edna.

"I thought you left town." She keeps her voice steady.

"I need money." Edna sways, then leans her hand on the wall. Her eyes are bloodshot and vacant, heavy with black circles. "Help me out."

"I don't have any money to give you."

"*Whaddya* mean? You must have a shit-load of money working here all the time. I hear you don't pay rent. I have to help pay for gas." Her head tilts in the direction of the idling tanker.

"I said, 'I don't have any money to give you.' I have to save everything I earn for university."

Edna straightens up, shuffles forward a step, and vaguely waves her index finger. "Oh, you're Miss Hoity-Toity university student already, are you? You're still in high school and you're too good to help your own mother?"

"My mother abandoned me a long time ago."

Edna says, "I named you Lourdes because you were supposed to heal my marriage. Supposed to heal me. You failed me and now you can't even find the compassion to help me out?"

The only thing Lourdes hears while she races for the motel lobby is the air horn of the tanker.

She runs down her corridor, past her room, and out the hallway exit. Slamming that door open, she sprints down the path toward the hollow. Once there, she listens to the wind through the birch and willow leaves. The thistle flowers peer downward, their purple heads bent and battered. The flowers on a new batch of thistles by the female crow's grave also droop. Lourdes spreads her arms and feels the damp and humid air on her exposed skin.

Calm now, she watches the field beside the motel. The purpling flax stalks wave in the wind. The wind swirls her hair around her face as she stands and stares up at the mine's plume.

The mine, where her father went to work after he graduated from Liverwood Comprehensive High School. What would life be like if he hadn't died in that mining accident? She feels an emptiness in the pit of her stomach that has nothing to do with food. She remembers her male crow with the purple sheen and his final flight from their hollow. She stares at the field of flax; the only sound is the wind. She tucks her hair behind her ear.

Back in her room, intending to change for a run, she instead fetches her laptop and returns to the hollow, sits at the picnic table there. Mindless of the darkening sky and nighttime chill creeping over her bare arms and numbing her fingers, she types and retypes until her laptop battery is fully discharged. Dashing back to her room, she plugs in the machine and continues to type until the sky reddens and morning light shines through her windows.

Silence In Wind

All I hear is endless
prairie wind
when the sun drops
in the west.

I turn my back
from where you were under a plume
watch night creep skyward
on an obsidian surge.

I turn back, call to you
hear only silence
in endless prairie wind.

∾∾∾

"Silence in Wind" was published shortly after Lourdes' eighteenth birthday. Over coffee and birthday cake in the Treadwell's kitchen, Helena congratulated her on her first publication, for finishing high school with high honours, and, of course, wished her a happy birthday

"Thank you, Mrs. Treadwell," she replied.

Helena waved her pudgy finger. "You call me Helena now. No more Mrs. Treadwell, for at eighteen you are a woman too."

That was more than a year ago. Lourdes did not attend the high school graduation ceremonies and felt nothing about them.

Now, she sits in the restaurant kitchen during a slow moment after the supper rush. She takes her spiral notepad out of her server uniform pocket and unfolds the two letters she keeps tucked between the back page and back cover. The first is her acceptance letter from the University of Saskatchewan telling her that she can register in the University's BA in English Literature program. The letter has been there since March but she has not yet acted. Over the past three years, she's saved enough money to finance her entire program if she's careful with her spending. Registering felt wrong at the time the letter arrived and still feels wrong at this moment. However, she keeps the acceptance handy as a constant reminder.

Helena always says, "Listen to your womanly instincts."

The second letter arrived just the day before from the University of Toronto Press. It tells her that four of her poems, including "Silence In Wind," have been accepted for publication in a yet-to-be-titled anthology of emerging Canadian poets. Lourdes consulted her womanly instincts and mailed her acceptance to the terms of the agreement within an hour of opening the letter.

She wonders if she should focus on her poetry manuscript instead of going to university. Acceptance in this anthology will surely help her chances of eventual publication when the manuscript is complete. At the same time though, she knows she is still a novice and should continue her education.

With this publication news, perhaps things are going too well. She doesn't necessarily believe in the idea of karmic balance, but in moments of indecision she does wonder if something bad will happen to balance all of the good currently in her life.

So for the moment, she decides once again to hold off registering for university. She's studied some online course material for an Introduction to Administration class and read that doing nothing is a viable option.

"Silence in Wind" started this whole current chain of events. She refuses to wonder how such good can come from her anguish. She only accepts that it does.

She tucks the two letters away and free associates. She writes, *Coincidence? Is the universe nothing more than a random series of electrochemical reactions? But if man is made in the image of God, and man is capable of committing the atrocities he does, what exactly has man been modelled after? How can the concept of a loving God take such a young life* . . .

The seedpod slithers in deep darkness. She squeezes her eyes shut and roughly brushes her hair with her hand. Inhaling, she wills herself to remember the smell of her damp hollow. She writes, *life continually comes up with contrivances, that would immediately be rejected as ridiculous, impossible in satire or even farce* . . .

Instincts tuned toward the customer, she senses someone enter the restaurant even though she's in the kitchen. Putting her pen and notepad away immediately, she strives for excellent customer service and quick-steps to the front of the restaurant.

A man casually leans on the cash register counter and patiently waits to be seated. The suppertime crowd is long past and it's seat yourself by this time, but he still waits. Lourdes guesses he is around twenty-five years old. His dark brown hair is spiked and his clean-shaven face has no five o'clock shadow. He is six feet tall and his tapered, white dress shirt reveals his well-formed, muscular torso. Shirt sleeves rolled up to his elbows, his forearms are tanned and veined.

He stares directly at her with his bright blue eyes and she has to look at the bridge of his nose while she approaches him. She feels her face flush. *What's the deal here?* she thinks.

She draws her focus away from his intense stare and looks at his left hand. There is no ring and no tan line showing where a ring may have been recently removed. Possibilities, quite unbidden and unexpected, flood her mind. *It's been so long since . . . No! Get to work, idiot.*

When she looks up again, he is examining the back of his left hand, fingers spread, with the slightest smile. She takes a deep breath, clears her throat, and asks, without any traitorous quiver in her voice — years of controlling feelings do come in handy sometimes — if she can help him with something.

He replies, with a bass radio announcer's voice, "Could I still grab some supper, please?"

She clears her throat and says, "Follow me." She turns and fumbles the menu she grabs from the stack on the counter. She has never fumbled before. It's always turn and grab in one fluid motion.

She feels him watching her while she leads him to a booth by the window farthest away from the counter where four regular cronies, all retired farmers wearing baseball caps, are gossiping and drinking coffee. She deliberately cat-walks, one foot directly in front of the other, like models on TV, even hopes her hips sway sensually, like Helena's.

Stop it! she scolds herself and purposely splays her feet as she takes the last few steps toward the booth. Jaw tight, she sets the menu on the table, points to the seat, and says through clenched teeth, "I'll be right back with some water."

If he notices that anything is amiss, he does not let on. His passive and bemused expression does not change. And damn the bugger. He's still staring.

Lourdes almost sprints back to the kitchen to compose herself. She realizes that she forgot serving protocol and did not ask him if he'd like some coffee. She rarely makes even a single mistake, let alone two in as many minutes. She leans against the food-prep counter, breathes, and recalls the sound of the breeze through the leaves in her hollow.

Snapping her head up, she glances around, sure that the baseball-cap cronies, who can see her through the food-serving opening, and Gus, the nighttime short order cook, are all watching her. She's sure they all know what she's thinking. But they are all fixated on a CFL game playing on the small television on the shelf above the opening.

She takes a minute to scribble two notes in her notepad. *Your eyes seared your image on my soul. Love at first sight is a clichéd, fictional fake farce, except in real life.* She scratches out that terrible first line and then pockets the notepad.

The cronies suddenly boo. So does Gus, shaking his fists toward the ceiling. He says, "Come on you bums. Get in the game." His hairnet flops on his forehead and his long grey ponytail whips back and forth when he shakes his head.

"Who's winning?" she asks.

"Not the Riders. As usual." He slaps his fist into his other palm. "Another two and out with a shitty punt. *And* they're down two touchdowns, no less."

"Who are they playing?"

"Thieving Edmonton. I can't believe their luck. Thirteen Cups and counting my aunt Fanny's twa—" Gus abruptly shuts his mouth and doesn't finish his epithet in front of her. Turning, he takes tomorrow's pies out of the oven while a half-ton truck commercial blares about how tough the vehicle is.

She doesn't care about football and everyone knows that. All the better: no one will pay any attention to her. Peering through the opening, she studies the man in that revealing dress shirt. He leisurely sits back, watching out the window, with his hands folded on the closed menu on the table top.

Lourdes pours a glass of water, takes a deep breath, and walks toward the faraway booth. Long before she is in his field of vision or even before he can possibly hear her coming, he turns toward her. Smiles. Stares.

She watches the glass in her hand, afraid she will slop water if she doesn't concentrate. She sets the glass down. Her mouth is so dry that when she tries to speak there is only a rasping sound. She clears her throat again.

"Thanks so much," he says immediately, touching the glass. "I was hoping I could still get something for supper, if it's not inconvenient."

"Not inconvenient at all." Her voice scratches, which she covers with a cough. *Enough of this, control yourself, infant!* She focuses on the work, gains control of herself, and remembers to ask if he wants something to drink before she takes his food order.

"Would a Pilsner get me with the in-crowd over there?" He nods toward the cronies.

"You're not going to drink and drive, are you?" The words are out of her mouth before she realizes she's said them. *Damn this man.*

He replies smoothly, "I have a room here tonight. Only a short stagger that won't involve motor vehicles. I promise."

How did he get under my skin like this? She cannot not reply. She coughs again to recover her composure. *Back to work, you.* She says, "Good to know. But I was actually thinking you don't look like a Pil guy. We have Keith's in bottles. You look more of a Keith's kind of guy."

"If you say so. Keith's it is."

"And I live here, so I can help you to your room." *WTF!?* Her face burns. She feels sweat on her forehead and a stickiness in her armpits. *Stop it. You wacko.*

The only sign of a reaction from the man is a slight widening of his eyes and a momentary ripple of his eyebrows. With that unchanging, damnably passive face and that constant stare, he says with an even voice, "A very kind offer. But I'll probably have just the one. Work tomorrow and all. Thank you, though."

He stares at the name tag on the upper part of her left breast. Abruptly extending his hand, he says, "I'm Lee. It's nice to meet you, Lourdes."

She instinctively takes his hand. His single shake is firm but not hard.

Betrayed again by her body, she feels a ripple in her lower abdomen. *Maybe if I stab myself, right in the eye . . .*

"I have to apologize," Lee says, holding her hand in his for more than a moment. "I called you by name without asking permission first. I'm sorry for that. Most inappropriate on my part. But that name is so unusual. I'm afraid I lost control and had to say it out loud. It rolls off the tongue. Many apologies." He finally, finally, breaks that stare and opens the menu.

"No. No worries," Lourdes rasps. Trying to gain a modicum of control over herself and the situation. She says, prattling, "The specialty tonight is chicken stir-fry, Gus's specialty, he can make it with his eyes closed, which might be your best choice tonight, I'd recommend it, with the way that silly football game is distracting him, I don't think he can focus on cooking properly." *Did I really just say all that without taking a breath? What am I, eight?*

"Stir-fry it is then." He slaps the menu closed.

"Stir-fry with rice and a Keith's, which I'll bring right away." She rarely has to write down orders; usually only when a horde of children is in the restaurant after church on Sundays.

She fetches the Keith's from the refrigerator and a glass from the freezer. Lee again turns to watch her the moment she emerges from the kitchen. He thanks her for the beer with that voice of his.

She flees back to the kitchen and feels she's scuttling like a weasel after pillaging the henhouse. She takes yet another deep breath to regain her composure.

The cronies and Gus shout in contempt at a bad call. Gus throws a fork into the sink. They have no idea anyone else is even in the restaurant and they pay no attention to her.

"One stir-fry special, please, Gus," she says.

"No problem," Gus replies. "I'm done with watching bums and losers play their peewee, scrimmage football." He immediately goes about his business.

She watches Lee through the food-serving opening again. He leans back, head turned toward the window, hands folded on the menu. She slaps her forehead with her open palm. Another mistake after all. She forgot to take the menu.

Okay, control yourself. This man is not coming on to her. Who wants chunky, damaged goods? Clearly, she's imagining things. She puts her palms on her hips. Admittedly, she's down to 185 pounds, but her uniform does nothing to hide her stomach.

There are also other customers to look after. Only the four cronies at the counter, granted, but she can't ignore them. All business, she pours them more coffee and offers them pie. They all accept and two ask for a-la-mode. She asks Lee if he wants another beer, which he declines. She retrieves the menu and returns it to the stack, placing it precisely, and turns back to the restaurant in one smooth motion.

Back in the game. She mentally high-fives herself.

She serves Lee his food when it's ready and waits the appropriate number of minutes before asking how the meal is and before coming for his empty plate. On each visit she completely ignores his intense, blue-eyed stare.

Things are back under complete control until he gets up to leave. She has been dawdling in the kitchen and didn't take him his bill. Did she do this on purpose? She is suddenly very tired.

She turns down the corners of her mouth when she gets to the cash counter. "Was everything okay?" she asks, with as level a voice as she can muster.

"Fine," he says.

She gives him the bill. "Cash or do you need the machine?"

"I'll pay cash." That damn voice, flawless and calm like a national news anchor, is so soothing. He pays his $18.65 bill with a twenty and a five, telling her to keep the change.

Stuffing his receipt in his wallet, he says, "Maybe see you at breakfast." He spins on his heel and leaves without a backward glance. The door to the motel lobby swings shut and she catches the flash of his white shirt — it's like the flash of the purple sheen on her hollow crow. She takes the change from the cash register and slams the drawer shut. Dropping the change into the shared tip jar, she takes the five-dollar bill to Gus and says, "That man wanted to give you this tip." She waves the bill at him.

"Great. Set it there." Gus points at his wallet and keys sitting on a sideboard in the cooking area.

Fine. He's gone. I don't need his money or him. Back to work. Damaged goods aren't on the menu tonight. But the smell of Lee's aftershave or body talc, much like Old Spice, lingers.

It is a quiet night for customers and the cronies are only interested in the football game. Lourdes tries to scribble some notes and finds she is uninspired. She's been blocked before but this time she encounters a white blankness, much like staring at the back of a crisp, white dress shirt.

The apple and cinnamon aroma of Gus' pies permeate the kitchen. At least the smell of Lee is gone but her stomach grumbles. She knows she is far from hungry and that she is only craving food. She will not submit to the craving and hangs on until her shift ends.

With only a cursory good night to Gus and the cronies, Lourdes speed-walks past them to the lobby exit. Outside, she breathes in the damp, warm evening air. Moisture clings to her skin and she feels exhausted. Her eyes dry and crusty, she rubs them vigorously, takes a cigarillo and lights it with her Bic, savouring the vanilla flavour. She holds the smoke in her mouth but does not inhale. The parking lot is still and quiet in the orange wash of its quartz halogen lights. She sees a flash of white and breathes in sharply, sucking smoke into her lungs and coughs. Her stomach flips, but not from inhaling.

Lee sits on a picnic table in the motel's rest area. His back is to her. Her heart races. Is he waiting for her? *Impossible.* She has had enough of her own foolishness and stomps toward the picnic table to prove it, gravel crunching under her shoes.

At the sound of her approach, Lee swings his legs right around on the tabletop and rests his feet on the opposite seat. He waves and his white teeth flash.

"Hey you," he says.

"What are you doing out here?" she asks, with an edge in her voice.

If he notices the tone, he doesn't let on. "Thought I'd check out the stars," he replies, "while I finished my smoke." He holds up an extinguished stub of the same cigarillo brand that she smokes. "I found these for sale in the lobby. The English dude running this place imports some quality stuff."

Goose bumps creep all over her skin. There is something about this man. She is attracted to him — or maybe just fascinated, like a crow drawn to a shiny object. An electricity emanates from him. An electricity that is hard to resist.

"By the way, I didn't tell you my last name earlier. It's Markham. I'm really happy to see you again, Lourdes. And I didn't even have to wait until breakfast."

She says, "My last name's Smith."

"Smith? Really?"

"I can show you my photo ID."

"No need. I believe you," Lee says with a grin, extends his hand and again, instinctively, she takes it. He says, "My god, are you ever cold."

Her hand is freezing. The feeling intensifies the warmth of Lee's hand. He sets his cigarillo butt on the table, takes hers from her trembling fingers and sets it down also. He takes both of her hands in his. "Are you okay?" He draws her toward him, careful to keep their entwined hands between them. She does not resist.

"I'm good," she says, her voice wavering. "I was just in the freezer." Her knees quiver and she isn't sure if she can continue to stand. She extracts her hands and says, "I'll just sit for a bit." She quickly sits beside him and grabs her cigarillo, taking a drag.

He gazes back up at the sky and says, "Beautiful night. I really like the way you can see the stars when you're away from the city."

"Which city?"

He leans backward on his hands. She can feel the warmth of his arm as it brushes her. *He did that on purpose,* but she does not shunt away.

"Regina," he says.

"What brings you to the backwoods burg of Liverwood?"

In that throaty radio voice, Lee tells her about himself. "I work for Bland Electronics, in service and support. The company bids on tenders for maintenance contracts on various control systems for a bunch of industries in the province. We've just won the tender for Liverwood Potash and tomorrow is my first visit to the mine."

She can't help but compare Lee to her father, who went right from high school to a helper trainee position at the mine. "Have you ever worked in a mine?" she asks.

"I have, but not the actual mining of ore or potash. Our contracts include hardware and software support and operating system and programming support and upgrades. I'll be working on the mine's control systems and computer gear."

"You have a Computer Science degree?"

"Actually, I have a Bachelor of Admin with a minor in CS. I'm also a Chartered Accountant. I got that designation taking night classes. And I took a leave of absence from Bland to take heavy-duty mechanics at SIAST too. I figured if I have to work with heavy industry, that ticket could only benefit me."

"So you've never been a miner?"

"Afraid not. I've worked for Bland ever since I graduated university. I'm more of a jack-of-all-trades and master of none. But I've been inside most mines in the province, including that gold mine up north. I've been anywhere from the Shand Power Station to the Tobin Lake generating dam. The job takes Bland lots of places and Liverwood is the latest in a long, long list."

Lourdes simply says, "Uh-huh," and takes another drag.

Lee sits up straight and turns to face her, making more space between them. She lifts her head to study the brilliance of the stars against the pitch black void of outer space.

After a moment's silence, he says, "You know, with all the places I've driven to, they're right about the wide open prairie."

"Right about what?" she asks.

"They say the flat prairie is like the ocean. I like to think of the places I stop at as my ports of call."

"Is there a woman in every port?" *WTF! For a second time tonight!* She should have asked if he'd ever been to the ocean. Or who "they" are supposed to be, at the very least. Instead, the words are again out before she realizes she has said them.

He chortles and says, without the slightest variation in pitch or tone, "Very clever, Lourdes. You're going places aren't you?" Without waiting for an answer, he says, "I'm not big on long-distance and/or occasional relationships. I'd be perfectly happy with a permanent, monogamous relationship. You wouldn't know of anyone who might fit that job description, would you?"

Now, is that a pick up line or what?

"And in answer to your question," he says, "There's no woman in any port. And I currently have a vacancy for that permanent relationship."

Yeah, right, a line and a half then. And a relationship as permanent as this cigarillo. "No, I don't know of anyone." She stands up, finishes her smoke, and drops the butt in a nearby disposal bin. "I have work tomorrow."

Lee stands also but keeps his distance. "Can I attend you to your room?"

Attend? Wow. This guy's growing corn now. "No thanks. I know the way."

"Well, goodnight then," he says, his voice not modulating even slightly.

She marches away and hears the strike of a match. He must have relit his forgotten cigarillo. He calls to her, "Maybe I'll still see you at breakfast."

"Maybe," she replies over her shoulder without turning. She has housekeeping duties in the morning and won't be near the restaurant. She crunches driveway gravel under her feet.

After a couple of tries to get her key in the lock, she hazards a quick glance toward the picnic table. Lee's back is toward her once again. A cloud of smoke billows upward.

She heads directly for her laptop and opens her journal file. She tries to write about what just happened. A summary is easy. Putting down her feelings is not. She can't come up with anything creative. Abandoning the laptop, she decides to go for a run. If Lee is still out there when she leaves, let come what may. She puts on her sweats, running shoes, and reflective windbreaker. After stretching, she ties her hair back in a tight ponytail, secures her key to her wrist with a key-coil, and exits her room running. Her door slams behind her.

He is gone. *Fine. I need to run and don't need the distraction.*

She jogs out of the parking lot, crosses the highway and runs toward the mine, facing oncoming traffic. Feeling the cool night air on her face, she inhales deeply, smelling the nearby flax fields. She catches a whiff of algae and stagnant water as she jogs down the incline toward Liverwood Creek. To her right, behind the motel, is her hollow in complete darkness. She spreads her crow wings but stays with the rhythm of her feet on the pavement, gets the scent of the prairie with every breath. Surrounded by the dark, she marvels at the bright stars so far above her. She watches the mine's plume drift lazily overhead. Her feet know the way and her body knows the rhythm. She doesn't need to think and she won't think of Lee.

After an hour's jog, she returns to her room, takes a quick, cold shower and crawls into bed.

Edna is not in her dream. Lee is there instead. He grows gigantic, grabs her by her hands and lifts her over the brown field of dead thistles. The gigantic Lee makes her feel like a shrimp. He puffs a Cuban cigar and blows smoke in her face. She chokes and looks down to see the seedpod slithering along the ground, searching.

There is no baby's cry when she blinks awake and she feels as empty as that barren field.

On autopilot, she completes her morning rituals and steps through her outside door. She needs some fresh air before starting work.

A business card flutters to the sidewalk. It must have been lodged between the door and jamb. She picks up the card and shivers, but not from the creep factor of someone lurking around her door sometime in the night. In a precise and blocky print on the back of the card is written: *Our meeting means a lot to me. I'd like to see you again — only if you would like to, of course. Lee.* His name is in a flowing script.

Work. She has to work. She hurries through the main entrance of the motel. No one is at the front desk so she is able to get to the utility closet in her quadrant without talking to anyone. Here, she focuses on her cleaning routine and, before she realizes the passing of any time, she is in the restaurant preparing for the noon rush, focusing on her server duties. However, she finds herself expecting, maybe hoping for, Lee to show up. She watches for him each time she hears new customers come in the restaurant entrance.

He won't come back. He is at the mine site.

So what? Why would he want to anyway?

The rest of that day and the next are a blur. She keeps feeling the nearness of his arm to hers. The Old Spice smell that reminds her of her father seems to permeate everything. Only Gus' pies can overpower that smell.

Lee doesn't call nor does she entertain the idea of calling him. She wonders if she should send a short note to the email address on the card but rejects the idea. Reaching out seems too much like chasing him. Too much like something Edna would do. She decides to leave it alone. If he's interested, he'll get back to her. If he doesn't, then all of his talk was just bluster and merely intended for that night's entertainment. She is certain a man like Lee flirts with every waitress in every "port."

Who's interested in damaged goods anyway?

By the end of the second night, there is still no word from him. When her shift ends, she steps outside for another cigarillo. Gus and his damn pies. She lingers over her smoke and watches the vacant picnic tables. She finishes and disposes of the butt. She rubs her arm and then brushes her hair behind her ear before turning to trudge back to her room. Strange little shadows dance in the contours of the sidewalk cement under the orange glow of the halogen parking lot lights. She slows to watch a water beetle scuttle out of her way.

Reaching her room, she has the head rush — as if hanging on the crow's branch by her knees and swinging backwards; she feels the call of her hollow and its peace: stuck between the door and the jamb is another of Lee's business cards. *Hey you. Room 105 — only if you'd like.* She has to steady her hand while fumbling with her key.

She dashes into her room. Slams the door and leans against it. Eyes closed, breathing deeply, she controls her rapid gasps as if she is running hard. Room 105 is across and down the hall and if she goes around her end of the motel, she will gain strength by walking close to the comforting darkness of her hollow.

Resolved, she steps back outside with her breathing and heart rate under complete control. She is only going to see this man to get him out of her system once and for all. He'll see her in her work clothes, smell her with the stink of a whole workday on her. Nothing can possibly come from this, so relax.

She raps on Lee's door three times and steps back a pace.

The door opens instantly, as if he is just leaving or is possibly waiting right on the other side. *Not waiting, don't be ridiculous.* She waves his card at him and says, "Hey, yourself. What are you doing here?"

"Hey, you," Lee replies. Grinning, leaning against his doorjamb, and crossing his arms over his chest, he speaks with the slightest amusement and without hesitation. "Well, I was called away first thing that other morning to an emergency system board failure at the Cory mine in Saskatoon. I'm sorry I couldn't let you know or say goodbye.

"Then I had to stay in Saskatoon until this afternoon. I intended to drive back to Regina. But what do you know? I zoned-out or something and must've driven here on automatic pilot. And now that I'm here, obviously it's too late to drive home but too early to go to sleep. So, I was thinking maybe a nighttime smoke or walk is a possibility, but I don't want to do that alone, so I was wondering . . . "

Her resolve is displaced like earth chewed by a boring-machine. Her control falters and her knees nearly buckle. She says, "Are you going to let just mosquitoes and moths into your room? Or can I come in too?" Her attempted sarcasm fails with the traitorous croak in her voice.

Lee, the bemused tone gone, says, "Of course, how thoughtless of me. Please come in."

With two giant steps, she is inside the room and Lee closes the door. The only indication that the room is occupied is that smell of Old Spice. She turns to face him and stares at his shirt. She knows she wants this man, desperately, but she doesn't know what to do now, trapped in the room. She must flee to her hollow. Her crow wings propel her to the corner of the ceiling.

49

While she watches, she has an immediate sense of how the Treadwells share thoughts. Lee steps forward and wraps her in his arms. Lourdes collapses like a water-bearing formation bursting through the mine's shaft and lets her unrealized need overwhelm her.

They're undressed. Lourdes lies crossways on the bed, Lee is on his knees. She can't hover up here in the corner while Lourdes writhes and burns. With a sudden arch of her back she is in her body and feels a flood of relief like coming into bright light from underground. Then, she feels nothing but Lee on top of her, pressing her, pressure building and building, until, again there is that bright light, and then she feels as if she should sleep and sleep when Lee gasps, moans, and falls limply on her.

She clings to him, pressing him down on her. She is in the hollow under the shady comfort of the trees. Cool, damp air clings to her skin, as tactile as mist rising from water. She thinks, *did this really happen?* But the tenderness inside her is real and confirms the physical reality. Lee's muscular body is against hers. Yes. It really happened.

They find their way under the covers and she lets desire for sleep take her down into the blackness of an unlit mine where the dreams cannot follow.

A short while later there's a yellow glow around the room; the bedside lamp is on and Lee is lying on his side, facing her. His head rests on his biceps, with his forearm bent so his hand can caress her hair. He takes long strands and lets them run through his fingers; his other hand is gently splayed over her tuft of pubic hair.

He opens his eyes when he feels her stir and says, "Hey, you."

"Hi," she replies, and strokes his jaw.

"Thank you," he says, and leans forward, lightly kissing her lips.

It's not quite a recoil, but she stiffens. Yes, this really happened but what does it all mean?

"What's wrong?" he asks, that bass voice of his so soothing.

"Why did you want a fat thing like me?"

He replies immediately, without taking a breath to think. "One, there's no 'did' about it. I still want you. And two, you're not fat."

"That doesn't answer my question." This is not a time to flee. It is a time to take a stand.

Lee pauses for a long time. He continues to let strands of her hair fall from his fingers. She waits and studies the shadows on the ceiling, searching for where her wings brushed the stippling and knocked it to the floor.

He eventually says, "I get what you're trying to ask. But believe me, this isn't meant to be a one night stand. That's the last thing I want with you. From that first moment I saw you at the restaurant, I felt this vulnerability about you. I'm not feeling sorry for you nor am I trying to rescue you. Because I also sense strength and intelligence. You're after something, there's a — desire, or maybe a need, for lack of better terms. As corny as this sounds, I'd love to be a part of that journey with you. Only if you'd like to, of course." He pauses and takes a breath.

She says nothing. There is no stippling knocked off the ceiling, but she does think of the dead female crow, inert and cold on the ground under that birch tree.

Lee continues, "I never felt so low as the other night at the picnic table, when you walked away from me. I've had serious trouble focusing on my work. But then you were here at my door tonight. I may not have shown it, but when I saw you I flew with the birds." He rubs his forehead. "Wow. How's that for a load of corn?"

Her pair of crows from long ago flew into danger every time they left their nest. Eventually, the male with the purple sheen headed out on his own. That's life, isn't it? Her father once told her that bad things happen, yes, but nothing will ever happen if you do nothing.

For the first time since she came to live with the Treadwell's, her heart feels tender. So tender that she feels she can trust this man; feel safe with him.

Taking a chance, she tells him her story.

ᴄᴠᴄᴠᴄᴠ

I lost my virginity to a boy named Barton just before turning fifteen. Before that I was popular because everyone thought Edna, my mother, was so cool. She could play a mean Madonna and other top 40 songs by ear on our electric piano. She drank like the men and she made us kids laugh until the booze eventually got the better of her. A girl named Susan was my best friend at the time. Her family had immigrated from Serbia when she was five and she spoke with a bit of an accent. I was the only one who was nice to her. Puberty struck us both like an air-launched missile. My coordination tanked with the coming of these honking big boobs. I lost all ability at sports and started to gain weight like Dad. By that time, too, Edna's reputation preceded her everywhere and friends started to shun me, no doubt at the urging of their parents.

It was then that I vowed never to be like my mother. I quit drinking, not that I ever drank much, and stopped going to parties. And what is there to do in a small town if you don't drink and can't do sports anymore? I focused on my school work, read as much as I could, and tried to record everything in my journals. I became a total geek.

Puberty was good to Susan though, giving her one of those fashion-model bodies. She was on the cheerleading team and became the star volleyball player. Barton was her male lead. He played hockey in winter and football in summer and curled whenever he could. Of course he excelled at all three. Those two were the match of the century at school while I pined away in Edna's trailer.

Then Barton came knocking on the door one night. Edna was off partying in the Steak House and he said he wanted to check up on me. Check me out more like.

It felt good to have him pay attention to me. To me. He said Susan wasn't putting out like a real woman should. He'd only gone out with her because it was expected at school. But me on the other hand . . . and I couldn't help myself.

We'd read Margaret Laurence's *The Stone Angel* in school, and Hagar, the story's main character, said her first time "hurt and hurt." It didn't for me. It felt really good. Even though it was quick and messy. Barton knew

53

enough to put towels down that first time. I burned them in the leaf barrel afterward.

He kept coming around and I gave in every time. After all, it was me he loved, he said. He only kept going out with Susan to get help with school work. He intended to marry me when we finished school, just so I knew. He wasn't really clever, especially when he was drunk. He said he'd pull out in time, every time, if he wasn't wearing a condom. Long story short, I found myself pregnant. When I told him, he simply said, "We'll have to do something about that. Let me check it out."

Susan showed up the next night. She'd been crying. Her face was streaked with mascara and that exotic, beautiful black Romani hair of hers frizzed out like a frayed rope. She accused me of coming on to Barton. He'd told her to tell me to stay away from him.

She was still my friend. By then my only friend. When she looked at me with her stunned, brown, cow eyes brimming with tears, my guilt felt like those endless heaps of tailings at the mine.

I told her it was one of Edna's men who got me pregnant. I wasn't coming on to Barton. I was only asking him for help. I didn't know where to go or what to do. He must have misunderstood.

Susan actually squealed with relief. She lunged at me, hugged me and burst into tears. As an afterthought, just as she was skipping out our trailer door, she said, "Oh, we'll find some way to help you with you with your little problem, too."

I lost Susan as a friend, but Barton and I were best buddies after that night. He said he'd do all he could to help me muddle through my problem, to keep my chin up. That's when I really started to eat. To smother my guilt. To smother my despair. When Edna asked how I could let myself get so fat, I said, "I'm not fat. I'm pregnant."

She was quiet for a long time, then said, "How the hell could you let that happen? I don't know how you're going to deal with it, but don't come crying to me."

I said it was her fault and called her a slut.

She was on me then, punching, slapping. I went for her throat but I was so gawky and clumsy that I tripped and ended up flat on my stomach.

There was a warm gush between my legs and then a horrible, stabbing pain all across my abdomen and I shit myself.

Edna shook me and yelled was she supposed to clean this mess up? and I threw up on her and she dropped me like a sack and I curled into a ball right on the floor. Weird — I remember there was some comfort in the warmth of the liquid soaking through my pyjamas.

The next thing I remember is waking up in the Yorkton hospital.

Two nurses held me down. The doctor used forceps. My baby came out in a red lump and made only one sound. Kind of like a crow does when it's all by itself . . . makes that single croak. She died right in front of me and they took her away.

Lee holds her tight. She feels smothered and wriggles out of his grasp. Sitting up cross-legged beside him, she is self-conscious about her bare breasts and covers herself with her pillow.

"My god, Lourdes," he says, "you told me all that with such dispassion."

"That was years ago, Lee," she says, annoyed. "I've stored all of that slag deep underground. It's over and done with." *Except during those uncontrolled moments between dream and waking . . . Stop it.*

"Okay," he replies simply, quickly. "Would you like to tell me what happened after?"

"I spent a couple of days in the hospital. I was told I could never get pregnant again.

"Then I had to name my little girl for the Statistics Department and some sort of death benefit because she was alive a moment." I named her Mary. 'Middle name?' They asked. 'Bliss,' I said. Bliss because it was over. I didn't say that part out loud. They wrote her name down and left.

"Then this willow-branch of a woman from Social Services and some fat Mountie with Sergeant stripes on his sleeve, came to see me. They said Edna had reported that I fell. I didn't disagree. They wrote stuff down. I'm sure the cop was fully aware of Edna and her antics. He had to have talked to the Liverwood detachment at some point. Anyway, they left and I never heard from either of them again.

"That death benefit payout was enough to cover a cardboard coffin while Edna went on a week-long bender in Yorkton. The Treadwells picked me up from the hospital, let me spend some time with them, and arranged a plot for Mary at the United Church graveyard.

"Pretty soon after that I ditched Edna, and the Treadwells let me live and work here. Susan got pregnant and couldn't finish high school. She and Barton got married and have three kids at last count. He got a job at the mine.

"And here I am today, in all of my big-boobed glory." She hugs the pillow. She says, "So what happens with us next?"

"I'm not ending this tomorrow when I leave here, if that's what you're asking," Lee says. "What happens next is I'd like to hold you again, if you'd like. And after that, I hope you'll stay with me tonight."

There is a strata of chalk in that vein of granite, Lourdes thinks. She watches Lee while he lies there, rubbing his curled right index finger and thumb together. At that moment he seems such a little boy, wanting approval from his teacher.

She puts the pillow back in place and slides up against him. He turns on his side and holds her tightly again.

This time she does not feel smothered.

After a few minutes silence, he says, "Can I ask you something that might be hurtful?"

Not sure where he intends to go with this, she says to go ahead.

"When I was at the mine site, I read a plaque in honour of Ted Smith. Was that your dad?"

The crow's wingtip brushes her hair — "Silence In Wind" was her first published poem. She smells musky water from the cool shadows of the hollow and finds she can't answer.

Lee says, "I'm so very sorry for your loss."

"Thank you," she replies. "I've mourned and I'm past it. Life goes on, right?"

Lee pauses at that comment, eyebrows furrowed. After a moment he says, "You're so stoic. There's that strength I was talking about. You've had so much loss. . . . " He doesn't finish his thought. After another pause he says, "You're a remarkable girl."

Girl? Not woman? "Is there anything else you'd like to know?"

"Well, now that you ask, what happened to your mom?"

Lourdes is tired. She tells Lee a condensed version of that story. "She burned the trailer down after I left. The fire investigation found that she was cooking something in a pot and left the burner on. Then she moved in with her boyfriend Herb, the guy who ran the secondhand store and pawnshop, until he was sent to the Edmonton pen for drug trafficking. Then she took off with a trucker who hauled product from the mine. I haven't heard from her since. And I don't need to hear from her again. Ever."

Lee's brow furrows again and his thumb and curled index finger rub together. "So why did your folks name you Lourdes?"

"My folks didn't name me. Edna named me. And she named me Lourdes because she's crazy. And she's crazy because she's a hopeless boozer and a drug addict. She's a nymphomaniac too. But she liked the singer Madonna who named one of her kids Lourdes. Mercedes was her alternative but Dad said I wasn't going to be named after a car. And I have no interest in changing my name. It's mine. So don't ask.

"How about we talk about you for a while now," she says.

"If you like," Lee replies. "It's pretty boring. I grew up in working class, east-end Regina, attended the same high school for all four years, was in the computer club, chess club, drama club's technical crew, and on the wrestling team. I was just an average, all round kind of guy," he says. "I just fit in and I wasn't bullied and I didn't bully anyone. We all seemed to get along at my school."

He repeats his university story and that he's only ever worked at Bland. A few years back his parents moved to Arizona permanently and he bought their house.

Then the conversation turns and they chat on about Liverwood, and Regina versus Saskatoon and other trivial matters until Lee suggests they turn out the light. He does not ask if she intends to stay.

In the darkness, while Lee breathes deeply and rhythmically, the Human League's song "Fascination" runs over and over in her mind. Yes, new connections are made and the conversation did indeed turn a number of times, well past sundown. But this is nice. A nice diversion. Perhaps momentary, perhaps not. Lee rolls over and she snuggles into his back, letting sleep overtake her.

He invades her dreams again. Just like in her dream the night she met him, he is gigantic and smokes that Cuban cigar. Lourdes sits cross-legged, naked from the waist down, in the brown, poisoned field of thorny-thistles. The seedpod lies nearby, encrusted with dried blood and other matter she can't identify. Lee picks her up in one hand. She sits on his palm facing him; he looms over her and blows smoke in her face. She doesn't understand the specific words of his questioning but the tone is intense and combative. It grows in intensity and hostility as she keeps saying that she doesn't know the answer or doesn't understand the question.

She startles awake with a gasp and thinks of Mary, even though the seedpod had lain dormant in the dream. She quickly recovers her composure because Lee is on his side, wide awake, watching her.

"Hey you," he says. "Are you okay?"

She smiles at him. "Of course." From constant practice controlling her breathing while she runs, her voice is steady.

Lee says, "I should apologize for all this sneaking around with cards in doorjambs. But I'm not sure about the owner's policy on workers dating customers. I should get your cell phone number."

"I don't have a cell," she says, happy he didn't ask her how she slept or anything about her dreams. "I've never needed one here at the motel."

"We should get you one."

"Thanks, but I'm good. Besides, I'm sure it's okay for you to call me either in the motel or restaurant. The Treadwells won't mind."

"That's good to know," Lee says, "because I'd like nothing more than to be seen with you. To hold your hand in public. Kiss you goodbye in the restaurant."

She puts her fingers on his lips, slides toward him, and feels his erection against her thigh. Although she flew high last night, this time she remains rooted to herself and savours the moment. This time, there is no flight to the ceiling, no escape to the hollow.

After a quick breakfast of toast and coffee right in the restaurant, Lourdes walks Lee to the parking lot. Standing by his grey Buick Lucerne they kiss goodbye.

When she steps back into the motel lobby, Helena is waiting for her by the counter, arms crossed, hands cupping biceps. Helena's grin lights up her whole face.

"What?" Lourdes says. She knows it's a feeble attempt at nonchalance. She also knows her face is red.

"You are a brat," Helena says. "They named that *Bratz* doll after you. You are Ell, the Fire-Haired-She-Devil model — taking advantage of that man like that."

"I just kissed him goodbye."

"After doing what else? You are glowing today. I knew it would happen because I checked Mr. Good-Looking in that other day and saw the way he talked to you."

"Well, he wants to build a shrine to me in the rest area. How would you like to see a naked statue of this body right by the highway? You'd lose all of your customers."

Helena says, "You are a voluptuous catch. Do I say that right? Voluptuous? Looking just like that Julianne Moore from the movies."

"I *do not* look like Julianne Moore."

"Okay, you might think you don't look like actress. But you are wrong. You are also glowing. You can not hide glowing from me. You can not hide passion from me either."

And with this, Lourdes becomes "the Lee Markham barometer" for Helena, the cronies, and Gus. They all say they can tell if Lee is in town by Lourdes' glow or, if he has been away for a while, her glower. They never hesitate to take a loud barometric reading, either. At least once a day — thank you very much, Mrs. Treadwell.

But when Lee is absent and Lourdes is left alone to write, she finds she is blocked. She sits with her laptop and stares at a white featureless wall that looks like the back of a white shirt.

~~~~

How easily she's fallen into a routine with Lee. She decided not to enrol at the U of S this year and it's now mid-September, just two months after meeting him, and she continues to be blocked by that featureless whiteness. Not only has he continued to invade her dreams, he is now encroaching on her living space.

Helena, presumably preferring her to be glowing, may not be a co-conspirator but she is certainly complicit.

Lourdes finishes her kitchen cleanup and goes to stand with Lee and Helena by the cash register counter. "What's going on here, you two?"

Lee says, "Maybe you should tell her, Mrs. Treadwell."

Stepping from foot to foot, Helena says, "We don't charge Our Boy here for a room anymore. You stay together so why make him pay?"

"I said you have to make the decision about me staying in your room," Lee says. "It's up to you, Lourdes."

She doesn't quite know how to take this. It is the first time she's ever been annoyed with Helena. The Treadwells took her in. Gave her a job. At one point they even said she didn't need to clean rooms anymore. But that was always part of the agreement to cover her board. So when they tried to pay her for room cleaning, she wrote *no thank you* across the cheque and put it in their mailbox. She was terrified that they might take offence but they only asked, over coffee the next day, if she was sure. They said she was the best worker they'd ever hired and they were only concerned that they might have offended her.

Now this. Helena is clearly excited, the way she grins and dances from foot to foot. And there's Lee, rubbing his thumb against his curled index finger. She ignores the weight of earth pressing down on her. *Why didn't Helena talk to me first? Or at least talk about this decision with me present?* She doesn't answer.

Helena stops shuffling.

Lee says, "The company still pays twenty-five bucks if an employee stays with a relative or friend."

"Oh, well, in that case," Lourdes replies. To Helena she says, "And that's a very kind offer. Very kind. Thank you. I think it's workable."

Helena beams. Lee grins, his thumb at rest. Lourdes tells herself that they made this decision with her best interests in mind.

A week later, she thinks, *Best interests, seriously?* when a treadmill is delivered to her room. Helena tells her that Lee said it would be safer for her than running on the highway. "Really, I can not argue with Our Boy's thinking."

Lourdes needs time alone in her hollow.

It's cool in the evening shade and dampness of the late September day. Studying the thistles' vibrant green leaves and stalks, not yet touched by frost, she sees that the flowers have gone to seed, some pods are burst dull white, some still closed.

Lee is suddenly beside her. "Hey you."

She jumps, startled. Annoyed. How has he found her hollow?

"Sorry," he says. "I didn't mean to scare you."

"No worries. What are you doing down here?"

"Helena pointed me in the right direction." He investigates the leaves on a willow tree, touching them. "I'll bet kids would love to play down here."

He continues to explore, running his hand down the trunk of the birch tree where the purple-sheen crow once lingered. He pokes the toe of his shoe in the mud and then tenderly lifts a seedpod. Abruptly letting the pod drop out of his hand as if stung, he says, "This would be a great place to make love. Out in the open air."

"Oh, it would, would it?" Lourdes says. "Out in the open, freezing air? Butts exposed to the cold and mosquitoes? We'd have to flip a coin to see whose bare ass gets rubbed against the table top."

She keeps her tone light but thinks, *this is* my *place. Maybe, if I invited you . . .*

"I guess you're right," Lee says. "Your room is far more comfortable for that sort of thing."

She says with a neutral tone, "And for running, it seems. Thanks for the treadmill. But I prefer to run outside."

"I know," Lee replies, using his soothing radio voice. "But winter's coming and I expect you don't run much when it's cold. Besides, I worry about you running alone on the highway."

He is right about the cold. She believes she should be touched by his concern. After a moment's thought, she lets it go and says, "How much do I owe you?"

"Nothing, *monetary*. It's my gift to you. But if you want to pay me back, I'm sure we can come to some sort of exchange of goods and services. GST-free that way." He wiggles his eyebrows.

The male crow with the purple sheen skips along a branch and watches Lourdes let it all go and lead Lee by the hand out of the hollow.

ᓚᓄᓇᓄ

She uses the treadmill because Lee wants her to. It's okay, and winter is cold with lots of snow anyway.

Lourdes lets the easy routine of visits continue. Christmas comes and goes. It's the new year and he spends more and more weekends in Liverwood, arriving sometime Friday night and leaving the following Monday.

They are comfortable with each other, right? This is the way it works. When two people seem to get along so well?

And they can talk for hours and hours. Their conversations range from the antics of Liverwood denizens to government to SCADA — an acronym for Supervisory Control and Data Acquisition; Lee goes on and on about these SCADA programs. They are used in many industries and something he deals with on a daily basis. He goes on hour-long monologues on the ingenuity of some of the programs' coding, programming languages, and the ever-present cyber-threats to today's infrastructures — it's all meaningless to her.

But the talks are always cordial and casual, she thinks, *because we're* simpatico, *right?*

And the university conversation starts innocuously enough.

One night, as they're lying in bed together, Lee asks, "Have you ever thought about the future?"

"You know I've been thinking about the U of S," Lourdes says. "Then I'll see where that leads."

"Does it have to be the U of S?"

"I picked it because it's closest to Liverwood. I can travel by bus. In case things don't work out, my backup plan is to come back here."

"So that campus is not definite?"

"I didn't register last year — because we met. And I haven't decided about this year yet. I received my registration acceptance just last week."

Lee takes a deep breath. "I want to give you more stability in your life. My first thought was moving here but I need to be headquartered near Bland's office. So, if you'd like, you could move in with me in Regina, go to the U of R, like I did, and I can pay for your university?" Lips tight, his thumb and forefinger rub together; the sound is like a mouse trying to scratch its way out of a live trap.

Lourdes' heart surges in her chest. This is an offer like Treadwells' when they told her she could stay at the motel. She hasn't been to the hollow since the day Lee found her there just after the treadmill was delivered. She remembers previous winters, her parka crinkling in the cold while she made her way through snowdrifts to the hollow. With the leaves on all the trees gone, there would be more sunlight. More light to reveal the frozen and blackened thistle leaves and stocks showing through low spots in the snow that couldn't quite pile up in the windbreak of the trees.

"That's a kind offer," she says. "As kind as the Treadwells'. But you hardly know me. We've only been together a couple of months."

Lee cocks his head. "It's been more than eight months, Lourdes."

Eight months already? How routine makes the time pass unnoticed . . .

Lee continues, "And that's a long enough time for me to know that I want to spend the rest of my life with you. You're one of the most mature people I've ever met. You don't end your sentences with that questioning inflection, like most girls seem to do these days."

Girl? Still?

Lee says, "You're intelligent and passionate. You have a wonderful sense of humour. And there's that strange mystery about you. That sense of longing, of things yet to be resolved. I'd love to take that journey of discovery with you, wherever it leads." He pauses, his thumb constantly active, and then says, "So are you absolutely determined to pursue this Lit Degree thing?"

It's mid-March, Lourdes thinks. *Where's the gust of wet spring wind that's supposed to rattle the windows with a loaded question like that?* She suspects where this turn of conversation will lead and returns from the snow of her hollow. This talk has to be rooted in the reality of the here and now.

"For now. It's something I'd like to try."

Lee shunts sideways. "There's no money in that line of work, you know."

"I know. But I'm going to try it. And, like I just said, I'll see where it leads."

Lee takes another deep breath. "You know the Treadwells never stop talking about how smart you are and how hard you work. Even I can see that. You graduated high school with high honours. I can say from experience that a degree in CS or Engineering would be a breeze for you. And with either of those degrees you could work anywhere you wanted."

"You mean work anywhere in mining, like you," she says with an edge in her voice. Trapped in that garage-sized cage, smothered under countless tons and tons of earth, she clings to her father when he picks her up, wrapping her in his thick arms. Face pressed into his chest, she smells his sweat. Her father does not cajole or tease or get angry about her fear. Instead, he tells her it's okay. They'll go right back up. Right back up to stand under the plume that hangs in the air like a question mark, that constant reminder of how the place controls, and sometimes destroys, lives.

She says, "I'm not interested in mining, the machines that run in the mines, the computers that run the machines, or the computerized accounting systems that pay for all of it and make gobs of profit for the mine owners, or the government in our case. The mine's tendrils are thick and invasive. Once they're in you, it's like trying to get rid of thistles. Even if you poison them to brown crumbling powder there's still living roots that eventually grow to claw at you."

She involuntarily scratches at her legs where, in her dreams, the gnarled stocks and thorns tear at her bare flesh.

"That's very metaphorical," Lee says, "if that's the right word. But does that kind of stuff actually pay bills? Besides you don't have to work *in* a mine."

"I'm not going to be an office drone like Barton's brother Buck either. Especially in some office tower."

"It's not all about mining," Lee says, his voice taking on an edge. "There's plenty of support industries. There's research. Just think, you could become an engineer and maybe find ways to make things safer for all miners. Or would you rather stay here and be a waitress and cleaner all your life? And continue to literally clean up other people's crap?"

She practises her breathing and metabolism control. She will not react like an Edna-banshee. There will be no plates smashing into cupboards here, either.

And she intends to stay here — she's fine, thank you very much; she has a plan; she does not need to escape to her hollow anymore. She calmly and quietly says, "I don't intend to, *literally*, clean up other people's crap forever. What I intend to do is try the U of S and see what happens."

"Okay," Lee says, his voice back to that passive, and now very annoying, tone of his. "Clearly I've upset you with my thoughts on your education. And for that, I'm sorry. I only wanted to point out that with your intelligence and drive, you could do anything, absolutely anything, you want. I'll be happy to help you with that, if you'd like. But it's late." He rolls over and turns out the light.

They lie on opposite sides of the bed, still slightly touching in the narrow width of the double. Lourdes runs their conversation over in her mind. She notes Lee did not repeat his offer for her to move in with him. He obviously won't do so until she complies with his choice of education. Her breathing and heart rate are under control.

Close to sleep, she wonders what ever happened to her crow with the purple sheen.

In her dream, Lee has shrunk to normal proportions. He has been shrinking a little every dream since he first invaded them. He still smokes the Cuban cigar, which is more toxic than ever. The smell reminds her of that painful and stinking half-hour on the trailer floor waiting for the ambulance so long ago. In this dream, Lee digs frantically with a short spade in the brown field of dead thistles. Going in circles, he shovels dirt, stalks, and thorns over his shoulder. Lourdes watches, unable to move, thorns scratching her legs, holding her in place. Lee tosses the seedpod toward her with a shovel full of dirt. The seedpod plops at her feet and lies dormant until she pokes at it with her bare toes. It lifts itself and lunges.

Heart pounding, she awakes with a gasp and sits up straight. She's covered in sweat. Mary is in her lap, and she throws the covers back revealing emptiness. She claws at her hair where the crow's wing brushed it until she regains control of herself.

Lee is in the bathroom getting ready for work. She is thankful he didn't see her jump out of sleep and can't ask her any stupid questions about her dreams. His absence gives her a moment to think. Why did she stay at the trailer so long after she lost Mary? Why was she unable to act? Dawdling like that. What a stupid thing to do. Will she be able to take charge when the time comes? Or will she simply submit to Lee's wishes? Is it fear of failure?

She thinks about how much trouble she has writing lately. She has trouble finding the right words for the most simple description. How is she supposed to complete university-level work then? The longer she is with Lee, the more that blank whiteness fills her mind. It's particularly bad when his arrival is pending. It takes her longer and longer to get back into the swing of writing after he leaves. But then he is due back and the cycle starts over again and, of course, it's impossible to write with him around. Last year she didn't register at U of S because she was afraid of change. This time, though, will she have the will to act?

Is there something more, something deeper, to Lee's "things yet to be resolved" comment?

No! There isn't. All those tailings are buried, including, *literally*, that of Mary.

Lee comes out of the bathroom wearing crisp, fresh work clothes. He smells of shampoo and Old Spice. "Hey you," he says, almost in passing.

Suddenly, concern furrows his eyebrows and he sweeps toward her, sitting right beside her on the bed. "Are you okay? I love your messy morning-hair but it looks absolutely dishevelled today. Did you not sleep well? Are you sick?"

He reaches over and puts one hand on her shoulder, the other on her cheek. "Are you ever hot," he says. "You're, you're not well?"

"I just woke up," she says. "It's just night sweats." She turns toward him and hugs him hard. He returns her embrace. If he is still upset about last night's university conversation he doesn't show it.

Normally she closes her eyes when she hugs him but this time she keeps her eyes open. The light shining from the bedside lamp is nothing like the dappled sunshine in her hollow.

∽∾∾∽

Lourdes is in the brown field of dead thistles. The writhing thorns hold her in place while she watches a shrimp-sized Lee erect a towering white wall of canvas between her and her hollow. Smoke billows from Lee's cigar and he puffs with satisfaction over his work and wipes his forehead with his sleeve. The smoke blows with force toward the mine's plume and joins it. The plume shifts and the sun shines on the white wall. The glare blinds her and she squeezes her eyes shut, turning her head away. Slowly opening her eyes to a squint, she begins to turn her head toward the wall and spots a slithery movement in the thorns at her feet. The seedpod.

Opening her eyes wide, Lourdes thinks of Mary. She brushes her hair with her hand and focuses on the discomfort in her lower abdomen. A whole night after drinking two eight-ounce glasses of water after her run just before bed, she really has to urinate. She sits up and throws the covers back. Shunting to sit on the side of the bed, she drops her pyjama bottoms on the floor and dashes quickly to the bathroom.

After a long, pressure-relieving pee, she reaches her arms straight up in a soothing stretch and arches her back, cracking it. Two buttons across her breasts pop open. Remaining seated, she takes off the top and tosses it through the open bathroom door. She holds her belly in both hands, grabbing only about two inches, and flops it up and down. She was 171 pounds the last time she weighed herself, and her belly flab continues to shrink. She manages a three to five kilometer jog six days a week now, although only on the treadmill. She misses running on the highway; miners driving to or from work would always honk and wave and she would always wave back even though she didn't know them. Some probably knew her father and their story.

Today will be a day off from running and she slides her hands up to her breasts, gently lifts them, and watches the skin wrinkle around her cleavage. She thinks of Lee and slides her fingers down to the end of her reddish nipples and gently rolls them between her fingertips. The warm pee relief is replaced by a delicious heat.

Enough of this nonsense, he'll be here soon enough.

She wants to try to get some new writing done before he arrives. She immediately gets up and steps into the shower and lets the cold spray wash away the sweat still clinging to her skin. She then turns the water off.

Scrubbing herself with a bath sponge and back-brush, it takes ten minutes to completely lather her hair and body. She turns the water back on and lets its coolness flow soothingly over her for another ten minutes. She hates wasting water like this but today is not a day to rush. She'll get to her laptop soon enough.

She dries herself, puts on her fluffy white housecoat that hangs to her ankles and goes to the refrigerator for a bottle of Boost. Chocolate flavour this morning. She pads across the shag carpet and opens the gold and green drapes. Blinking against the bright sunshine, she lets her eyes adjust. Sunlight glares from the field of ripening purple flax. For a moment, she watches the plume drift lazily across the sky. Sitting at her round wood laminate table she flips open her laptop, waking the machine up, and opens her dream journal file. Even though she's blocked, she still writes in the journal every day as a warm-up exercise. This morning she will describe the Lee dream with the white wall.

She fondles her manila file folder marked "University" but doesn't open it. Lee has not broached the subject of her choice of faculties since the one time they talked about it. Inside the folder is the acceptance letter from the U of S. She no longer carries the letter in her notepad. She has until July 15 to accept and register, which can be done online. A dorm room is also available if registration is completed and a credit card deposit is made before the deadline date, now only five days away. It would take a few clicks and she'd be registered. How hard can this be?

Very hard, it seems, but now is not the time to get mired in that quandary again. There's work to do. She finishes her description of yet another *Threading Through Thorn-Fields* dream, and saves and closes the journal. She opens a new word file and poises her fingertips on the keyboard.

And it happens again: her mind is like that blank whiteness. *Well, I'm not just sitting and wasting precious time.* She turns toward the window and stares intently at the plume. She thinks of the mine's four-rotor boring machines deep under the earth, soil hoisted to the mill where her father worked with the centrifuges, separating various ores from tailings. She turns back to the laptop, types:

The mines of men rend
and tear Gaia's pearl
ripping, shredding, ripping,
well, shit

She slouches back in her chair, arms tightly crossed on her breasts. She lunges forward, seizes her bottle of Boost, and chugs the contents. Normally she would savour the drink, make it last for at least part of her writing time. She clunks the bottle on the tabletop and then types — *bottle's clunk on table so much like my words.*

She leans back again. Stretching her legs straight out, she crosses her feet at the ankles and stares up at the white stippled ceiling. Turning her head back to the window, she again stares out at the plume. How exactly did her father manage from day to day, first so deep under the earth and then with the grinding tedium in the mill? Her one and only descent terrified her so much they never talked about it again. And then he died when she was so damn young . . .

She abruptly reaches for the laptop and types:

I barely knew my father. He was a big man. "Fat Like Me." The title of my nonfiction story starring daughter, co-starring father. He worked at Liverwood Potash mine until he died. Before he died, he worked at the Liverwood Potash Mine . . .

She has heard so many snippets of conversation over the years about her father's accident and death, her adult mind has galvanized the story. She knows the story by rote and can tell it — like Lee said when she told him — with *such dispassion.*

Weighing in at over 250 pounds, well over six feet tall, the father dwarfs the mother and makes the daughter feel like a shrimp. He is not overweight, just big, and the man has stamina. The daughter is a wisp of a child — not gaining her father's kind of weight until puberty — and her father calls her "Tiny Lady Lourdes." He holds her up over his head with one hand. She keeps herself straight, arms and legs spread like a ballet dancer, and he flies her until her body folds over and they both tumble to the ground, laughing.

But this happens so rarely. Either at the mine working overtime or playing poker with his buddies, often all weekend, he otherwise lies in bed. It seems to the daughter that he is an occasional visitor with sleeping privileges instead of a member of the family. In the beginning of the time of the father's long absences, the mother would quietly get drunk at home. Eventually, she started to drop the daughter off at the eccentric neighbours and hang out at the Liverwood Steak House, sometimes until late; sometimes the daughter saw more of the neighbours than of her mother and father.

The little daughter scribbles notes and draws pencil crayon pictures for her father, leaving them under his pillow. She hopes he will at least communicate with her that way. But he never does. This makes her sad, and her mother scolds, "Don't mope like a Sad-Sadie." So she begins to smother her feelings so she won't, heaven forbid, mope.

It's not until after Mary Bliss is gone that she fully understands why the three of them lived in a drafty and decaying trailer in a mobile home park. The daughter understands why the father, after a weekend of playing poker, needed to stay in the bedroom with the shades drawn. Why they had to eat peanut butter sandwiches every day until next payday. These parents couldn't help themselves, let alone each other. The daughter pines over Mary Bliss in her bedroom. She floats in the corner of the room watching herself eat large bags of chips and jumbo chocolate bars, listening to her father's same old Human League and Flock of Seagulls albums over and over on the MP3 player.

If only she was a real writer, she could write poems that would make her father happy and bring him up from the metaphorical mineshaft so he wouldn't have to play poker. Lourdes types:

I see you sink and I throw you lines you choose not to see.

Her father said that new contracts with Asia were a godsend. They meant unlimited overtime. Although exhausted from playing cards and working too many hours to begin with, he took as many shifts as he could. The intense production schedule sent down from the executives at head office, as dictated by the Ministry of Mining's directives, permitted maximum work-hour rules to be conveniently overlooked.

And then, a freak accident. The accident wasn't the freakish part—constantly rolling conveyors in the vicinity of workers' arms and legs were, according to Long-shanks, vindictive goblins waiting to pounce on the fatigued toilers of the mine. It was the way he fell. His arm was broken at the wrist and elbow, the shoulder dislocated. Witnesses said they saw him take off his hardhat to wipe his forehead. Then they saw him sway, stumble, and fall forward over the safety rail of a centrifuge platform.

He tried to break his fall and his hand landed flat on a tailings conveyor, whipping him forward. He cracked his forehead on one of the rollers. Had his head hit anywhere else or at any other angle, he would have had a severe concussion at worst. But with that precise angle of fall, at that particular speed, on that particular edge of the roller, his skull cracked like a melon from the bridge of the nose to the base of the skull. He was pronounced dead on arrival at the Yorkton General Hospital.

The mine's First Responders had him secured and stabilized within minutes of the accident. A credit to the miners' fellowship and safety and emergency procedures. But the Liverwood Hospital's emergency department had closed months earlier due to lack of funding and a reduction of medical staff in rural areas. It took more than a hour for an ambulance to respond and get him to the nearest open hospital.

Edna wept and drank and passed out, leaving Lourdes to mourn alone with a vague understanding that Daddy will never come home again. The Treadwells looked after funeral arrangements and the installation of the survivor payments, both at company expense. They invited Lourdes to stay with them for a while.

It was when she was with the Treadwells that she found her hollow while wandering behind the hotel. The hollow was a comfort. Her crow with the purple sheen was there to share their respective losses. Surely her father's death was her fault. If only she had tried harder and written better, her father wouldn't have had to work all that overtime.

When she returned home, she found Edna passed out in bed. She made up her mind. She couldn't help her father but maybe she could help her mother. She crawled into bed with Edna. It was now up to her to look after Edna. This was no time to grieve. She should not to be allowed such privileges.

If only she had not been scared in the service elevator. Her father had said, while she snuggled into his barrel chest, "It's a happy accident we named you Lourdes. You'll do what you need to do, to make yourself all better once we're back in the sunlight." Fear was misbehaving. If she hadn't been afraid, she and her father may have been able to talk things through. But that descent in the elevator was like plunging into a bottomless ocean.

Lourdes, frenzied now, types, retypes, and retypes. If only her words could at least bring him out of his dark, undersea bedroom. Maybe put some colour into that big-cheeked zombie face. Get rid of the circles under his eyes . . . She types until the 11:15 AM alarm turns on CBC One. She reads what she has written:

Heavy water
  rolls in
    dousing you in your dim room

where pale light frames drawn shade
you're shackled in an armoured diving suit

I see you sink, throw
lines you choose not to see
me frantic on shore, I can't wade in
breach the deep pitch enveloping you.

Her words bring a dangerous surge of emotion. She couldn't save her father after all. And now, not even on the page. The crow's wingtip brushes her hair and she closes her eyes. She breathes out, her whole body loose, her arms hanging at her sides. She then closes her laptop, putting it back to sleep. With the click of the lid, it is time to focus on motel work. She will not be one of those surly servers who lets personal life affect customer service. She is above this.

She is done with these old feelings. They are silt and clay, crushed, and dumped in the tailings heaps. Discarded, they surface only in emotional moments when she is not on guard.

Besides, Lee might already be in town and surprise her by showing up unannounced at lunchtime. He does this on occasion and she won't let him catch her in a soppy mood.

At 11:30 Lourdes changes into her server uniform, turns off CBC One, and makes her way to the lobby of the motel with a bounce in her step.

"Mornin', Lass," Mr. Treadwell says from behind the check-in counter. "I need to pester you a moment."

"Good morning!" She veers away from the restaurant entrance toward him. She notices that the royal-blue carpet in the lobby is wearing thin, reminding her a bit too much of the old trailer. A picture of a young Queen Elizabeth, from the 70s maybe and faded with age, hangs askew in its wooden, gold-painted frame behind the counter. The counter itself is dark oak laminate, 80s style.

It also shows signs of wear from decades of customers rubbing against it.

"What's up, Mr. Treadwell?" she says, leaning against a worn spot. She wonders how many others have rubbed their bodies here.

"Got a phone message for you from Markham." Long-shanks always addresses men formally by their last name — Gus is "Marin," as in Cheech Marin, the facial resemblance between Gus and the actor quite remarkable. "I couldn't get through to your room."

"Sorry." She had unplugged her phone from the wall outlet the night before. "I was working on the computer."

"Ah, I hope you got a bit accomplished, then."

"Some."

"Jolly good. Anyway — " he takes a folded sheet of Motel 6 notepad paper from his shirt pocket and consults it. "Markham says he had to fly to Edmonton to retrieve a system board. Then he's off to the Cumberland House Dam to install it. It'd take too long to courier the lot and they wanted to make sure it was received and installed in short order. They actually chartered him a small plane to Edmonton and then back to P.A. He has to drive the rest of the way here. He says he won't be about 'til tomorrow night at the earliest."

"Thank you, Mr. Treadwell," Lourdes says, thinking she just might do some more writing.

Long-shanks stands silent, folding and unfolding the notepaper.

"What is it?" she asks.

"Ach, I'd hoped you be off. I didn't write down the last part of his message in hopes I'd forget, but . . . " he trails off.

"But what?" Lourdes says. "Is he still on about that cell phone?"

"Quite right, Lass. That's it. I told him you'd get one when you're actually in need of one." Long-shanks nods, crumples the paper and tosses it into the dented grey wastepaper basket under the Queen's picture.

"Three points, Mr. Treadwell."

"I have to ask, Lass," Long-shanks says. "What's troublin' you?"

"You know I've applied to the U of S, right?"

"O' course. I'm wonderin' why you're still hanging about and why you weren't gone at eighteen. It'd break Helena's heart if you left, but offspring gotta move on sometime."

The word "offspring" tugs at Lourdes' heart. She feels warm and comfortable with this man. "I have been accepted again."

"Truly? Wonderful. When do you leave?"

"The truth is, I haven't registered yet."

"Why not?"

"I'm just not sure about the move. And then there's my work here. How would you make out?"

"You're a good worker and all," Long-shanks says with a grin on his face. "We've said so, many times. But I hate to break this sort o' thing to you," he leans forward, gangly torso almost folding in half at the waist. He rests his elbows on the counter, winks, and whispers, "You *can* be replaced."

She is not stung by the comment. In fact, she senses how encouraging Long-shanks means to be. She says, "Yeah, replaced by three other women. And I don't mean just to match my weight."

Long-shanks laughs out loud. "Now you stop that fat natter, woman." He shakes his bony finger at her. "It's just not true. Never was. But what I am saying is, if you're ready to move on, you just go ahead and move on. We'll manage jolly well.

"Besides, if you left," again he whispers, "it might be the final straw and I can finally convince the Old Bird to pack it in. Helena's back is getting worse. I'm getting tired of these long days, seven days a week, and these winters." He shakes a fist at the ceiling. "We're both in our sixties. Might be high time for a breather in Arizona or Florida. We haven't had a vacation since I quit the mine to run this place. And with all that oil development moving this way, now's the time to sell. We're too old to add a bar and rent rooms by the hour. The new owners can compete with the Steak House bar and motel for that sort o' market.

"Lord knows she's always so whacked-out at the end of a day as it is."

Long-shanks stands up straight. Crossing his long arms across his chest, fingers reaching around to the back of his biceps, he says a little too loudly, "You should think about that *celly*, just so's Markham doesn't keep pestering me and the Missus. Mornin', Helena."

Lourdes turns to see Mrs. Treadwell struggling to get the room-cleaning cart through the fire door of the far corridor.

"See what I mean?" Long-shanks whispers, not taking his eyes off his wife.

Helena limps slightly while she pushes the cart across the lobby. There are bags under her eyes and her cheeks sag. But when she sees Lourdes, a grin spreads across her face.

"Helena!" Lourdes scolds, exasperated. "Didn't I ask you to call me for housekeeping if someone doesn't come in?"

"How could I call you, with your telephone off?" Helena says. "Our poor Boy's frantic when he can not reach Ell the Fire-Haired *Bratz*."

Lourdes closes her mouth, lips tight. *Don't hurt her feelings, idiot.*

"Aha, you see. Your face tells you feel bad. You let him buy you cellular soon so Our Boy's not frantic. It's cheaper on his plan for two phones and you pay nothing."

"Maybe I should do that, Helena."

"Good for you then. Now, you call on his cellular. Tell him you have his message and you are waiting."

"As soon as I can. But I better get to work before management fires me." With a fake laugh, she turns to leave. She does not want to call Lee.

She hears Helena say, "See. Ell. She-Devil. I keep telling you, Old Coot, that *Bratz* tortures the Boy."

"Only in your mind, woman. Only in your mind, " Long-shanks replies.

Lourdes enjoys their lighthearted banter. But light-hearted or not, the cell nagging takes a bite out of her day. It does not, of course, negatively affect the way she performs her server duties. It actually improves her performance because she focuses on perfection. Any feelings or thoughts not related to serving her customers just hone her focus.

Yet always focusing on duty means it's harder to obtain and maintain a creative edge. During slow moments, as the afternoon wears on, Lourdes sits in the kitchen with her spiral notepad. The pad's pages continue to remain blank; so much whiteness. But she is pleased with her accomplishments this morning. It's been too long.

When her shift ends at 8:00, she asks Gus to make her a Greek salad with a chicken breast. Long-shanks himself takes over as server until closing time. The only other customers in the restaurant are the cronies. Lots of miners eat here but head elsewhere to drink, if they are so inclined. Lourdes eats beside the cronies and attempts to be interested in the televised CFL game. Anything to ignore the spiral notepad hanging heavy in her pocket like a decade's worth of mine tailings.

On her way out, after returning her dish to the kitchen, she hears, "I sure hope that Markham fellow gets back here soon."

"Yup," another of the cronies says, "Too much glowering and not enough glowing around here."

The cronies all guffaw and agree.

"Listen, you lot," Long-shanks says. "As long as your coffee cup's filled and you got your pie to gobble, keep your comments to yourselves. No more *barometric readings* for the likes o' you."

Another says to Long-shanks, "You got a point there, Treadwell, but us geezers prefer the young woman glowing. Makes us feel so much younger."

The cronies again guffaw and agree.

Young *woman*, Lourdes thinks. She tugs at her hair while she laughs along with them.

Grabbing the coffee pot, Long-shanks says, "Knock it off, you old buggers. Quit nagging my best serving lass. I don't want her packing it in 'coz o' you. If she does go, I'll have you whole lot working back here to make up for the labour shortage."

Turning his back on them, coffee pot still in hand, he catches her eye, nods once, and mouths the words, "Do what you need to do."

Giving him a finger wave, she remembers climbing off her father and stepping out of the service building into the sunshine. "You'll do what you need to do to make yourself all better once we're back in the sunlight." Walking toward the car, his big hand enveloping hers, she did make herself better, even though she was right at the source of the mine's plume.

The guffawing grows robust at Long-shanks' expense, four against one, but he holds his own. Stepping into the motel lobby, Lourdes does not hear what else is said. She makes her way outside for a cigarillo and glances only once toward the picnic tables in the rest area.

Back in her room, after only a few minutes of editing her morning's work, she finds her mind drifting. Did she really dream about Lee building a wall or did she make it up some place between sleep and waking? She reaches over and opens the University folder. She rereads her acceptance letter. The laptop is running. The Motel 6's wireless service — the only update to the motel since she started living here — is always available. Registration is a few clicks away. She book-marked the registration page in her web browser long ago. She has more than enough money now, after saving her server wages another year. Just click here and here.

She closes her laptop lid and stands up. Whatever self-doubt she has about her plans has been amplified by Lee's suggestions. Edna is a booze and drug addict. Her father had a gambling addiction. The word "enabler," never spoken, was just under the surface of day-to-day life like the stumpy root of a pulled thistle; always a little chunk left behind to grow again.

Needing a distraction, Lourdes strips off her clothes, including bra and panties, and gets into her sweatsuit, all the baggier now as she continues to lose weight. After tying her runners, she unfolds the treadmill and decides to reread one of her favourite novels, *The Stone Angel*, while she jogs at a ten-degree incline. She loves the novel and admires Hagar's determination and strength of conviction, regardless of the tragic consequences of this part of the character's nature.

She will call Lee when she is done with the treadmill.

Five minutes into her run, she hears a knock. At first, she thinks she's hearing things. But a second, firmer knock follows, definitely on her door.

Thinking immediately of Lee, the heat between her legs overwhelms her self-control. But she is cautious. She peers out the window and inhales sharply.

Susan. Of all people. After all this time.

Susan hesitates an arm's length from the door, her hands in her pockets, then leans forward and knocks a third time.

This is as unexpected as Edna's surprise visit when she wanted money. But there is no bile burning in Lourdes's throat — she is only curious, wondering exactly what her ex-friend might want.

She adjusts her sweat-suit top needlessly, swings the door open, and says more harshly than she intends, "Susan? What are you doing here?"

"Lourdes!" Susan says with a girlish squeal. She vaults forward, wraps her arms around her waist and squeezes, at the same time planting a slobbery kiss on Lourdes' left cheek. The reek of booze hovers like a late night summer mist on the creek by the hollow.

While Susan clings and snuggles, Lourdes slowly and lightly returns the hug. Susan doesn't let go until Lourdes manoeuvres her arms between them and gently pushes her away.

Susan giggles and says, "Look at you." Her eyelids hang heavy from too much booze. She speaks with a drunken slur. "I can feel how much weight you lost."

You haven't seen me since high school. How would you have any idea?

"Let me look at you, skinny. Girl, you look just like Julianne Moore. Well, you're shorter, I think? And you're plumper. And you're . . . " Susan holds her open hands up and out from her petite breasts and doesn't finish her sentence. "But other than that, you look exactly like her!"

"I doubt that, Susan. Maybe close the door before mosquitoes get in."

"Well, I think you do," Susan says, swaying. "Not like me. I don't look like anybody. I'm so fat. Look." Susan lifts her white T-shirt and pinches less than half an inch of skin from her flat abdomen.

Lourdes thinks she hears a buzzing sound.

Susan hangs her head.

Lourdes gets a direct view of her scalp and is startled to see how much pink skin shows at the part. Glancing at her own shoulder, she pulls two strands of Susan's hair from her sweat shirt.

Rolling the hem of her shirt up, Susan tucks it under her breasts and says, "Pretty gross, huh?"

Lourdes stares at Susan's ribs. Her low-rider jeans reveal her hip bones protruding from her flesh. After three children, there is not a single stretch mark to be seen. "No, Susan. Not gross. Why would you say something like that?" She takes Susan by the arm and guides her far enough inside so she can close the door, slamming it shut.

Susan says, "You really don't think so?"

"Really." In the light, Lourdes can see that Susan's hair lacks body. How stringy it is, and it falls over her face, covering both cheeks when she lifts her head.

"Well, Barton always says skinny is best."

"He shouldn't."

"Oh," Susan replies. She stands, swaying slightly until there is another buzzing sound which Lourdes is sure she hears this time. Susan looks down at herself and then rolls the back of her T-shirt up so the hem is even all the way around her upper torso.

After a few more moments of silence, while Susan continues to hang her head and sway, Lourdes says, "Why are you here, Susan?"

Susan looks at her and says, "Hey, girl. How are you? Do you have anything to drink?"

"I've got grapefruit juice, diet-caffeine-free Coke, Boost, and water." She points at the dispenser beside the refrigerator.

"I mean the good stuff, silly."

"Sorry. Nothing like that."

"Is the restaurant still open? We can get a case to go."

"I left the restaurant at eight. I'm done there for today."

"Oh. Too bad they close early."

"Yeah, too bad," says Lourdes. She hears that buzzing sound again.

Susan plops down in the chair by the table. Her elbow clunks dangerously close to the laptop.

Stepping quickly forward, Lourdes shunts the computer away to safety. She crouches down in front of Susan, takes one of her hands, and says, "Where is Barton?"

"I left him at the Steak House. Shooting pool. This was supposed to be our night out. The money he loses on that game." She suddenly grabs both of Lourdes' hands.

"But he mostly wins. Don't get me wrong. He tells me it's his only vice. So it's okay. So don't look at me like that?

"We can afford it. Barton's already a shift supervisor. Only with a little help from his brother Buck at head office. All the kids are normal and healthy and we're in a split-level in that new development. It's all good. Isn't it?"

"I'm sure everything's fine, Susan."

Susan only tries to focus her bleary eyes.

Lourdes says, "You didn't drive, did you?"

Susan blinks. "Of course I didn't drive, silly. Barton takes away my fob when he knows I'm drinking. I walked."

"You walked? All the way from the Steak House?"

Susan nods and giggles.

"Why did you come here?"

"I'm not lonely, if that's what you mean."

Lourdes hesitates. "That's not what I mean."

"Barton has not driven off all my friends. We all just kind of drifted apart, you know? With babies and all. Parents have other priorities, Barton says. You'll know what it's like once you have babies of your own. Then you'll understand."

Unbidden, the seedpod snakes its way through the brown thorn-field. She lets go of Susan's hands and stands. She says, "You didn't answer me. Why are you here after all this time?"

"I just wanted to come by and tell you, you should marry that man. Barton says he'd die without me, you know?"

The seedpod is gone as quickly as it came.

Susan continues, "You have to marry that man so you won't be lonely too, I mean so you won't be lonely, just pining away in this room all your life. We never see you at the Steak House."

You've never invited me to the Steak House.

When Susan slumps in the chair, Lourdes hears music, recognizable only as some sort of heavy metal ditty. Susan wiggles in the chair and pulls a cellphone from her back pocket.

"Hey," she says into the phone with a hesitant quiver in her voice. Wide eyed, she puts her free index finger to her lips.

The loud voice coming through the phone's speaker is plainly Barton's, but the actual words aren't clear. Susan says, "I just needed some air and went for a walk." There is another indistinct comment and Susan replies, "I guess I didn't feel the vibration. I made it to the Motel 6. I'm at those picnic tables by the highway?"

Susan grimaces at the tirade that follows. She says, "What would I want to see her for?" Then, after another tirade, "Yes, of course I'll wait for you and won't move. See you in a minute." Pale now, she disconnects the call, stands, and shoves the cell back into her pocket.

Staggering toward the door, she says, "We'll have to do this again, real soon." She flings the door open and suddenly turns. Lourdes stops just before they collide. "I mean it," Susan says. "And please remember what I told you about marrying that man."

"His name is Lee, Susan."

Susan doesn't pay attention. She lunges forward, grabs Lourdes' cheeks in both hands, and gives her another slobbery kiss, this time on the mouth.

She's out the door before Lourdes can recover her composure. By the time she wipes her mouth and steps outside, Susan has weaved halfway to the rest area.

Lourdes gets a cigarillo, lights it, takes her key, turns off the lights, and steps outside. She dashes around the corner of the motel and lurks unseen in the shadows, watching Susan lean against one of the picnic tables. It's the same one Lee sat on a year ago.

She watches Susan plop down on the bench and look up at the stars, in feigned nonchalance; her anxiety is obvious.

Moments later, a large SUV — maybe a Chevrolet Suburban or Tahoe, it's hard to make out the exact model in the glare of headlights on high-beam — skids to a stop, spraying gravel. Susan jumps up, runs to the vehicle and tries to open the passenger door. The SUV lurches forward and stretches Susan's arm before she can let go. She stumbles forward and tries the door twice more. The dimming of the headlights indicates the driver has finally unlocked the doors. Susan jumps in and slams her door. The SUV accelerates hard, making a 180-degree turn, leaving a shower of gravel in its wake.

Lourdes saunters toward the picnic tables and slowly finishes her cigarillo. The image of the snaking seedpod is long gone, but she remembers the dream where Lee erected the white wall blocking her way to the hollow.

True, she hasn't been to the hollow in while. She doesn't need to go anymore, does she?

Reaching the skid marks, she pokes at the little gravel ridges with the toe of her runner. "Shit," she says out loud. Her shoes glare white in the quartz wash of the parking lot lights. These are the runners meant only to be used on the treadmill. Little stones and fragments of gravel will now be caught in the shoes' treads.

She throws her cigarillo into the valley of a skid mark. Little sparkles of red flash from the butt. She's about to turn and leave but instead reaches down and picks up the remainder of the cigarillo. Dropping it in the disposal bin, she turns toward her room, intending to finish on the treadmill. A breeze lightly blows her hair out behind her. She brushes the strands where the crow buzzed her. She smells the creek and the purpling flax.

Treadmill be damned. She jogs out of the parking lot and follows her old route toward the mine. She'll complete tomorrow morning's run now and have more time to write before she starts another day of cleaning up other people's crap. She has missed the feel of the cool air blowing her hair, blowing through her clothes, and chilling her skin. The smell of the fields and the stagnant water. She hasn't looked at the stars in a while. Even the mine's plume, as hateful as she sometimes feels it is, is a reminder of normalcy.

Breathing and heart-rate in time with her stride, she runs almost four kilometres toward the mine before turning back. The plume reflects bright moonlight in the dark sky and Lourdes again remembers the plunge underground. But she's running, her breathing is under control and she does not feel the oppression of the earth pressing down on her.

When she returns to her room, comfortably numb from near exhaustion, she's too wired to sleep. And instead of showering, she stays up with Hagar, finishing the novel sometime after the morning's light frames the closed drapes. She then lies on the bed on top of the blankets and falls into a short sleep.

ᴕᴕᴕ

The four-year-old girl in the brown field is her Mary. The seedpod slithers up beside the young girl and she reaches for it. Lourdes lunges. She must stop Mary from picking up the hideous thing but she doesn't get there in time and awakens with a start at the usual time.

She wants desperately to hold her baby. A pressure builds in her chest. *Breathe. Calm.* She visualizes the hollow in last night's darkness. The purple thistle flowers are partially closed, drooping in the night's cool. One thistle, near the shore, hangs its flowers in mourning . . . *I'm not the only one suffering.*

As much as she feels she should at this moment, she does not cry. Reason takes over and she accepts what is.

Getting up, she plugs her phone into the wall outlet but still doesn't call Lee. Instead, she sends an email to his work address, where it will be downloaded to his cellphone. She apologizes for not calling and briefly mentions Susan's unexpected visit. The story is too long for an email and she'll explain when they next meet.

Utterly fatigued, she cruises through her unusually hectic day on autopilot. She is thankful for the busyness and doesn't even try to write in her notepad. Instead, she sits in the kitchen with her eyes closed whenever work allows.

And, although her server performance is excellent, not even one mistake the whole day, she finds herself growing tense as evening approaches. Back in her room after her shift ends, she discovers an email from Lee telling her things are going well at the dam site and he should be in town later in the evening. He ends by saying, "Helena said you have Saturday off so let's take the day to ourselves. Maybe go for a drive."

She writes a short reply saying that plan works for her. Maybe he'll send another message saying he can't make it after all, so she does not close her email session and opens another tab in her browser. She clicks on the U of S bookmark.

Opening a third tab, she searches for The Human League music and watches a video for the song "Don't You Want Me", followed by "Fascination". From there, she follows various threads until she stares vacantly at Electro House videos and finally a rave from Ibiza.

It is near midnight when she hears a car pull up outside her door.

Cracking the curtains, she sees Lee close his trunk and walk towards her door with his suitcase. She flings it open before he knocks and embraces him at the threshold.

The heat is back as soon as Lee drops his suitcase and returns the embrace. They kiss and she closes her eyes.

After a moment, they separate and he steps inside. "Sorry I'm so late. I had to stop a few times to exchange text messages with the support desk." He pulls his phone from its belt holder and reads the screen.

Lourdes watches him thumb-click. She waits a long moment and eventually says, "I didn't realize Bland Electronics has a support desk."

"Not Bland," he says, still clicking. "Liverwood mine's technical support desk at their head office." He finishes clicking but continues to watch his screen.

She continues to watch him in silence until the cell chimes.

Lee clicks once and reads something else. He smiles and a dreamy expression briefly sweeps over his face. He clicks frantically, focused on the screen.

"Must be very, very important, communicating this late on a Friday night," she says.

Still clicking, he replies in that absent tone, "Just Deirdre from the help desk." He presses one final button and quickly replaces the cell in its holder. "Just closing the log for that system board I installed."

"You said 'support desk.'"

"What?"

"First you said you're messaging the support desk and you just now called it the help desk. Which is it?" She is not going to ask why he is in contact with Liverwood's technical support when he supposedly was installing a system board at a power generation dam. Perhaps Long-shanks got the information wrong. Or maybe he's dealing with a Liverwood mine service call at the same time.

"The full name is Systems and Technical Support Centre. Help desk, help centre. They're both shorter and easier to say."

"As is support centre," Lourdes replies and turns around. Over her shoulder she says, "It's been a long day for both of us, probably. I think we should get some sleep." With that, she strips naked and crawls under the bed covers. Lee slowly does the same, neither of them saying another word. She turns out the bedside lamp.

After a few moments in the dark, he reaches over and gathers a handful of her hair. She hears him breathing deeply and succumbs to her body's call. She climbs on top of him.

When they've finished, they kiss briefly and she says, "Good night then." She rolls over on her side of the bed. She hears him fiddle with his phone again but there is no annoying clicking. He sets the phone on the bedside table and is breathing rhythmically in minutes.

The sleep of a guiltless child, she thinks. She recalls him saying, on the day the treadmill arrived, that kids would love to play in the hollow. He has only brought up children one other time since. Once, shortly after sex, he abruptly asked, "So after Mary and all, would you ever want children? I think you'd make a great mom."

She said calmly, "I can't have children. I think you know that. We've had so much unprotected sex."

Lee stiffened at her response and didn't say anything.

"Why do you ask?" she said after a moment's silence.

"No real reason." He just lay there and stared at the ceiling, one hand behind his head, the other on his chest with thumb and index finger rubbing. "I was just thinking about children. I was an only child, which was okay, but all of my friends had big families. When I have a family, ideally I'd like four kids. And I'd better get on with it, considering how old I'm getting to be."

"You're not that old."

"I'm thirty-four, you know. I'm reaching the far end of fatherhood."

Thirty-four? I pegged you at twenty-five. And four children with me? Something prickled at her feet and she left for the bathroom, that conversation never finished.

Now, that prickling returns and she shifts to scratch. Lee only rolls over, his breathing still deep and rhythmic. She finishes scratching and pulls her hair behind her head. *I feel fourteen years older than he is and he wants four children?*

She is not sure if Lee believes she is unable to have children. This annoys her. If that irksome dream seedpod was real, using it like a blackjack on him might be in order, might feel really good.

Her fatigue finally pulls her into darkness and sleep.

There is an image of that completed wall of white blocking her way to the hollow so she retreats to her room where, in the brown field of thorns, she watches Lee in the distance with his cigar, the smoke flying upward and merging with the plume. The seedpod is outside her window, tapping on the glass. The clicking sound, harder and harder . . .

Lourdes opens her eyes to Lee sitting upright against the headboard, knees drawn up, hands and phone resting on his legs, clicking away.

"Hey you," he says, fixated on his cell. "Just messaging mom and dad. Give me a second." A minute later, he presses a final button and, smiling, sets the phone on the bedside table. Shunting to face her, he says, "How did you sleep?"

Lourdes sits up beside him and sees that the phone lies display down. "Not bad," she replies, "You?"

"Great. That fresh northern lake air up at the dam always induces fantastic sleeps."

She says, "You mentioned a drive in your last email. What did you have in mind?"

"Dunno. We'll figure it out. Tell me about Susan's visit first, though. You said it was a long story yesterday and I'm intrigued."

She relates the story but omits the locked SUV scene in the parking lot.

"How did you feel about that blast from the past?" he asks.

"What could I feel? I haven't been friends with Susan since the Treadwells brought me home from the hospital. She was obviously too drunk to know what she was doing. I doubt if she'll even remember the visit today."

"Were you at all concerned about Barton making an appearance?"

Lourdes can't help herself. She grins an evil grin. She feels her face burn with sadistic glee. Helena is right about her being a fire-haired she-devil. "Not in the slightest. I suspect the horn-dog has had more dalliances than with me. All it would take is one comment and it would be all over town. Simple as a whisper. Then the innuendo takes over and there's suddenly corroborating witnesses. I'd love to see all of his little adventures come to the surface. I'd love to lord it over Barton and he knows it. And I hope he suffers from worry every single day at the thought of losing his trophy wife. He deserves it. I didn't tell you what else he did when he picked Susan up."

She goes on to describe the door-lock antics in the parking lot.

Lee is studying his hand while he rubs his thumb and forefinger. His action is a deliberate and calculated pause but she is in a wicked mood. She will wait him out.

Eventually he asks, "What else haven't you told me, Lourdes? That door story is a prime example of details omitted until you feel like telling them. I think there's other things in your life you haven't told me. That lack of trust hurts me. A healthy relationship isn't one with untold stories. How much more is there about you that remains secret?"

She says, "There's nothing more about me you don't already know. Why would you even ask a question like that? What could you possibly think that I'm hiding?"

"Well." He pauses. "You've never told me everything about Mary. Like maybe how you feel about her."

"I've already told you how I feel about her. Every time you've asked. Are you going to keep picking at me until you hear something you want to hear? That doesn't make for a healthy relationship either."

Lee looks directly at her. She meets his stare directly.

He says, "You told me the *story* about Mary. But you never told me how you feel. Just a minute ago, when you were talking about your lost friendship with Susan, you said 'since the Treadwell's brought me home from the hospital.' You didn't say 'after Mary died.' I think there's so, so much you're not telling me."

After this, she doesn't want a seedpod blackjack, she wants him deep down in the mine. In the lowest crosscut with a single, sputtering candle so he can see the earth give way just before the flood from the water-bearing strata reaches him, drowning the last of the light and him. She says, "All that was buried long before you came along with your amateur, internet-based psychoanalysis. Why are you digging in mineshafts sealed up ages ago?"

"Because they may be sealed but things haven't been dealt with," he says. "If you've dealt with it, why do you never talk about it? Why have you never taken me to see Mary's grave?"

"I don't need to see Mary's grave. Ever." Lourdes suddenly wants to leave her body, the first time in a long time she's felt that, but she stays rooted.

And for the first time Lee does not back off with his passive, "Okay" response. He says, "If it's all buried and dealt with, prove it. Take me out to Mary's grave. If you even know where it is."

His face is without its neutral, yet smug expression. It is strangely shadowed, with eyes narrowed and forehead furrowed.

Lourdes folds her arms across her breasts. She studies the way her cleavage forms as she presses her arms against herself. She studies the freckles on her upper chest and then those on her arms. The light red hairs on her arms are like fine, prairie weeds. She says, "I just told you. I don't need to go out there."

She also feels suddenly guilty about wishing Lee drowned in a mineshaft. She knows that terror of the deep. Why would she wish that on anyone?

He says quietly, "But what if *I* need to see the grave?"

"Go ahead."

"And what if I need you to go with me?"

"Won't happen." She twists around and swings her legs off the bed. She stands, covers herself with her housecoat, and strides to the bathroom. After closing and locking the door, she steps into the shower and turns the water on cold. She entices The Human League's "Fascination" into her head and recalls the lyrics. She lets them play in her mind over and over while concentrating on the feel of the cool water on her skin.

When she emerges from the bathroom, Lee is still sitting in the bed, that damn phone back in his hands. He quickly sets it, display down, on the table, and folds his hands on his knees. His face is back to its normal, passive expression.

"I thought you were going to the graveyard?" she asks, in an attempt to sound harsh.

"Not without you. I see clearly now that there's more to the Lourdes' story. You have unresolved issues. I'd like to help you with them so we can get on with our lives together."

"I have 'unresolved issues,' do I, Doctor Markham?" She is so frustrated with these machinations. He is trying to prove something. If she goes with him, he wins; if she doesn't go with him, he wins. He could say that he talked her into it or that she couldn't face the grave; either way he could *lord* it over her forever.

Lourdes pauses in mid stride. But, she thinks, if they do go, she can prove these supposed unresolved issues are a fallacy. Her so-called secrets are nothing more than a confabulation of an immature mind, an attempt to gain some kind of control over her. The way Barton controls Susan with his constant messaging and phone calls and locking and unlocking of car doors.

She will poison any such plan. She says, "Let's go then. Right now."

Dropping her housecoat to the floor, she flounces naked to the fridge and makes her buttocks sway and breasts bounce with each contrived and focused model-like step. She takes out a bottle of Boost, downs it, and flounces back to dress. "I'm not waiting for you in the car. Keep up, if you want to go out there."

Lee throws the blankets back, gets up and quickly dresses. They are ready at the same time. He is even quick enough to grab his cellphone.

Damn him again and again, she thinks, stepping onto the gravel parking lot.

The day is already hot and humid. The early morning sun hits hard. Crows caw in the pine windbreak and distantly from the hollow behind the motel. Marching directly to the passenger door, she waits until she hears the locks clunk before she tries the handle. Opening the door she sits and buckles in one fluid motion.

Lee gets in leisurely. He puts the key in the ignition. He adjusts his inside mirror. He slowly reaches forward to start the car. Leaning back, he adjusts the driver side mirror, then the passenger side mirror. Eventually he clicks the seat belt in place and jiggles his shoulders, like he's settling into a chaise lounge. He adjusts the inside mirror once more, puts the car into gear, checks over both shoulders and then slowly backs up.

Moving forward at idling speed, the car makes its way to the exit at the highway. He says simply, "Which way?"

"Left," Lourdes replies levelly. "Left again at your first intersection. Follow the road to the far side of town. Turn left again past the grain elevator at the T-intersection." She folds her arms and looks out her window. The plume is a stark white in the bright sky. "Can you follow all that?"

"Of course," Lee says, with his annoyingly calm voice. He follows her directions exactly without further comment.

∾∾∾

At the typical small-town intersection of Main Street and Railway Avenue, Lourdes looks at the Steak House which, in the light of day, seems benign enough. It is housed in another typical small-town landmark — an old, brown-brick, former hotel. The second storey has been converted to an upper deck for the bar on the main floor. The third storey has rooms for rent, generally by the hour.

She stares at this social nexus of Liverwood. When rallies aren't happening at the Liverwood Sports Complex, absorbing all interest, the masses congregate here, usually after these rallies. How many locals have dug through their daily lives at this place? How many lives are buried here, under a mineshaft flood of booze and drugs?

Lee gradually accelerates down Railway Avenue and proceeds past the former Pool Elevator, its faded orange dull in the sunshine. A new inland terminal is out of sight, located on the highway near the mine and railway spur. Turning left at the T-intersection, they leave the town limits where the asphalt road turns to gravel past the railway tracks.

Lourdes glances at Lee. He focuses on driving. She says, "Follow the road until you see the church."

"Okay." He replies without averting his eyes.

The road curves southeast after a kilometre of gravel and descends into a low rocky vale. The vale, not suitable for agriculture, is overgrown with prairie grasses, thick with Canadian thistle. Here, the thistles' purple flowers reach skyward toward real sunshine. They don't need the surrogate light of the mine's plume the way they seem to in the hollow.

Liverwood United Church and graveyard sit on a slight rise in the middle of the vale, which is pressed on all sides by the unbounded growth of prairie grasses and weeds.

Lee drives into the dusty parking lot and stops by two low cement cairns that mark the entrance to the graveyard.

Lourdes exits and slams the door. She's not going to dally while Lee fiddles with his seatbelt or mirrors or whatever he feels compelled to do in his *post-drive debriefing*. She stomps past the cairns and Lee is suddenly and quietly one pace behind her, asking, "Who maintains Mary's grave?"

She doesn't slow down. "The Treadwells. And they don't drag me out here because they know I have no *issues* to get over."

Continuing down the path between graves, she says without turning, "Not only do I know where the graveyard is, contrary to your snarky insistence, I know exactly where my baby's grave lies." She again hears crows *caw-caw-caw* distantly. And with this she can't resist. Now, she will fly with them in their green and blue and purple-sheen glory. She lifts off on her crow wings, leaving her physical self to deal with Lee.

She feels a head-rush from the acceleration. She flies high. The wind rushes through her hair — billowing it behind her.

She sees herself march with purpose to the far boundary of the graveyard. At the last row, she turns off the path and moves toward the farthest grave markers. She stops at the second last grave in the corner and looks down at the square, simple, flat fiberglass marker that resembles pink granite.

Lourdes' father does not lie beside his granddaughter. His was cremated and the urn containing his ashes was lost in the trailer fire. But from up here in the ether, she is aware of the mine's plume in the distance. Its source is the last place her father stood. *Did he think of me when he died? He must have because his words echo in my ears — You'll do what you need to do to make yourself all better.*

She plummets from on high and crashes into her body just as she falls to her knees. She is in the hospital. What she thinks is a bloody lump the size of a grapefruit is actually a fully formed little girl. Mary lets out one small croaking cry. Then Mary is silent. Then Mary is gone.

Gone to this place. Buried just within reach but Lourdes still can't hold her baby. Slowly, she falls forward on her hands in the fine, thin natural grass and the fern-shaped weeds spouting up here and there. She touches the delicate leaf fibres of the liver weed. Liver weed is found only in grassy areas, only in this part of the prairies. Mary is buried in a cardboard coffin under a thriving patch of the little weeds. Is she bringing new life to these delicate plants?

Lourdes falls on her side and curls into a ball. Her forearms rest on the fine grasses and weeds. Her hands touch the grave-marker, forefinger traces the single word: MARY.

She moans only once. The little patch of liver weed is wet. She lets her strength ebb with the flow while an exquisite agony washes over her. Washes out of her.

She becomes aware of Lee beside her. His hands gently stroke her hair exactly where her purple-sheen crow brushed it. She lays her head on the marker. Eyes closed, she is aware of only the marker against her forehead.

There is peace now. Comfort in this utter exhaustion. She kisses the marker and whispers, "Goodbye, Mary."

Lee helps her stand up. He supports her, his strong arms wrapped around her waist, holding her up. Holding her close. She puts one arm across his shoulder, manoeuvres the last few steps to the edge of the graveyard. Leaning against him for a few moments, her eyes close, and she feels only the sun warming her face.

When she opens her eyes, she sees the vale's wild growth and the Canadian thistles with their purple blooms stretching — reaching skyward.

"Lourdes," Lee says, his voice low, near cracking, "I'm so, so sorry. How can you ever forgive me?"

"It's okay, Lee. I know now. I was only out here once. I didn't allow . . . "

Lee holds her tight. He doesn't reply.

Confused, she gently takes his arms from around her and steps back a pace.

Lee's staring at his feet, thumb rubbing his curled index finger incessantly.

Her heart ripples and she says, "Lee, everything's all right now."

He shakes his head, still looks down. "I don't think so." He pauses and takes a long breath. "I didn't believe your Mary story, Lourdes. I thought you didn't want any children with me and were making it up because you didn't want to commit to me and my plans."

This hurts. *God this hurts.*

But the pain re-energizes her. She says, "You didn't believe me?"

He doesn't respond. He touches his cellphone holder on his belt.

Lourdes plainly sees and says, "Maybe your friend Deirdre from the help desk can give you the support you need."

Lee looks up quickly, sharply. "She actually works in accounting, but it's not what you think. We're just friends. She's been with too many men just like I've been through too many women. She's desperate for a stable, monogamous relationship and wants a family. We have that in common."

"Why don't you marry her, then? It sounds like she wants *a million* of your babies."

"It's not like that," Lee repeats, his voice shrill. "With Deirdre, that's all there is. You and I — we can always adopt if you really can't have babies. Maybe a surrogate would . . . "

Lourdes turns away and no longer listens. She gazes over the purple thistles, the vibrant field growing wild. Maybe he's right, perhaps Engineering is the way to go but *I will try it my own way first.*

She turns her face into the prevailing wind that blows the plume away from Liverwood and blows her hair behind her. She will once again lift herself on her purple-sheen crow wings. But she will no longer look down on herself. Nor will she merely drift with the breeze. Her wings will carry all of her where she chooses. She will pump her wings and fly in that prevailing wind, fly past and away from the plume.

Lew LeBelle Loogin
in the Land of the Looginaires

Loogin: derogatory slang for someone with any sort of mental health issue; or old prison slang meaning mentally ill prisoner

There's standing room only in the chaple of the Liverwood Funeral Home. Potash production at the mine is stopped for the duration of the memorial service. Lewis LeBelle is comforted that Ang is right beside him. She leans her head on his shoulder and her hair brushes his cheek. Arms intertwined and pressed together, they hold hands, hers warm and calming in his.

From a side room, the funeral director leads four people to the front row. A tiny woman with pocked cheeks and thin hair shambles beside the director and falls into her seat. Following behind them are a tall, bald man and short woman with pudgy arms. They each hold a hand of a red-haired girl, about ten years old, who walks with tentative steps between them.

After they are all seated, the director makes his way to the podium beside a stand with a bouquet of lilies and a plain porcelain urn.

112

Lew thinks of the first time he met Ted. It was at his initial orientation session after he was hired at the Liverwood Potash Corporation mine. Minutes into introductions at that session, he finds he's saddled with the nickname "Lulubelle."

He says, "I prefer Lew, thank you very much."

His response earns him immediate jeers and guffaws. Someone yells, "Won't work. Can't call you lewd names."

Ted says to him, "Lulubelle it is."

Lew is on a mentoring team with three other men: another Helper Trainee named Ashley, and two Senior Miners, Ted and Hal. He studies the miners and repeats their names to himself so he won't forget them.

Ted stands four inches over Lew's six feet. Weighing at least 250 pounds and without an ounce of flab, Ted has thick forearms that are heavily freckled and have a thin covering of reddish hair. The red hair on his head and face is trimmed to a uniform stubble. The man reminds Lew of a wrestler but Ted's grin immediately puts him at ease.

Hal is also over six feet but he is a beanpole of a man and seems to be built entirely of muscle and cartilage. His thinning black hair is combed straight back. His grey-blue eyes seem to penetrate to the back of Lew's optic nerve; his stare is intense, just like a shark's.

Lew maintains eye contact only briefly.

Ted slaps him heartily on the back and says, "You'll soon enough get used to Lulubelle and hard work. Let's check this place out."

The backslap stings, even through overalls. However, he does not stagger forward but twists his own sinewy frame, deflecting most of the impact of the blow.

This earns him the slightest double nod from Hal.

Ted leads them to the entrance of the service elevator. Other mentoring teams are already mustering; they are all to see underground operations for the first time. While waiting for the elevator to come to the surface, Ted and Hal focus their attention on Ashley.

During a break in testing for potential employees the week before, Lew learned Ashley also grew up in Saskatoon and went to the University of Saskatchewan, enrolled in drama. Ashley attached himself to Lew over the dozen or so other university students seeking summer and temporary mine employment. They were both in arts, Lew being an English major, but they had never met each other on campus. Lew was the only one who listened to Ashley complain about how every single U of S Education program "sucked and blew," which is why he had changed his major to drama. They were physically similar: twenty years old, tall, slender, both sporting dark, spiky hair, and both with a total inability to grow any sort of facial hair other than a bad *cheesestache*. All the other students hoping for work were built like CFL linebackers.

Lew found he had himself a twin or a shadow, who was now assigned to his mentoring group.

Under Ted and Hal's scrutiny Ashley hunches his shoulders. Shuffling his feet, he moves back slightly and stares at Ted's freckled arms.

Hal says to him, "We'll come up with a nickname for you soon enough."

Ashley shuffles his feet again.

The service elevator door opens and the miners coming off shift stream out. The shift production supervisor joins the orientation teams and barks out that hardhats and safety goggles are to be put on immediately.

With hardhats and goggles in place, overall sleeves are rolled completely down and zippers zipped completely up. The supervisor slides into a litany of safety protocols, bellowing them out like a war movie drill instructor.

The senior miners don't need safety gear prompting and Lew gets that the safety protocols are for the benefit of the new workers. Which is too bad, because even though the supervisor yells, he can't hear everything he says through all the back talk, fart jokes, and actual farting.

He thinks, *well what do you expect with a bunch of men working together? First, they come up with that stupid Lulubelle moniker and then they all try to be comedians. Why did I take this job, again? Oh, yeah, money to finance my post-secondary education.*

As a general arts student, he had taken two geology courses to fill his degree's science requirement. Mid-semester, during a class in the second course, mine recruiters came in search of summer and temporary employees. New contracts with Asia meant substantial production increases and serious staffing shortages. He applied for a summer job right at the end of that particular class.

He wrote on the application under general information that he was considering a degree in Geology. He then passed all of the preliminary testing and now he finds himself among a legion of miners.

Or a legion of loogins, he thinks. Loogin, a common epithet for anyone who fumbled or made any kind of mistake in high school Phys Ed. *Yep, I'm stuck with a bunch of looginaires.*

He misses most of the safety protocol lecture because of the ongoing back-talk but hears enough to realize that one of the reasons for three days of orientation before actual work is so the senior miners can get the new workers up to speed on safety.

The off-shift miners have finally exited the elevator and the new shift crowds on board.

When the elevator car moves, Lew feels an immediate rush. With a top speed of twenty feet per second, the garage-sized car descends silently, the flow of air whispers around him. On this first ride down, he ignores the crowd of miners and the clutter of equipment. He watches millennia of strata whiz by through the upper wire-mesh walls of the car.

Ashley finds his way to a corner. Lew glances at him. Firmly ensconced in the perpendicular, solid lower walls, he is rigid and wide-eyed, with his arms tight at his sides. He grips his cooler and thermos jug, knuckles white.

Other veteran miners nudge each other and cast nods in Ashley's direction.

Hal slithers to his side, leans over him, and says, "Scared?"

Ashley answers too loudly and too quickly. "NO. It's just, this isn't exactly the summer job I wanted."

Lew thinks, *wrong answer.*

Hal says, "Oh, I'm sorry *Purrfesser.* You were supposed to be in the corporate Info Department, yeah? But somebody made a mistake."

Ashley hangs his head. "I applied for an office job."

Rubbing his chin, Hal says, "But it's below a Fine Arts student to hand out key rings and promo binders. So you abandoned head office and came to toil with us kobolds, yeah? What a grievous miscarriage. As shop steward, I'll launch an immediate grievance on your behalf."

Ashley raises his head, expression suggesting he half believes Hal. The men in the car erupt in laughter. Ashley's face turns crimson and he hangs his head once again, chin on his chest.

Lew does not laugh.

Hal then turns his head to face Lew, slowly, like some sort of indestructible reptilian monster targeting his next hapless human victim.

Lew empathizes with Ashley; they are both poor misplaced arts students among engineers and tradesmen. He thinks, *yep, I'm next,* and immediately holds up his free hand. His other hand loosely holds the handles of his cooler and thermos jug.

Open palm toward Hal, he says, "Hey. I'm happy to be gainfully employed. And I just learned I seriously love riding this crazy fast elevator."

Lost in the rush of the elevator's descent at that moment, Lew can't help but gaze around again, a grin on his face.

"That so?" Hal says, his eyebrows cocked.

Lew no longer feels those grey-blue eyes boring into the back of his brain.

"'Gainfully employed,' eh?" Hal continues. "Well, well, aren't we all. Well spoken *Monsewer* English Major. Too bad your ultimate destination is the tailings heaps."

Ted laughs and says, "So don't cream your jeans, Lulubelle. This trip underground is only for operations orientation. It's the first and probably the very last time you get to ride this speed-demon."

Hal adds, "Yeah, and the most complex piece of machinery you newbs get to use this summer is a shovel."

The elevator decelerates and stops with a smooth whoosh.

∾∾∾

After finishing the morning-long orientation of underground operations, the mentoring teams return to the surface. Stowing their coolers and thermos jugs in a lunch area attached to the mill building, they enter the milling operations area proper.

After everyone puts in industrial ear plugs, Ted has them wait a moment to acclimatize to the noise in the mill. He drapes one arm over Lew's shoulders and the other over Ashley's. With that huge grin on his face, he yells, "If you got a hard-on for the roar of big machines, this is the place you wanna be. 'Coz this is where you're gonna be. Like it or not."

Glancing behind him, Lew sees Hal staring directly at Ashley, who is grimacing and holding his hands up to his ears even though he wears plugs.

At this, Hal hovers around Ashley, patiently yelling out the milling processes.

Ted stays close to Lew, nudging him every now and then.

During a break, the mentoring teams gather with other senior miners in the lunch area, a relatively quiet place partitioned away from the noise of the mill. It has rows of long tables with plastic chairs, a microwave, a refrigerator, and a counter with a sink.

Hal's hand rests between Ashley's shoulder blades while he guides him to a chair at the end of one of the long tables.

Ashley plops into the chair, which collapses, and he falls flat on his back to uproarious laughter.

Hal says, "Well, now how did that happen, *Purrfesser?* Here, let me get you another chair." He does so in the most apologetic manner and then asks Ashley, "So, how long are you going to stay a virgin?"

After that, general and relentless Ashley-bashing about his lack of sexual ability lasts for the duration of that break.

In the bathroom afterwards, Ashley sidles up to the urinal beside Lew and says, "I'm not a virgin, you know. I lost it when I was fourteen and I've been with at least a dozen different girls since then."

Lew nods and says, "Let it pass. Don't show they're getting to you."

On the walk back toward the centrifuges in the mill, the next stop on the orientation, Lew thinks about his own limited sexual experience. He's still with Angie, Ang for short, his one and only grade ten sweetheart. They met in high school in Saskatoon while playing in tournaments for the collectable card game Magic. She too is a "ginger-kid" with freckled forearms like Ted's, and is lanky and as tall as Lew. The bangs of her shoulder-length russet hair usually hang over her eyebrows. She's one of the most hilarious people he's ever known. Her humour is infectious and they always make each other laugh. Even after a fight, they both giggle and chortle their way into bed.

He can't imagine his life without Ang — can't see any possible reason to change that.

Back in the company of the two senior miners, Ashley, with a nasally whine, says to Hal, "I've been with dozens of girls, you know."

Lew thinks, *so much for my advice.*

Hal immediately replies, "Name them."

Ashley snorts and clears his throat. With a croak in his voice he says, "I'm not telling. It's none of your business."

It's none of your business, Lew thinks. *Not their names or even a first name?*

Ashley opens his arms in a plea to Ted who, grinning, says, "I'm not hearing any names."

Lew quickly asks, "Just how big are those centrifuges? *They're fricken huge.* What's their capacity?"

His questions distract the older men from Ashley and get the group back on its orientation track.

❧❧❧

After the three days of orientation are complete, they start their first day of actual work.

Hal says with a sneer, "You newbs have a job so simple, even the *Purrfesser* here can handle it." He goes on to explain that they are merely to watch a monitor's display of flow rates of the tailings' conveyors. Lew and Ashley are not allowed to touch the monitor's controls. They are only to advise a Senior Miner if the rates drop below, or rise above, the limits clearly posted, in red, on laminated sheets attached to the display.

"Otherwise," Hal continues, "You watch your assigned tailings trails from the final centrifuges. The tailings spew from the centrifuges' discharge chutes onto conveyors. Now, these open conveyors only run inside the mill. Just on the other side of the mill wall are the enclosed trunk conveyors that send tailings to the tracked spreader-derricks. I trust, *Purrfesser,* you remember our two-kilometre drive to the tailings piles the other day?

"Now remember, 'gunk' builds up here," Hal points to the discharge chutes connected to the open conveyors, "and there." He points to the area where the open inside conveyors flow into the external, enclosed trunk conveyors.

"So remember. Your only job is to 'de-gunk.' I don't want to hear any alarms and I especially don't want you two running to me or Ted because you let things get out of hand. Got it?"

Ashley's face falls when he learns Hal wasn't kidding when he said the most complex piece of machinery they would use was a shovel. He nods, his head tilted downward. Lew gives Hal a thumbs-up.

The whole morning is spent learning how to operate the shovel most efficiently, with the least contact with the constantly moving conveyors. Ashley, clearly bored by his unwanted summer job, complains to Lew, "My life is reduced to a kilometre or so of conveyors and a red digital display."

Lew considers it a challenge to keep the monitor's readings at optimum levels. He sprints to the discharge and trunk chutes to clear the gunk when he sees the flow rates fluctuate.

Ted yells at him from the centrifuge platform, "Hey, Goddammit! No running! Fast walk only."

Subsequently, he fast walks in a pattern from chute to chute and back to the monitor display, always moving, always watching.

Ashley is red-faced before the shift is even halfway done, and he sweats profusely. He leans on his shovel while he watches the flow monitor from under droopy eyelids. Lew begins to watch Ashley's conveyors also and calls to him when he notices a gunk buildup. Ashley can barely drag himself to the problem areas.

Soon, Lew finds he has doubled his own workload trying to keep Ashley's flow at optimum too.

Only once does he notice Hal sneering down at them from a centrifuge platform, his body rigid and arms tightly crossed.

He can see those shark-eyes boring into Ashley.

But Hal doesn't say anything to either of them.

When that first shift ends, Lew is exhausted. He has never been so physically active for such an extended period in his life. On his six kilometer bicycle ride from the mine site to the Motel 6 in the town of Liverwood, where he rents a room with a kitchenette by the month, he has to stop twice to catch his breath and rest his legs.

∾∾∾

The next day, Ted tells him to watch only his own readings and his own conveyors. Stiff and sore from that first day of work, he doesn't argue. Hal consistently hangs around Ashley, which seems to motivate him, seems to improve his attitude, and his efforts are slightly more than half-hearted.

During a break on the third day of work, everyone settles to eat at the rows of long tables. Ted sits next to him. Ashley plops down across the table on an end seat. There are bags under his eyes and a pale, drawn expression on his face. When he flings open the lid of his cooler a brown rat squeals and launches itself out at least three feet vertically.

Ashley screams. Lunging backward, he overturns his chair and crashes into the wall behind him. He screams, "You assholes destroyed my lunch."

He covers his crotch with both hands and runs from the lunch area.

A moment later, someone yells over the laughter that the rogue rat is still at large.

Crouching in a corner, the rat defecates and hisses at everyone in general and at Lew in particular because he is closest.

Lew reacts immediately. He is mortally afraid of hantavirus and hates rodents, believing all are potential carriers. He dumps the contents of his cooler and slams it bottom-down on the hapless rat, breaking the handle completely off.

He plops back on his chair, hangs his head, and tries to stop shaking. Bright lights flash at the periphery of his vision. Now he feels bad about killing a helpless creature, regardless if it's a hated rodent, *but it's the rat or me.* He tries to take deep, slow breaths.

A couple of miners are civil enough to dispose of the rat's body and both coolers in black garbage bags stored in the lunch area. A guy wearing dishwashing gloves cleans up the rat's remnants with lots of dish soap and half a roll of paper towels.

While the cleanup proceeds, Lew senses a figure looming over him and raises his eyes. Hal offers him a garbage bag and says, "To stash your food containers for now."

Lew nods, lips pressed, and takes the bag.

Hal moves his cooler and thermos to the abandoned end seat and settles in.

Ted says to Hal, "Nice one."

Mouth full of food, Hal replies, "Found it in a live trap over by the maintenance sheds when I parked this morning."

After taking a long drink directly from his thermos jug, Ted says, "We still on this weekend?"

"You bet," Hal replies. Facing Lew directly, he says, "Hey, Lulubelle. Do you play poker?"

ৡৡৡ

At first, Lew resists going to the regular weekend poker games. He then wonders if maybe that's not such a good idea. With Ashley gone two weeks now, replaced by a Senior Miner in his sixties and nearing retirement, he thinks these guys might get bored and may need a new target to harass.

Sitting for lunch in what has become his spot at the end of one of the long tables, he notices that his new cooler is heavier than it was in the morning when he stowed it in the lunch area. Something has definitely been added to the contents.

In the yammer and banter and laughter, no one seems to notice his caution. Hal, across from him, and Ted, beside him, are arguing about some improbable poker scenario.

He gives his cooler a shake and leans forward to listen. He can't hear anything inside, which doesn't mean much. Nothing would be audible through all of the surrounding din. Splaying his hands on the sides of the cooler, he attempts to feel for any indication of movement inside. He gives it another shake and turns his right ear towards it to try and listen once again. He glances around. Everyone seems to be in an intense conversation and completely ignoring him. He slides his hands up to the top of the cooler and slowly pushes the handle down. Stretching out his arms so the cooler is as far from his face as possible, he grips the sides of it with his fingers, takes a deep breath, and slowly pushes the lid upward with his thumbs.

"Lulubelle!" Hal yells.

Lew lurches, sliding his chair backwards. The cooler falls off of the end of the table. He grabs his head with both hands and yells, "For *Guy Fawkesakes* — don't do that!"

Laughter fills the entire lunch area.

"Yeah, funny," Lew yells, half-laughing from relief. "Let me find another rat and some duct tape for you guys. You're obviously bored and need a distraction."

Ted reaches down for the cooler and slams it back on the table.

"Thanks." Lew opens his cooler and proceeds to remove his lunch like nothing out of the ordinary has happened. It's a litre bottle of root beer inside which gives the cooler the extra weight.

He checks the safety seal on the cap. Even though it is still intact, he says, "You guys trying to poison me? Or is this laced with cocaine or another controlled substance?"

Hal says, "The rat trick only works once a summer. We'll find something more devious if necessary. And that," he says, pointing a stick of celery at the root beer, "is to help you work your way up to real beer."

"I'll drink this for sure," he says, waving the root beer bottle. "As for real beer, consider it under consideration."

There's no possible way he'll ever drink booze again.

He drank his first beer near the end of grade eight, which is the time kids all over Saskatchewan do that. But it only caused him an acute hangover and the numbness while drunk didn't break down any inhibitions.

He tried several times in isolated parks and vacant fields and lots in Saskatoon, but booze actually made his inhibitions worse. Specifically, his murophobia, which he'd had his entire life and didn't know the cause of, rose to paranoid levels so intense he couldn't even walk into trees or bushes to urinate. He would hear scurrying sounds and feel rodents climbing up his legs. When drunk out of control, his imagination confabulated giant, rabid rats, skulking about on their hind legs like in some low-budget horror movie.

Part way through grade ten, shortly after he started dating Ang, she convinced him to avoid booze totally. She said, "If it makes you sick, why do it? As for me, any booze reminds me of pig shit. And I don't do pig shit."

Besides, he didn't want to end up like his father, Lewis Senior. A binge drinker who somehow scored long-term disability early in his work career, his boozy abuse was all about neglect. Lew Senior missed many school concerts and Christmas plays and was "sick in bed," even for Lew's grade eight farewell. But the time that stands out most in his mind is *Schindler's List*.

As part of a grade twelve Social Studies project, his class was supposed to watch the movie with a parent, "for guidance," and then prepare a group report. Ang was in his group.

The high school had procured a number of VHS copies to be signed out and Lew and Ang watched with Lewis Senior. Passing out about a third of the way through, his guidance had consisted of comments like, "Who is this guy? Is this guy real?" and, "Why is a modern movie filmed in black and white?"

The next morning, Ang came to pick up Lew for school and to get release forms signed for the project. Without reading the forms, Lewis Senior asked, "What am I signing here? For what movie, now?"

Ang's raised eyebrows and exaggerated smile told Lew Junior to grab the signed forms and get them the hell out before an inundation of stupid questions. On the way to school, he wondered aloud what the point was in having a parent present when he didn't even understand the story? "And what sort of possible guidance does the school think we can get from a hungover parent signing a release form after passing out during the project?"

Ang shrugged and said, "School is generally pointless. But what can you do? It's all about compliance and marks. Thinking has nothing to do with it."

Now, here at the mine, Lew thinks, at least the orientation sessions and tests have practical applications. Here, the student gets a modicum of respect from instructors who actually try to teach something, as opposed to making sure rows of desks are perfectly aligned.

His thoughts are interrupted when Ted says, "And considering that consideration, don't let Hal talk you into shit. Shit only leads to worse shit."

Hal takes a large and noisy bite of celery and chews with his mouth open while staring directly at Ted.

Although not physically afraid of Hal, Lew is intimidated by the man's seemingly limitless knowledge. Hal knows way too much about everything and has no qualms about sharing his wealth of information. During an earlier break, Hal compared the salt content of the human body to the shallow, prehistoric sea that once covered part of Saskatchewan. He pulled comparative salt parts per million out of his head. Without pause, he then segued into a pontification on the history of Liverwood Potash Corporation. In one of the areas that would have been a deep part of that prehistoric sea, sat the town of Liverwood.

Hal said, "So when potash was first mined around here in the 60s, local interests, headed by the Asp family, invested in Liverwood Potash. The mine was nationalized by the province in the late 70s, with healthy, healthy profits for the owners," he added with his sneer. "Then, when all the potash mines were privatized in the 80s, shares were sold back to the Asp family at distressed prices. Then come the 90s and the government of the day changes yet again. Somehow all of the Asp family shares are sold back to the government at market prices making Liverwood Potash the only crown-owned potash mine in the province. Funny the things you can accomplish when you contribute heavily to the main political parties, hey?"

On his next day off, Lew verified Hal's facts at the Liverwood library.

He didn't doubt Hal's voluminous knowledge or his intelligence. Especially considering he had somehow divined what Ashley and Lew both majored in on that very first day at the mine.

Later he asked Ted, "Who would keep all those facts in his head and why?"

Grinning, Ted replied, "Hal's like the computer from that movie. He knows everything about everything, however useless the information."

"The super-computer HAL from *2001*?" he said.

"You got it," said Ted. "Hal's a space odyssey."

Lew just hopes that there is no intentional, malicious programming in this particular version of Hal: the Hal who chews celery with his mouth open.

"Anyway," says Hal, "the root beer is an incentive to play poker with us this Friday. We need new meat to slaughter. Most of these losers," he waves his arm in a broad sweep around the room, "just don't got the chops. They're all too cowardly to take us on again."

The room erupts in general Hal bashing and a floret of broccoli flies in his direction. Without turning his head, Hal grabs the floret in mid-flight with his left hand and pops it into his mouth. Chewing the broccoli, he says, "I heard you say your girlfriend is gone with her parents to see relatives in Manitoba and you have a free weekend." Swallowing, he continues, "So I know you'll be bored in five seconds. Come play with us. Give it a try."

Ted says, "I say again, don't let him talk you into shit. But if you really want to . . . " He trails off without finishing.

Lew thinks, *Hal's right. I will be totally bored without Ang.* He says, "I think I am convinced. Where and when?"

∾∾∾

Lew has heard that poker nights could turn into weekend-long affairs with some people playing for forty-eight hours or more straight through. He has no intention of hanging around Hal's basement that long.

Walking to Hal's house from the Motel 6, he gazes up at the mine's plume reflecting orange in the setting sun. The sky reminds him of nuclear winter and a horror story he once wrote for a high school English course. The teacher had her class complete a fiction submission to a magazine as the major project for the course curriculum. His story was about life underground after a nuclear war where humans fought large rats for the scant food resources. He sent the story to a Canadian science fiction magazine but it was not accepted.

He received his best high school marks in English and picked it as a university major for lack of a better subject. But he's clearly not a writer of any sort and school can be so brutal with papers and exams and too many books he's not interested in reading. At least at the mine, when the shift is over, work is over for the day or for the weekend.

He shifts his backpack higher on his shoulders and the two six-packs of Stella Artois clink inside. He has brought the Belgian beer and a sack of pretzels to share. The gift bottle of root beer is stowed, still unopened, at the bottom of the backpack.

Turning onto Hal's street, he takes one last look at the plume. He just might skip school for a couple of years and work at the mine until he decides on another major. Or maybe he'll work in the mine until Ang graduates U of S from Veterinary Medicine and then he could be a kept man and learn to write horror stories. *She'd totally let me get away with that. As if.*

Reaching Hal's modest, older bungalow close to the centre of town, he remembers that he was told to go around back. There, other miners are clustered around a picnic table in the backyard smoking cigarettes and cigars.

He's met with, "Hey, Lulubelle," and, "Lulubelle made it."

"Hey, guys," he replies. He opens his backpack and pulls out one of the six-packs. "Where can I put this? Consider it a bribe to let me win."

There are a few guffaws. Someone reaches out a hand and says, "You can put one right here."

He passes over a couple of bottles and someone with a bottle opener on his jackknife passes that tool around. He is told to stow the rest of his beer in the fridge in the basement.

He yanks open the wooden screen door without knocking, steps onto the worn brown carpet of the landing, and descends the wooden stairs. Hal's basement is partially finished, with drywall painted only with a faded undercoat. The cement floor is painted grey with varied throw-rugs covering most of the area. Single shade lamps suspended from the open floor joists illumine six round tables. Four of the tables are occupied.

He notices that he's the only summer student or temporary employee and is definitely the youngest person there. He puts his remaining beer and root beer in the refrigerator and sets his pretzels with other snacks on an old kitchen table beside the fridge.

The players are too intent on their games to notice him.

Ted and Hal are at one of the tables with two other men he does not know. Judging from their heavily bearded faces and mullets, he doubts that they're miners. Making his way to that table, he discreetly stops a step away, with Ted on his left and Hal on his right. The game is Texas Hold'em and he can see each of their hole cards when they lift them. He makes absolutely sure he does not kibitz and stands silently and without expression. However, he can't stop his eyes from going wide when he sees the number of hundred dollar chips in the pot.

Intending to lose a limit of twenty, he'll last only for the first bet. It will be a short night.

Hal yells, "Cocksucker. I'm out." He flings his cards down, stands up and stomps past Lew.

Betting continues until Ted is finally called. He grins and says, "Straight flush, *genitals.*"

The other men shake their heads and one repeats Hal's epithet.

The other says, "That calls for a smoke break."

Both of the men stand up and head for the stairs.

Ted gathers his chips with both hands and yells, "Thank *youuuu.*" His grin breaks the tension of the moment. He turns in his chair and says, "Lulubelle. You're here."

"Hey," Lew replies. "Looks like I'm just watching. I can't afford those stakes."

Ted stands and stretches his thick arms straight up, almost touching the ceiling. "We wouldn't do that to you," he says and slaps him on the back. "Fish have to work their way up to the shark tank. Small stakes are over there." He points at one of the vacant tables. "As soon as those ass-clowns outside finish their smokes, you newbs can start. And remember, don't go over your limit."

"I don't intend to. Uh, Stella in the fridge, for anyone who's interested. Can I grab you one?"

"You bet," says Hal, sitting down again and re-stacking his remaining chips.

"Ted? Stella? Or does your drink need a top up?" Lew points at Ted's half-full glass of dark liquid.

Ted's grin has disappeared. He replies, "Sure, grab me my *pussy-man* Coke if you're heading for the fridge."

Lew shakes his head. "'Pussy-man Coke'?"

"Diet, caffeine free," says Hal with that half sneer. "Only a pussy-man would drink that carcinogenic, tasteless, slough water."

"Sore loser," Ted says with a laugh.

"I get it," says Lew. "Stay sober while playing."

"Don't bet on it, Lulubelle," Hal says. "You're not the only one with an aversion to booze."

"You don't drink?" Lew says to Ted, surprised.

"One addiction at a time." Ted turns abruptly and heads for an interior door.

Hal says, "Yeah, that's the pisser, Lulubelle. You don't need to watch to see if he gets there okay. I'm gasping here. Where's that Stella?"

Lew takes Ted's glass to the fridge, tops it off, and grabs a beer for Hal, the root beer for himself. By the time he returns, the smokers are trundling downstairs.

He joins a table of relatively younger men, all from the mine and all in their mid-twenties. Each hand is dealer's choice and Lew always calls five card draw. He manages this game fairly well and plays for a good few hours on his initial fifty-dollar buy in. *So much for only twenty bucks,* he thinks.

Betting conservatively and never bluffing, he has a few big wins. However, his play pattern is too predictable and the pots become successively smaller every time he has a good hand. It's midnight when he reaches his limit. A fifty down the toilet. But he has had a reasonably good time holding his own against his peers.

There is only one other active table left and he wanders over. Ted and Hal are still seated with the two bearded strangers. Another miner and a third bearded stranger are also at the table, making the game a six-hander.

Lew sees fifty and hundred dollar bills in the mix of high-priced chips. The tension at this table is almost tangible. He absolutely does not want to chance even a glance at anyone's hole cards, so he keeps two paces back this time. With such high stakes, he would risk life and limb if he interfered in this game. Even the slightest facial tick could prove dangerous, especially considering that the bearded strangers remind him of badass bikers from those '60s and '70s Roger Corman movies he and Ang watch on retro nights.

Two older miners on the opposite side of the table are also watching the game from a distance, absolutely poker-faced.

Ted takes the pot with another straight flush.

Hal slams his open palms on the table, making chips jump. "You fucker. Two straight flushes in one night? I should kill you with a butter knife so I can stab you a gazillion times. You busted me, you fuck."

With that, Hal storms away. He bangs around in the fridge a moment. Grabbing another bottle of Stella, he stomps upstairs.

Ted and the other players re-stack their chips and one of the bearded strangers calls seven-card stud. They don't talk or joke or even look at one another.

One of the watching miners across the table leaves without a word. The second circles the table and whispers to Lew, "Pretty intense, hey? I'll bet you weren't expecting this."

Lew replies, "Their expressions definitely suggest they could stab each other."

"No stabbings to date," the miner mumbles and then shushes Lew when betting starts.

Ted loses that round and the next deal starts immediately.

Lew whispers, "Who are those other dudes?"

"Professional moochers, occasional bouncers, and sometime card sharps. That big mother is a drug dealer."

Lew doesn't know to which "big mother" the miner refers, with all the players about the same size as Ted.

"They all hang out at the Steak House, you know that brown brick ex-hotel corner of Main and Railway?"

Lew nods. Ted's straight flushes must be luck then. No one in their right mind would dare cheat against a badass biker, let alone a drug dealer. He whispers, "This high-stakes stuff is too serious for me. I'm gone. See you at work."

He grabs his backpack. At the top of the stairs he peers into the kitchen to say thanks to Hal, but the host is nowhere to be seen. With the backyard totally deserted, he heads for home.

The intensity of those last rounds has soured the overall relaxed feeling he had built over the course of the night. He has never seen Hal that hostile before. There's always a malignant intensity about Hal but that near violence is definitely something he could do without.

While walking in the silent, windless night, with the mine's plume reflecting white in the moonlight and obscuring the bright stars in that part of the sky, he wonders how long Hal will remain angry.

He also wonders how long Ted's luck will hold out.

ᴓᴓᴓ

Monday, before the start of the four-to-midnight shift, Lew drinks coffee with Hal in their usual spot at the long table.

Hal is regaling him with his brilliant play during Friday's poker game. Lew is not listening because he is wondering where Ted is. Ted is usually on site long before he is.

Maybe Ted played all weekend? Did his luck hold? Or did he lose big time? And if he did lose big, how big?

He can't get those humongous stakes out of his mind.

Hal abruptly stops yammering and watches past Lew's shoulder. His eyes wide, he actually chews on his lower lip, brow uncharacteristically smooth.

Lew turns in his chair to see Ted shuffling towards them, carefully watching his feet, his hardhat way back on his head. He sits with a cursory, "Hi guys," and proceeds to drink directly from his thermos jug. The smell of strong coffee permeates the air.

Hal says, "Remember, coffee's a diuretic."

"Two litres of water before I left the trailer. Two more litres in the car waiting for my break. Don't worry, I'll stay hydrated, doc. Right now I need caffeine." There are dark bags under Ted's eyes. His eyelids droop and his face is haggard and pale. He sets his thermos down and turns to face Lew. "How was the rest of your weekend?"

Lew hopes his expression doesn't show the alarm he's feeling when he says, "Boring as feces. Exactly like you two predicted. I spent most of the weekend studying mine procedures like you told me to."

Before either of them reply, he takes the plunge, and says to Ted, "You don't look at all well. If you're sick you should stay home. At least that's what you both always tell me."

Hal says, "We're the mentors. We make the rules. We therefore can break the rules. Mind your place, Lulubelle, until you replace one or both of us."

Feeling momentarily complimented at the thought of replacing either man, Lew says, "Yes, boss."

Hal says to Ted, "And you'd better eat something before work."

Ted opens his cooler and removes a sandwich of rigid white bread and a single, nondescript cold cut.

"You grabbing extra shifts?" Hal asks.

"What else is new? You too?"

"Of course. I still got a mortgage."

Lew asks, "How come there's so much overtime available?"

Hal says, "It's simple. The Ministry of Mines tells Liverwood exec's that we gotta fill those new Asian contracts. The exec's go, 'duh, okay, let's get 'er done.' 'Get 'er done,' regardless of consequences. So somebody asks, 'what about maximum work-hour legislation?' To which the Ministry of Jobs and Employment says, 'duh, Mines says we gotta fill them contracts so we won't enforce the max work-hour standards.' And it's a done deal. Consequently, us toilers of the deep roll in the bucks. Somebody's gotta take them to court to stop them and I definitely ain't because I like rolling in the bucks."

Lew says, "So, why does the union allow maximum work hours to be ignored?"

Hal says with his typical sneer, "Whaddya think?"

Ted says, "The union takes a percentage of our total salaries. I don't know if that actually has anything to do with it. I'm just saying."

Hal flicks his finger against the side of his nose.

ᏨᏨ

Ted jumps down past the last two steps of the metal ladder on the centrifuge platform. His legs buckle and he falls to a sitting position.

Dropping his shovel, Lew runs toward the older man, who removes his hardhat, sways, and flops flat on his back.

Lew arrives and flings his own hardhat, goggles, and ear plugs aside just in time to hear Ted say, "Goddammit."

He does not think. His first aid training during orientation possesses all of his faculties. Checking extremities for breaks first, he next firmly squeezes Ted's thighs and asks if Ted can feel the pressure.

"Of course I can," Ted says. "I just slipped down these damn stairs."

"Don't move 'til I'm done," Lew says. He firmly but gently grips Ted's head and slowly turns it left and then right, all the while watching for the slightest grimace of pain.

"I'm fine, I tell you," Ted says. "No stars, no flashes. No pain anywhere. Move. I'm getting up."

From behind him a voice says, "Do what he says, Lulubelle."

Hal leans over them, face pale and taunt. He holds a first aid kit.

Lew's amazed at Ted's speed and agility. The large man is up in an instant.

"You good, buddy?" Hal says, grabbing Ted's neck.

Slapping his arm aside, Ted says, "Fine. Nothing broken. Now stop being dawdling old wet-nurses. We're not slowing production for a slip on the stairs."

Ted's face is plainly more pale, his eyelids still droop; his hardhat sits askew when he puts it back on his head.

"So, how do we report this?" Lew asks.

"We don't," Ted says. "I just told you we're not slowing production for a lousy pratfall. Back to work."

Lew is about to spout ingrained safety protocols when a sharp squeeze to his deltoid muscle makes him flinch.

Hal says, "As one of the senior miners here, I determine if we report it or not. And I say we don't. Do you concur, other senior miner currently present on the scene?"

Ted nods in agreement and says, "Absolutely."

The old miner who replaced Ashley approaches, listens, then simply turns away and walks back to his conveyors without a word.

"Besides," Hal continues, "it takes personnel eight months to do a lousy work-accommodation evaluation. And that only gets started after you open a Worker's Comp complaint. They don't care about production or workers and it'll take them a decade to process the paperwork. And we need to work. So to your shovel, Lulubelle."

Ted says, "It's all good. Now seriously, back to work."

Retrieving his safety gear, Lew watches the two older men shuffle away, their heads tilted toward one another in intense conversation.

When the shift ends, Ted tells Lew that he and Hal are taking the next midnight-to-eight shift.

"Should I stay and take an extra shift with you guys?" he asks.

"Be great to have you," Ted replies, "But more senior guys already filled any available slots. Relax while you can. See you tomorrow afternoon."

He starts to walk away, hesitates and then says, "Ted?" Waiting for the older man to turn, he crosses the Rubicon and boldly asks, "Are you really okay to pull a double?"

Ted rests both his hands on Lew's shoulders. He says, "I'm sure I need another shift. Thanks for your concern but don't worry about me. Go home and get some sleep."

∾∾∾∾

Riding his bicycle to the Motel 6, Lew worries that Ted looked too pale and had the blank stare of a horror movie zombie when they parted company. How much sleep did the guy really get over the weekend? This is like that sleepless, final exam time. *God, I hate finals. I'm really glad I don't have to deal with that shit. At the moment, anyway.*

The night is cool and windless and the near-full gibbous moon is bright enough to create shadows and partially light the road. It's bright enough to see thistle and other weeds crowding up from the ditch. The silence, now that the miners' cars of that last shift have all passed, enhances Lew's sense of peace and he wonders how much he's going to miss Ted, and maybe Hal just a little bit, when the fall semester starts and he's back on campus.

He recalls Ted telling him, after his one and only trip underground during orientation, that the deeper you go, the older the rock. Those underground strata have been there for millions of years. What constancy. As constant as Ted has been in his life these scant few weeks. What's he going to do without Ted? He's the antithesis of school teachers and even university professors. No question is too stupid, no matter how many times it's asked. No answer is ever condescending or sarcastic, no matter how many times it's given. How many times has Ted shown him exactly how to use that shovel with the least strain on the back?

Once, during a break when they sat alone at the long table, he said to Ted, "I want to thank you for all your guidance."

"That's what I'm here for."

"You spend so much time watching over me, I wonder where you find time to do your own work." He couldn't bring himself to ask specifically why Ted spent so much time with him. He hoped the older man got the gist of his question without being offended.

Ted did get it and wasn't offended. He said, "It's all part of the process. Safety is number one priority. Watching over you newbs is built into my schedule. Besides, Lulubelle," using the nickname with a kindly tone of voice, "you remind me of me. I see oodles of potential if you decide to stay. And I'm not just saying that because we're supposed to encourage you to stay, after investing all those resources training you."

"Thanks for that," Lew said, feeling his face flush.

"Nothing to be embarrassed about. I was mentored by old man Treadwell, my daughter's surrogate granddad, so the least I can do is pass on his sage advice to the up and comers. He got me in the mill while he stayed underground the whole time he was here. You'll do the same when your time comes. Besides, it's nice to work with someone who's interested and wants to do a good job. You've outlasted more than half of those linebackers that started with you. And that Ashley dude. Not only was he as useless as a sack of broken doorknobs, he was terrified of everything. The service lift, the machines, even the noise in the mill."

Lew's throat is tight. The veteran passing on his wealth of battle knowledge to the greenhorn. He manages to croak, "Yeah, I can't believe how much trouble he had even using the shovel. He barely had the stamina to last through his first shift. The things some people won't do for money."

Ted tilted his head toward the table. He shrugged and said, "Yeah."

Lew felt his face flush even hotter. His attempted Ashley-bash and feeble joke were a complete fail. He quickly said, "So, you have a daughter. Do you have any other kids?"

"Nope," Ted replied. "Lourdes is the only child of two only children. Took her on the service lift once when she was way small. She freaked, poor little thing. I felt so bad for her."

"I'm an only child too. Do you carry a photograph of her?"

Ted patted his overall pockets and said, "No photo, but she draws me some pretty good pictures." He pulled a piece of pink construction paper from his overall's inside pocket.

The pencil crayon rendering of a large man and small girl was well proportioned and not the usual childish stick figures. Two people, both with flaming orange hair, stood holding hands on an obvious shore.

"Not bad," Lew said, but he was more intrigued by the couplet written in gel pen under the drawing: *If only you and me/could dwell beside the sea.*

"'Dwell?'" Lew said. "Pretty adult word. How old is she?"

Taking the drawing back, Ted stared at it a moment. "Eleven. Reads, writes, and draws all the time. She leaves these notes under my pillow. Poor little thing — with all these double shifts and busy weekends I hardly get to see her. Once the new contract quotas are filled though, I'm going to change my ways and I'll spend a lot more time with her."

Goddammit is right. Lew's throat is again tight as he bikes into the gravel parking lot of the Motel 6. *The older the rock the deeper underground you go.* Yes, that old rock is constant like the bonds between veteran and raw recruit, journeyman and apprentice. *I don't know what I've done to deserve a mentor like Ted, but I'd definitely watch* Schindler's List *with him, anytime. And cherish the moment.*

Unlocking the door to his room, he turns on the light and strides to the telephone. Listening to the ring indicator, he prays Ang is back from her Manitoba trip and that she won't be too mad at him for calling her past midnight.

∾∾∾

Lost in his own thoughts, Lew pays little attention to the memorial service that is nearing its conclusion. Ang is his lifeline. He clings desperately to her.

At the start of his bus trip to Saskatoon after his last afternoon shift, he'd stared vacantly out of the window at the rolling, brushy, prairie landscape and the last of the dispersing plume from the mine. He'd felt as if the service shaft's tubing had ruptured and the water-bearing strata between the surface and underground mine site was inundating him; drowning him.

Ted had intended to work overtime straight through, with maybe one day off between the switch from afternoon to midnight shifts. Even though he had wanted to stay with Ted and Hal and work the overtime with them, he needed the four-day break. That last rotation on afternoon shift had been a stupidly long eight-day stretch and he hadn't seen Ang for more than two weeks. But all during the bus ride and even from the moment Ang picked him up at the bus depot, he was distracted, thinking about Ted. His distraction even resulted in them falling asleep in each other's arms that first night.

Next day, when they heard on the CBC news that there had been an accident at the mine, a fatality, he immediately thought of Ted.

Ang called both of her part-time jobs and said she wasn't coming to work due to a family emergency and drove them both back to Liverwood.

A swirl of activity followed. He remembers Hal's grey-blue eyes, vacant and moist. Hal said that Ted had collapsed and tumbled over the railing of the centrifuge platform. He had hit his head on one of the conveyors and then was taken by ambulance to Yorkton. "We did everything we could. But the ambulance was too slow."

Ted's ashes are carried out of the chapel by the funeral director. The tiny woman shuffles beside him and the tall, bald man and the woman in her old-fashioned long black dress, again holding the hands of that little girl with the flaming red hair, follow.

Then mourners, row by row.

Lew leans against Ang, his arm around her waist, as they make their way outside.

Aware only of the sunshine and the mine's plume reflecting bright white overhead, he sees Hal standing alone in the crowd, his eyes glistening like a hopelessly lost child; perhaps in a pit deep underground.

They approach Hal and he says in a humourless monotone, "You staying on at the mine? There's an opening now."

He replies, also humourlessly, "Of course. How could I possibly give up the name Lulubelle?"

They stand in silence until Hal starts to shake. He drops his head and grasps his forehead with both hands. "He was so tired from all those extra shifts, trying to get out of the red. I told him not to take off his hardhat. I told him, Lulubelle, but he didn't hear me . . . "

Lew can't speak. He simply opens his arms and Hal looks up and they embrace. He feels all of Hal's muscle and sinew collapse into saggy tailings.

Lew is upright, steadfast, while the miners hold onto one another tightly for a wordless minute.

Leaving With Lena

DILLON POKED AT THE SCUM floating on his coffee with a stir stick. He then leaned back in his chair, an ergonomically correct, high-backed tilter that did not match the hideous beige of his 48" cubicle panels. The two guest chairs, intended for visiting external sales people, also a vague and worn beige, sat in front of his dark brown, teak-laminate desk.

Rubbing his eyes, he signed into the Procurement Request system on his computer. His first requisition was for drills and drill bit sets for the general maintenance department at the mine site. He sat back again and wondered if Lena was already at her battered secretarial desk across the office, out of his line of sight. Maybe he should clean the coffee maker instead of filling orders. "Or not," he said out loud. "Not in my job specs."

"What's that you're muttering there, *Dial-on*?" said Buck, a co-worker in internal supply and distribution and sometime drinking buddy. He plopped down in one of the guest chairs. His convenience-store thermal cup, with the vendor's name worn off, was so full, coffee slopped out of the holes in the lid.

"Exactly. Just muttering, *Puck*," replied Dillon.

"Geez, sitting around talking to yourself, pally? You really need to get laid. Anyway, have we got a story to tell you. You know Johnathon the summer student?"

"Never heard of him. The only summer student I know around here is Lena, doing some sort of Religious Studies master's degree. I *do* know a Johnathon who's a co-op Admin student slotted as a junior buyer for his work term."

Buck took a noisy and exaggerated slurp of his coffee. "Dick-less, *Dial-on*. How could I forget that rhetoric is not in your repertoire. Mr. Liter-alley himself."

"Well, at least I have a marginal command of the English language, unlike some Bumbling-Bucks I could name. Do you even know what rhetoric means?"

"Doesn't matter. I came to tell you that we all went for beers last night and got kinda goofing around and got into the dare thing. So, we dared Johnathon to smell Lena's chair seat and he did it."

"Lame. You're losing what little talent you never had." Dillon took a swallow of his own coffee. "Try harder."

"It's no joke. It's totally true. And totally weird. Like, I mean, he got down on his knees and really took a whiff. A normal guy would just jerk around and then pretend to sniff and come up laughing when everybody groans. But he stayed there. And when he came up, he kinda had this look on his face."

"What look?"

"A weird look — on his face. He wasn't laughing. He just kinda smirked. The guy's on something or he's a total jerk-*meister.*"

"And you're not all of the above? How many beers did it take you idiots to come up with this?"

"No, you moron. I'm serious. Give Elmo or Billy a blast. They'll confirm."

"Oh, sure, let me *confirm* with Mr. Buck Van-Pretense's not-so-stealthy stooges. I'm supposed to call your co-conspirators to lend credibility to the fables of Aesop sitting across from me here? Good luck."

"Shit, Dillon. You're such a boner since you and Tiffany hit the skids."

∾∾∾∾

Tiffany and Dillon had been an item for over three years. They met when Tiffany was a sales rep for a stationary company selling office supplies to Liverwood Mines. When she started working for an insurance agency and any perception of corporate impropriety was eliminated, Dillon asked her on a date. Six months after that, he moved into her condominium, hoped he could calm her down, steer her away from her self-destructive binges; for example: spontaneous bar-top stripteases down to her underclothes. He'd wanted to get her away from the Buck-like slouches who leered and slobbered over her runway body and exotic, shoulder-length black hair. In return, she came up with venomous and unjustified accusations when he even looked at another girl. This cycle only ended with him learning to match her drink for drink. They both spiralled downward, with booze-saturated puke on the bathroom floor or in the kitchen sink, and one or the other sleeping on the couch, and after a 500 ml container of margarine splattered on the wall inches from his head and his fist flew past Tiffany's face and punched a hole in the drywall, he moved to his own place. That was a couple months ago.

∾∾∾

Buck swirled the coffee in his cup. "You're better off without her, you know."

"That much I've figured out. Haven't you got work to do?"

Buck stood up. "I don't know why I bother with you. My advice still stands."

"What advice?"

"Get laid. I saw Deirdre on my way in. She's wearing that sweet, lowcut top."

"Duly noted, *pally*. And hey," Dillon waited until Buck turned back, "come up with a better story."

Buck shook his head and said, "You're boring. I gotta check out what Lena's got on today."

∾∾∾

Lena had been at her desk when Dillon met her on her first day. She gave him a friendly and welcoming good morning and a warm smile. He stood still and took in this thin, but well proportioned, plain-faced girl with freckles on her upper cheeks, and strawberry-blonde hair that hung in a curled mess down to her shoulders; her petite nose wrinkled slightly with that smile.

He introduced himself and immediately retreated to the break room for a desperately needed cup of coffee. He was in shock and awe; Lena, he perceived, was some sort of angelic antithesis to Tiffany.

Back at his desk, he decided that Lena's friendliness was the total opposite of the overt hostility underlying the whole department. He wondered if she actually was an angel.

That afternoon break, he went to find Buck and the others. The three of them were swarming around her desk like wasps at an open pop can.

"Come on *chumm . . . ps*," he said, attempting to deflect attention away from her. "Break time. Let's go."

"Hey Dillon," replied Buck, putting his hand on Lena's shoulder, "Have you met our new acquisition?"

"Come on." Dillon marched toward the exit but the others didn't budge. Lena kept typing, her shoulders taut, expression neutral.

He turned back to grab Buck by his shirt collar but Johnathon appeared. He yelled, "Hey, Lena. You know stuff about spreadsheets." He elbowed his way between Lena and Buck. "Can you open file manager and go to the budget shared drive? I think I screwed up a range of cells in one of the files." He leaned over her shoulder and directed her to the appropriate network drive.

Lena's shoulders visibly relaxed. After a minute, the wasps leisurely drifted off to join Dillon for coffee break. He never saw that angelic smile again.

❀❀❀

He shook his head to clear thoughts of Lena and drained his cup. He proceeded to work through requisitions for hand tools, bearings for roller assemblies, and a portable 6.5 HP generator. He called different vendors and checked online prices and got delivery costs to the mine site.

He soon found himself thinking about Johnathon. The guy was in his early thirties, the same age as him and Buck and their office cohorts. But unlike he and the others, who all had gone right from high school to Admin degrees and turned into some sort of office-drones — which is what he felt he presently was — Johnathon had spent ten years working fast food kitchens and nighttime security jobs, including a year-long stint as a "swabbie" on a container ship. It was only after his time at sea that Johnathon signed up for his Co-op Admin Degree. He was therefore a mystery. He occasionally tagged along for after-work drinks but only when cajoled.

Dillon wondered why they'd all gone for drinks without him last night.

He scanned the break room. Johnathon was by himself, tapping on his Android tablet, a half-empty orange juice bottle on the table beside him. Dillon poured himself a cup of coffee and approached the table.

Johnathon looked up, nodded. "Solo today?" he said. "Where's Buck and buddies?"

"Who cares. What's this I hear about you going for brewskies with those clowns?"

"We went over to The Cavern for a few drinks and a bite to eat, yes." Johnathon hesitated. "I expected you to show up."

"I was on suicide watch last night."

"Your ex still?"

"Tiffany seems to think I owe her money for unequal contributions to living expenses over the years."

"I'm sorry to hear that."

"Not your problem. So, Buck told me about the chair. What's the scoop?"

Johnathon turned off his tablet and set it down. "That's straight to the point. I did not smell her chair when they dared me."

"And?"

"And nothing. I am so tired of their stupid jokes. Why don't they just shut up about Lena and leave her alone?"

Dillon pushed thoughts of Lena from his mind and studied Johnathon. He had a mass of dirty blond hair, always in disarray, and his slightly bulging eyes had an open innocence about them. He stood six-foot-two, with huge hands and shoulders, just as broad as Buck's, but he had a spongy body. "You really expected me to show up last night?"

"Why wouldn't I? Buck said you were coming. And I've been wanting to talk to you about a couple of things."

"Oh?"

"One, I've been meaning to thank you."

"For what?"

"For not indulging in the constant dirty tricks they play on me. It's nice you and I can have a half-assed, decent conversation about something other than the latest sporting event or the contours of some woman's breasts."

"Uh huh." Dillon drank some coffee. "And two, you were going to admit you have a thing going with Lena."

Johnathon cheeks reddened and he smiled. "Not exactly." He took a drink from his juice bottle.

"Whaddya mean, 'not exactly'? You hang around her desk all the time, like some sort of sentry. You almost rest your chin on her shoulder when you look at her screen." He poked at the scum on his coffee with his finger.

Johnathon stared at his bottle. "They hit on her all the time." He paused a moment. "What would stop them anyway?

Dillon shook his head. "Those guys will fish off of any dock, including the company one."

"And they're all married or attached too, aren't they?"

"Just Buck. Billy's single. He is too stoned to stay with any one girl for more than a night. Elmo just split with his wife."

"He doesn't seem bothered by it."

"Not like it bothers me, you mean?"

"That's not what I meant."

"Yeah, sure." Dillon stood up and turned to leave. "I'm done here."

"Drinks tonight?" Johnathon said.

❦❦❦

Dillon was at a table in The Coffee Cavern bar finishing his chicken burger. He took a swallow from his pint just as Johnathon appeared at the entrance. He waved his glass.

"Hey, Dillon," Johnathon said and sat down. "Thanks for meeting me. That's mine?" he pointed at the sweating glass of tonic water with lime.

"Hope it's not too warm," Dillon replied. "Anyway, now I don't have to drink alone. You know what they say about that."

"I do," replied Johnathon. "Are the guys going to show up?"

"The clowns are off to an NHL pool draft. It's never too early for an NHL pool draft, yeah?"

"I guess." Johnathon took a long drink.

Dillon said, "Where's Lena?"

"Choir practice."

"So, tell me, how long have you two been an *item*?"

Setting his glass down, Johnathon thought a moment. "Quite a while, actually. She was the lab instructor in a Psych class I took as an elective last year. We were coffee-buddies on campus and hung out together. You know, the usual stuff. She was doing directed reading last semester, so we didn't see each other much. Quite the shocker when she got a job at Liverwood. It got serious a couple of weeks after that."

Johnathon wiped his lips with his fingers.

Dillon finished his pint and caught the attention of the server. "Lena's a Christian, yeah?"

Johnathon's entire face flushed. "She's not that radical. She's a caring, giving person who happens to have strong beliefs. She also acknowledges, you know, physical needs."

"Well, good for you two. Tell me though, isn't she going to Niger or Timbuktu or someplace when her summer job's done?"

"Ethiopia. She's going to do some mission work."

Dillon smirked. "Gee, that's only three weeks from now. You'd better get what you can in the meantime."

"We're not splitting up."

"Right. Good luck with that. Let me tell you about distance relationships. They don't work."

"I'm going with her."

Dillon stared at Johnathon, mouth wide open. A religious studies person taking off for mission work was one thing. But an admin student-cum-office-drone? When he could finally speak, he said, "What the hell would you do that for? You've only got two semesters left for your degree."

Johnathon shook his head. "I can get a degree any time."

Dillon just cocked an eyebrow and waited.

Johnathon cleared his throat. "I want to do something maybe meaningful. I don't need the kind of crap that goes on around here. The guys at the office are either procuring objects or girls any way they can." He shifted, his face red again. "Present company excepted, of course."

Dillon felt a heaviness. He said, "So you're just going to drop out and head for Africa? For a woman, no less? You're a ding-dong, you know that?"

"Lena is the first person I've ever met who is totally selfless. She makes me feel . . . like I owe her something."

Dillon shook his head. Wow. Here was a guy who easily managed his small part of the departmental processes, not because he was happy doing it, but because he had an escape plan. An escape with a near angel who didn't need to drink or strip or argue.

Once, in a boozy stupor, he had mentioned to Tiffany that he was afraid of becoming *the scum that forms* — a vague metaphor for concerns he couldn't quite fathom. Tiffany had tried to focus on him with her booze-bleary eyes and told him to suck it up and stop being an infant.

The server arrived with his next pint. He seized the glass and drank.

Johnathon asked, "Do you believe in fate?"

"Not particularly," Dillon replied, "But don't tell me." He touched his forehead with his fingertips and closed his eyes, "It was fated for you to meet Lena and then set off on some African adventure."

Johnathon shook his head. "I had a dream. And that's what I wanted to talk to you about. Without the *clowns*."

"You've lost me."

"Why don't you come with us?"

Dillon snorted. "Are you kidding? You sound like Martin Luther King. 'I had a dream.'"

"The missions always need people. And they don't have to be Christian. I'm not."

"Why the hell would I want to go to Ethiopia?"

"Because you're sick of the 'mindless morons' you deal with everyday? Including Tiffany and that girl from Accounting, Darla, Deedee?"

"Deirdre. And what's your insane dream got to do with me?"

"In it, you seemed very, very unhappy. You were on a wide, thorny plain, staring into an overcast horizon."

Dillon shook his head and drained his glass.

Johnathon said, "Anyway, I think you drink too much."

That crossed the line. Dillon clenched his jaw. "Well, Friar *John-oh-thon*, thanks for your concern." He stood up. "My drinking is none of your business. And keep me out of your idiot schemes. Dreams. Whatever the hell. I gotta blast."

"They're taking volunteers until early September," Johnathon said.

On his way home, the night was calm and cool. He was furious with that pretentious cock. And what about Lena? What was her real motive? She hated his guts. Didn't she?

∾∾∾∾

Dillon didn't despise his job. It was something he was good at. The salary was acceptable, about ten percent higher than the industry average for purchasing positions. He enjoyed talking on the telephone with the workers at the mine site. He liked dealing with outside vendors.

He stared at the flashing *message-waiting* indicator on his telephone. Why would someone dream about him, never mind consider his wellbeing? If he dared ask anyone in his current circle — miner, vendor, co-worker — they would undoubtedly be waiting for the Buck-type joke, the punchline, so they could snigger and . . .

He sighed and reached for the phone.

There was a voice message from Deirdre in Accounting. "Oh, *mygawd*, Dillon. I'm so sorry I haven't called you lately. I just couldn't find the energy. I have some news. I'd love to go for drinks, get caught up and, you know, whatever. Let's cut out a half hour early and get that back table at The Cavern. I've got something to ask you, too. I think I totally need a change."

This relationship, if you could call it that, was off again, on again, and they hadn't seen each other for a couple of weeks. She might be a distraction. He called her back and ended up leaving a message on her voicemail saying her plan worked for him.

ᕦᕤᕦ

Deirdre was late. The din in the bar increased while people filtered in after work. The Cavern's dark, hardwood floor was polished to a shine but the equally dark, exposed support beams and pillars and the brown brickwork gave the whole bar an oppressive feel. The subdued lighting, probably to hide the crappy brickwork, added a dinge factor and the black marble of the long counter did nothing to brighten the place.

But the drinks were cheap. He was well into his third pint when she finally rolled in; he watched her head directly to the bar. She had an ample and well-proportioned body, but the really attractive thing about her was her waist-length auburn hair. She ordered her drink and then turned and gave him a finger wave. Waiting for her drink, she twirled her hair. It was annoying, her tendency to twirl her ringlets in the fingers of her left hand.

She slid into the booth across from him and gently set down her Paralyzer. She clunked her purse, a purple and mauve shoulder bag with long straps, in the middle of the table.

He recoiled and snatched his glass, saving it from a tumble.

"Sorry I'm late," she said. "Some receivables didn't balance. To the order of nine cents, no less. The boss wouldn't let us leave until he got his reconciliation. It probably cost 900 dollars to find the stupid inverted cents entry that caused the difference in the first place. Nine cents! Just write it off, I say, but who listens to me? I hate that place."

"Yep," Dillon replied. "How's life in general?"

"Oh, *mygawd*. That's exactly why I called you. I need someone to talk to. This crappy life so sucks. I can't even begin. My *gawd*, he's taken up with a nineteen-year-old. Like, how sleazy can you get? Some newb little chicky he found when he was coaching community association basketball. Barely out of high school. I hope he gets the clap. And oh, my, *gawd*, you know what he says? He says, 'It's nothing personal.' He says he needs to live before he can be tied down with marriage and kids. So I spilled my drink in his lap and I said I hope his pecker falls off. But I got it together and you were there for me when I needed you. You've come to my rescue." Elbows on the table, she rested her chin on her interlaced fingers.

"Well, Deeds," he said, while she smiled coyly at the familiarization of her name, "Tough news. I'm sorry to hear it."

"Don't be. All the self-help books say we have to make the best of adversity, which is what I wanted to talk to you about. We should try and be selfless. I am. And I think you and I should do something radical. Totally for the selfless part of ourselves before we finally settle down. Something they'll talk about for years to come."

"A suicide pact?"

Deirdre's braying laugh was so loud some patrons were looking over at her. "You're hilarious." She let her hair go, dabbed at her eyes with a napkin, careful not to smear her mascara. "Seriously, I think we should run away to some exotic, unexpected location, you know, just for the long weekend?"

"How about Ethiopia?"

Furrowing her eyebrows, she shook her head once. "Do they have all-inclusives there?"

"Not exactly." He drained his pint and waved his glass at the server.

Deirdre shook her head. "Wait a minute." Her fingers twisted deeper into her curls. Her acrylic nails, purple and adorned with little black flowers, disappeared from view. "Isn't there, like, pirates in Ethiopia? And, *mygawd*, isn't it one of those places where women can't wear bikinis?"

He didn't bother to tell her there were no pirates because Ethiopia is landlocked. Instead he said,

"Someone suggested I should try a new job there for a while."

"Ewww." Her finger gyrations slowed as her head leaned over and rested on her hand.

Dillon was thinking about Johnathon's proposition. Johnathon and Lena and him, all together.

Deirdre stared vacantly until her eyes grew wide, as if at that perfect tropical, all-inclusive paradise. "Oh, my, *gawd*. I get you. You're pulling one of those silly Buck jokes, aren't you? Stop it right now. That's not even a little bit funny."

He laughed without humour. "Hey, you caught me." He wondered where his next drink was.

He was mired.

But if he was mired at that moment, Deirdre looked adrift and rudderless, a soul lost, out of sight of the coast of the Horn of Africa.

He said, "So, what places do you have in mind?"

"Well, now that you ask." Deirdre wiggled her eyebrows and pulled a stack of internet printouts on office paper from her purse. While pints and Paralyzers flowed she presented a plethora of getaways and he listened.

They left at closing time and he pushed Deirdre into the back seat of the first cab, and said, "I need some time alone."

"I thought you were coming over?"

"Not tonight." He slammed the cab's back door.

Staggering home, putting one foot in front of the other, trying not to trip on weeds growing through the sidewalk cracks, his mind remained completely blank.

∾∾∾

He finally managed to unlock the door of his downtown condo and stumbled inside, leaning at the entrance until the spinning slowed. The *message waiting* indicator was flashing '2'. Dali's *Temptation of St. Anthony*, the only thing on any of the walls, loomed above the answering machine.

He walked a reasonably straight line to the machine and pressed the *play messages* button. Johnathon said he and Lena had talked to their church pastor and they were holding a place for him in their upcoming mission. Before he could absorb an iota of Johnathon's words the next message chimed.

"Dillon. This is Tiffany. I want you to know that I don't blame you for our split and I don't hold a grudge, even though it is all essentially your fault, but . . . " His bladder protested and he rushed to the bathroom. " . . . too much smothering. Too much for me anyway. Perhaps a lesser woman . . . " He proceeded to brush his teeth, went back to the hallway and put his shoes and jacket in their places in the front closet while Tiffany's voice droned on, slurring occasionally, " . . . we agree our pensions won't be touched by the other person but when I think of the costs over the years, I really think I got the short end given that Saskatchewan marital law states that after a year of living together everything is a 50-50 split, and I know I make more money than you, but you shirked on daily living expenses and I've calculated you owe me . . . "

Maybe he should subscribe to voicemail so he can simply delete messages without having to listen to them all the way through. He pressed the delete button twice, eliminating both messages, then eased onto his black leather couch.

He thought briefly of channel surfing on his 42" flat screen TV, just to unwind a bit, but instead tossed the remote out of reach on one of the two matching leather armchairs, reached for the cardigan he kept on the back of the couch, covered himself, and passed out.

ᕼᕼᕼ

He sat up, fully dressed and checked his watch. Standing, he felt reasonably rested. Making his way to the bathroom, he wondered how much booze it would take before he started to suffer from hangovers — or maybe if he quit now he'd suffer withdrawal? That rested feeling only lasted until he finished urinating, then his conscious mind powered up. He felt like he was standing in the lowest level of the potash mine. A lump throbbed in his lower abdomen in all that heavy darkness. He hung his head and leaned against the wall above the toilet. He massaged his forehead.

Standing up straight, he was hit with a sudden resolve. He simply went with the impulse and made two telephone calls.

One was to his manager's voicemail to say he wasn't coming into the office. The second was to make an emergency appointment at a twenty-four-hour clinic.

The doctor on call there wrote a note prescribing, at his suggestion, three weeks off and some heavy antacid drugs. He also strongly suggested that Dillon stop drinking.

Scanning the doctor's note on his scanner/printer, he attached it to an email to his manager and, after another phone call to him, a three-week medical leave was agreed to.

Johnathon would cover for the duration of the absence. By the time Dillon returned to work, Jonathon's work term and Lena's summer job would be finished.

∾∾∾

Dillon did not believe he had a drinking problem. To prove it, he spent his entire absence avoiding all alcohol. This included wine with meals. He simply made up his mind not to drink, and he whiled away the hours cleaning and re-cleaning his austere and spotless home. He reorganized the kitchenette until nothing sat on the countertop; all small appliances, including the coffee-maker, grinder, mixer, sat behind closed cupboard doors with the plastic containers of flour, ground coffee, sugar.

He drank warm water with lemon or cups of fresh coffee to satisfy any urge to drink. The only time he ventured out was to buy groceries. Otherwise, he watched movies or TV series online, and never turned on the television other than to watch the news. He checked his email daily but deleted all messages unread.

He tried not to think of the office, Deirdre, Johnathon, Lena, or Ethiopia. He rejected the thought of the upcoming mission each time it emerged from the dark mineshaft. There was simply too much to leave behind. He couldn't even entertain the possibility.

He ignored a number of phone calls from Tiffany. He played messages with the answering machine's volume turned down and deleted them immediately.

He began deleting numbers from his telephone's directory and call list, including the pastor's and Johnathon's.

∾∾∾∾

On Dillon's first Monday back at work, Johnathon and Lena were gone; they would be in preparation for their mission to Ethiopia; they were to leave the following Friday.

A new girl, blonde, with heavy black mascara, and a body type that reminded him too much of Tiffany, sat at Lena's desk. He walked past her with a cursory "Good Morning," and headed to the break room for a cup of coffee before starting work.

He set his cup in its usual spot. A plain white envelope was almost completely tucked under his keyboard. It was addressed to *Dillon* in Johnathon's handwriting. He tore it open and found a single white sheet with names and telephone numbers: Johnathon's, the Pastor's, and Lena's, all handwritten. He stared at the sheet a moment, then rubbed his index finger over Lena's name, slightly smearing the ink.

Pursing his lips, he folded the page in half and ripped it four times. Balling the paper shreds together, he threw the wad into the garbage can.

He powered up his computer and stirred his coffee. He'd done it — dry for three weeks. Perhaps a treat — a celebration — was now in order? He'd head to The Cavern after work for sure. He set the stir stick across the rim of his cup and signed into the Procurement Request system.

Buck plopped down in a guest chair. "So, *whaddja* do on holidays there, pally? Thanks for not letting your buddies know what was coming down, by the way." He slurped coffee from his overflowing thermal mug.

"Watched movies. Cleaned the apartment. Told Tiffany to fuck off. And now I'm all ready for my brand new life."

"Geez, *Dial-on*, you're a machine, but you still need to get laid."

"What do you want, Buck?"

"Drinks after work? But if you're going to be all pissy, well. . . . " Buck trailed off and slurped again.

"Now look who's pissy. Of course I'm going for drinks."

Buck hesitated a moment and said, "So, have you heard about Deirdre?"

Dillon crossed his arms and leaned back. He waited for Buck to continue.

Buck blew on the lid of his cup and didn't say anything.

"Heard what?" Dillon finally snapped.

Buck took another long, loud slurp. "It's a sad, sad loss to all us healthy, red-blooded men here."

Dillon thought of his suicide pact joke and what a horrible turn such a thing could take. "What's your point, Buck?"

"Now don't make that face, pally." Buck slurped again. "She hauled that gorgeous ass off to Cancun. She gave two-week's notice and got an accounting job at some swanky five-star hotel. They gave her a suite — right on the beach, no less. The girl's gonna have a tough life down there. I sure hope she doesn't suffer too much."

"You're kidding me, right? This is another joke. It has to be."

"Try her number. She won't be answering that phone no more. She quit and moved away." Buck's cup hovered in front of his lips. "To Mexico no less."

Dillon put his hand on the telephone's handset. "I suppose there's worse places to live."

"Yeah, like Ethiopia."

Dillon felt his face flame. A hole burned through his stomach. He couldn't remember everything from that night, and that truly scared him.

Buck lowered his cup, exposing a twisted smirk, and burst out with a roaring *Bwa-ha-ha-ha*. "She told me all about your Ethiopia vacation joke and how you ditched her. You must've been like a baby monkey playing with his dink." Buck pointed at Dillon with his mug. "But what's really funny is you falling for that Cancun story. '*Oh, my gawd*,' Deirdre can barely talk English, let alone Mexican. You can be such a moron."

Buck looked at his watch and jumped up. "Well, gotta go pally. They hired a new temp-schlub to replace that Lena chick. I gotta go break in the new meat. Great body on that one. Later."

So this workday starts the same as all the others. If he goes drinking after work it will end the same. He really is the scum floating on his coffee.

Leaning over, he picks the ripped and crumpled page from the garbage and begins to smooth out the pieces.

Godsend

THERE WAS SOMETHING I NEEDED to remember. It wasn't work, I was already there staring at my bloodshot, bruised-looking eyes in the washroom mirror. I'd even made it on time because I had crashed at my friend Darryl's apartment, a ten-minute walk away. My clothes were a bit wrinkled but I'd been at work in worse shape before. Darryl even let me use his extra toothbrush. So what was it I had to do?

I had already called Esther. The answering machine at her house said *leave a message*, which I didn't. Her work voicemail said she was away. I didn't leave a message there either.

The last time we spoke she told me I whined like a mule. "That's creatively original," was my less than creative response. "By the way, nice mixed metaphor." Not that I know what a metaphor is, but I'd heard her say the same thing.

We had stayed married for about twenty years. The things we don't do for our children. Or only daughter in this case.

A recollection had just started to crawl up from the depths of my addled brain when Darryl found me.

"Miller, there you are. Lorne's looking for you and he's pissed off."

"How does he know we're hungover again?"

"You shouldn't slobber down a co-worker's cleavage first thing when you come into work. Especially if she goes to the same church as the boss, you dumb shit. And not we. Just you. I'm not the one who looks like he's still wasted."

"You always drink more than me and look at you." I blinked at his reflection in the mirror. Darryl's glaring-white, tapered shirt, crisply tucked in, revealed his broad-shouldered upper body. His black hair was perfectly groomed, without any of the grey which spread like a fungus from my temples.

"It's all in the genes," he said. "I told Lorne I'd go find you — I kind of figured you'd be here puking — so at least I could give you a head's up."

"I'm not puking. It's the dry heaves." The near constant pain in my stomach surged and I leaned my face toward the sink. Nothing happened.

Darryl clicked his tongue. "Whatever. Just get moving."

I turned toward the door and tried to properly tuck in my wrinkled Walmart dress shirt, which stretched across my belly and ballooned across the lower back.

He grabbed my arm. "And, hey. Keep me out of this. I'm not the one stupid enough to get caught. Again." He passed me his apartment keys. "Just in case," he said.

I made my way to Lorne's office. He immediately made eye contact with me and dropped the sheet of paper he was reading on his spotless, uncluttered desktop. He did not stand up or offer me a chair. Maybe he surrendered the psychological advantage because he was a large man and would have towered over me had he stood. Especially if I sat down.

Instead he leaned back in his chair and folded his hands across his massive midsection, his thick arms resting on the chair's arms. Without preamble or the usual lecture on company image, he said, "You are being suspended without pay for the rest of the day. The reason: inebriation in the workplace after multiple warnings."

"You can't do that." I vaguely waved my finger in his direction. "You can't even talk to me about this without a union representative present." I heard movement behind me and turned to see a uniformed contract security guard and a barrel-bellied retired cop from the internal security department hovering at the open door.

Lorne glanced at his watch. "I am intimately familiar with disciplinary procedures . . . because of you. You can have your say to the union at a hearing on Monday morning in the Staff Relations office in Personnel. Now that's Monday three days from now. This coming Monday morning, at 8:30 AM."

"All right. Monday. I'm not stupid."

"I want to make sure you don't have one of your convenient 'misunderstandings'." He picked up the sheet again and held it toward me. "This note reiterates what we've just discussed and, in bold, indicates the time and location of the meeting. Don't forget to report via the security kiosk. Until then, please leave." He nodded to the two men at the door. The ex-cop, whose name I would never remember placed a gentle hand on my shoulder.

"I'm launching a grievance, you know."

"Fine." Lorne did not move.

"Come on, Rex," said the ex-cop, and squeezed my shoulder lightly.

My security entourage followed me to my desk and watched me fumble through the telephone directory. I wanted the union office phone number but couldn't immediately find the listing. "Screw it. They're in on this conspiracy anyway." I threw the directory aside.

Darryl was nowhere to be seen when I was escorted out. The ex-cop asked me if I intended to drive home; he could call a cab if I needed one. "I intend to walk," I replied, "to my buddy's place, where my stuff is, and have a sleep. Thanks for the send off, boys."

They went back inside without another word.

I headed to Darryl's, fondling his keys in my pocket, for a well-deserved nap before going for a well-deserved drink.

の

I sat with Willie, the permanent resident of The Coffee Cavern, across the street from the building. He scratched his chin under his scraggly beard and flakes of dead skin drifted down onto the table.

He drained the glass of Guinness I'd bought him. "Jeez Rex, that bites. Sounds like them bastards are out to get you. You should get a lawyer or something. Especially if them union guys are in on it. You could probably sue them for a couple of hundred grand, eh?" He waved his empty glass at the server. "Do you mind?"

"What are friends for?" Although I hoped I wouldn't need the money for something else.

He attracted the attention of the server on station at the black marbled bar. I waved two fingers at her.

Willie said, "They're not going to send you to rehab again, are they?"

"So what? Darryl helped me out last time sneaking in the occasional flask. The Rehab staff was way overworked and I was a model attendee. Yeah, Esther dropped me off that time but I couldn't deal and I pretended to buzz in. Then came here. Remember that night?"

He nodded, staring down at his glass. Of course he remembered, even though I didn't completely. How many times had I told that Esther story?

I've never told what really happened the next day.

I woke up in Victoria Park beside a little playhouse. A young girl with a snotty nose was poking me with a stick. Her mother, sitting on a nearby bench and rocking a baby, kept yelling at her to leave me alone. Funny the things you do remember. I heaved myself up by clinging with both hands to the window opening of the playhouse.

"Good thing the cops didn't find you, eh?" The mother said with a smirk.

"You bet," I said and staggered to a coffee shop next to the park.

Suddenly there was this guy sitting across the table from me. Dressed like a tree-hugger in a vest with a million pockets, he was my height and his face was smooth with no crows-feet or black rings under the eyes. His dark hair, without a hint of grey, was pulled back in a ponytail much like the way my hair used to be twenty years back in those carefree university days. Those days before the grinding tedium set in under a perpetual plume of sales quotas and shipping schedules.

The guy extended his hand and said, *Kingsley.*

With hesitation I reached forward. My fingertips tingled from his firm grasp.

What would your daughter say if she saw you now?

"None of your business, jerk."

Are you sure?

"Daddy?"

I swung around and knocked over my coffee. "Christine? What are you doing here?"

She stood over me, lower lip quivering. Her entire body was tense and hunched: so vulnerable. "I thought you were in rehab."

"I am. I mean, I'm on my way. I just wanted a coffee." I looked around. Kingsley was gone. "Christine? Did you see that guy?"

She was already sopping up my spilled coffee with a handful of paper napkins. "Why do you do this?"

I gently touched her shoulder. "I'm sorry, honey. Can you drive me over there right now?"

She blinked hard, but did not tear up, and nodded.

I held her cheeks with my fingers and kissed her forehead.

She threw the napkins in a garbage can and apologized to the staff for my mess. It was then I decided I'd better do the whole stint at rehab. And a good thing, because I've never been stalked by creepy Kingsley since.

After my release though, it took Esther less than an hour to discover nothing had changed. She packed up and took the dog. We'd been apart ever since.

Willie said, "You okay there, Rex? Kinda zoned out."

We had a few more before Darryl joined us. "Close call there, buddy." He waved three fingers at the server. "I thought they were going to fire your ass."

"It's not over yet. I have a meeting with Personnel on Monday."

"Pah, you'll just get another disciplinary letter. Maybe suspended for a week or something. Come on, pal. It's Friday night. We got all weekend to party."

"Wait a minute. I have to call Esther. There's something I'm supposed to do."

"What do you want to talk to her for? She'll just bring you down. Willie, my man, here's some coin. Fire up the jukebox.

"And look, here's our brewskies."

∾∾∾

The phone rang. Lorne. I was an hour late for the meeting in Personnel.

"I've got the flu," I told him. "I took some heavy medication last night — from the doctor — and I don't think my alarm clock is working."

"You were able to see your doctor over the weekend?"

"24-hour clinic. If you don't believe me, call his office."

Lorne sighed. "When can we expect you?"

"I'll be there in an hour."

I sat on the edge of the bed and tried to orient myself. The pain in my stomach was constant. I showered quickly and skipped shaving. The dress pants I had been wearing for the last week had mud and grass stains on the knees and butt. I kicked them behind the toilet. Snippets of the weekend were coming to me.

I had drunk a lot. Puked a couple of times. Slept Friday and Saturday at Darryl's again and spent Sunday afternoon at his place watching football and drinking beer. I'd then walked to Wascana Lake and weaved along the shore. Chucked a rock at some geese on the water. My throw landed nowhere near the birds but it did spin me around and I fell to a sitting position in the wet grass and new thistles. I'd felt a hand on my shoulder.

The guy with the pretentious vest and my old ponytail loomed over me.

"Kingsley?" I said.

Well, well. I am amazed you remember me.

"What the hell do you want?"

Do you remember what you are supposed to do?

I drew a blank. "What do you know about it?"

I know more than you might think. It's simple. I want what's best for you.

I staggered to my feet. "What if the best for me is to smack you in the face?"

Go ahead. Remember though, you missed those geese by a mile.

I tried to plant my left foot to deliver a right hook, but only stumbled.

Kingsley stepped forward, grabbed my shoulders and steadied me. *Serious memory loss. You will have a revelation when you least expect it. And you will be filled with remorse.*

"Remorse?"

Someone called my name. Darryl. He strode toward me, swinging his arms, hands balled into fists. "You idiot. Do you want to get tossed in the drunk tank?"

"How did you find me too?"

"Too? What are you babbling about?"

Kingsley had disappeared again. "Did you see the guy I was just talking to?"

"Come on, let's get you out of here. You look like a freaking rummy. It's a good thing I found you."

"Why do you bother, anyway?"

"When I saw your car still parked in front of my place I knew you were on the lam. I was the last person you were seen with. I don't need hassle from the pigs if you get into more trouble."

We didn't say anything else to each other when Darryl drove me home.

I put on my cleanest pair of pants and headed to the appointment I was more than two hours late for. The meeting itself lasted about an hour. Lorne, the union representative, and the Manager of Staff Relations talked about me in the third person. I was addressed directly only once by the union rep when he asked me if I agreed to the terms.

I said, "Sounds good to me." Then I signed some forms, made a quick stop at the bank, and I was at The Cavern shortly thereafter.

"I tell you, Willie, it's the best thing that's ever happened. They terminated me with a week's pay for each year of service plus all outstanding vacation pay, plus one month's pay in lieu of notice. And they handed me a cheque right on the spot. I've got full access to my pension. I just have to call a broker and get a RIFF set up. One of the forms I signed said I wouldn't sue, and she's a done deal. I didn't even clean out my desk."

"That's a real godsend, pal. Work was interfering way too much with our drinking anyway." Willie licked his lips when our order arrived.

After our second round, I phoned Darryl and told him to join us after work. And then I went and threw up. That continued for a while. I'd drink, then throw up. The stabbing pains in my temples steadily worsened and my vision blurred. I sent Willie out for painkillers and antacid tablets.

Then finally, finally, after a few boiler-makers with scotch, I achieved that euphoria that had eluded me. I was back to normal and ready for some action.

The bar had filled to capacity and Willie had disappeared into the crowd.

Darryl was at another table chatting up a lanky blonde in a short leather skirt and white blouse with the top two buttons undone. A swarm of young, seemingly drunk girls came shrieking into the bar. I was trying to get a good look at them through my blurry vision when Darryl sat down across from me.

"I'm going to be cutting out of here pretty soon with my new friend over there. She's got a 'BFF'," he quoted with his fingers. "How about it?"

"That's what I like about you, Darryl. Always looking out for me."

"That's what I'm here for, buddy."

"I'll let you know in a couple of minutes."

"Whatever." He stood up. "Don't take too long. When our drinks are gone, so are we."

At that point I found myself interested in the girls, particularly one sitting on the periphery of the group. She was hunched over the black marble bar and seemed detached from her friends and just a bit out of place. There was a sense of vulnerability about her.

I approached and squeezed in between her and the wall.

I said over the din, "Hi. I don't think I've ever seen you in here before."

"Daddy?"

I staggered backward, the bar disappeared, and I was alone in a circle of light, surrounded by blackness. Christine's eyes were wide but dry, her lower lip quivering; the same expression I had seen countless times before.

Kingsley stopped me from crashing to the floor. *Coveting your own daughter now?*

My head ached. My stomach burned. My heart hurt. I remembered when Christine was born. Esther said she was our Godsend.

How much more do you think she's going to take?

Christine's nineteenth birthday. I had promised to spend it with her.

"What have I done?"

You know what you've done.

I heard Darryl telling me to hurry. I raked my fingers over the stubble on my face. Willie was at the edge of the light staring at Christine, licking his lips.

"Come on, Miller, hustle up," Darryl said. "These wenches aren't going to wait all night."

There was a ripping hurt all across my chest. "Scuttle back to the hole you came from and die," I said to Darryl. "You too, you lecherous old bastard."

Willie faded into the blackness.

"Suit yourself," Darryl said to me.

Your daughter. Enduring you all these years. At the very place you've called home longer than you've been at home with her.

"Help me fix this."

Only you can fix this. Kingsley did not let me fall. His face reflected mine, unblemished, like mine used to be. Like Christine's. He made sure I was standing upright. I returned to the bar, the noise, the stink, and Christine. Silently enduring me, yet again.

I stammered, "What are you doing *here?*"

"Celebrating my birthday with my friends, bar-hopping."

"But you don't drink."

"Yeah. Designated driver at my own legal drinking party." She turned away from me and indicated to her friends that she was leaving.

The girls kept glancing over at me; expressions of contempt obvious and unbridled, while they gathered their things and prepared to leave.

That ripping had to end now. I touched Christine's shoulder. She didn't turn but did say, "What?"

"Do you think your friends would mind if you drove me somewhere?"

"Isn't there enough booze here?" Then she did turn to look at me, the way a child would examine a poor misshapen worm caught on concrete after the rain, trying to decide whether to nudge it onto the dirt or put it out of its misery.

"No. I need help, Christine. Can you help me? Please."

ᏜᏜᏜ

I pressed the emergency buzzer and muttered my name into the speaker. After a few moments, the lock clicked and I opened the door. I turned to wave goodbye to my daughter, watching me from her car.

Bring It On

Once upon a time
when the last world of Christ
came and went
we feasted on diodes and silicone
in a polymer Eucharist

— The Gryphonic Techno-Bastards

A SONIC ASSAULT OF LYRIC GUITAR percussion disruption slams him. Arrhythmia's reverberations vibrate his chest. Humidity clings to his face. Strobes and Fresnel lenses dark red deep blue flutter his pulse. The *Master-Blaster* soundboard and *Wonkin* speakers tower stelae-like in the shadow on the raised stage. DJ Q-Tipp's spectral visage pogos to baseline time phases in and out of the laptop screen's glow. He resonates with Q's modulations. Becomes one with the amalgam. Gyrates. Breathes deep, regains equilibrium, smiles at the writhing mass of humanity.

He has not forgotten the bag-lady. She wore a brown kerchief tied with a bulbous knot under her hairy chin.

Her too-small tweed coat, ravaged by seam-rending stretches, enveloped her stumpy bulk. She stopped her disposal-bin excavations and made an open-palm plea. He passed her a fiver, passed on wordless, and opened the spit-stained, bare-metal, alley entrance door to *Dark Electronica*. Made his way down the twelve steps to the dance floor. The bag lady made him think the black-lit orange arrows pointing down the purple stairwell were glowing reptile slither-prints that had preceded him.

Now he is immersed in penny-waisted wares of midriff revelations. Short hems and barely-there-butt-covering short pants aglow in burnt-orange and lime-green, all clinging to hard bodies. Head bobbing, smirking, he surveys a bit of girl-on-girl, hip-grinding, deep-kiss action in a semicircle of alpha males. Tight black pants, satiny-smooth white shirts, spiked hair slicked with *Axe*-endowed contours ripped to perfection. The pack watches the girls. He presses by, receives spiky recognition nods from two alphas. Life is good.

He moves to the red-neon-washed, crimson marble bar. Slides cool onto a stool.

"Hello, Joe."

"How's it going, Billy." Joe's gravelly voice disperses.

He and Joe read each other's lips. "Boilermaker, Joe. Black Label."

Joe's *Electronica* black-T strains to contain Herculean arms. Billy's own spiked-to-perfection head nods once. Joe's stodgy fingers pour with poise. Coors on tap and scotch shot flow in Joe's magic hands. Apple juice-coloured elixirs proffered to Billy. Beer glass cold, wet, drips condensation, stinging foam passes lips, cools throat. First swallow. Second. He splashes the scotch for a tingling-tangy third swallow. He shivers. Scrumptious. Boilermaker-enhanced, nose-candy delight. Life is very good.

He toasts Joe. Swings around, leans on the bar. Elbows at countertop ease, beer glass inert between thumb and two fingers, he surveys his people. Tempo decelerates to one-ten beats per minute. Masses cling, swing in digressed rhythmations. He proceeds with his heuristic browse of the female of the species. All hair shoulder-length or longer, ebony or bleached, in ringlets or tightly permed, some cascading down, midriff-exposed, brushing butts that sway. He tingles.

Slim pickings tonight, though. He parses the clusters of hippie-blondes and trippy black ravens. Catches that one watching him, she quickly glances floorward. Lanky, smooth legs in flat black shoes, black skirt, hem at the knees with revelations of a petite-butt wonder. Dark-brown, straight hair, beige blouse unbuttoned to reveal . . . enough for a runner-up.

His recursive search reveals she's with him and he's with her, and she's hers, and the knots of males have grown exponentially. Her gaze lingers on his second pass, her head turns away. He determines she is fall-through, else-choice. He downs his ambers, she chats amiably with her friendly cluster. He's conscious of her struggle to keep her head not-his-way. A nanosecond smirk she does not see and he sets his glass behind him.

Joe knows the empty glass semaphore and the second set of juices is already ready. He reprises his two swallows, splash, third swallow, sees her glance once again his way. He smiles. Spontaneous wave turns to hair-tugging exploration, she peers at her skirt. Adjusts her hem.

A farewell nod to Joe, he sees himself in the bar mirror. Alpha-male-style brown spikes, black in this light, smooth-faced, Joe-tall six feet. Black shirt, pants, and Prada slip-ons. Armani vest many-pocket-equipped with various stashes of the rave trade. Spikes firmly in place he flows toward his target, sidles canonical to her. She smiles, with a quiet-quick, "hey" before she evaluates the parquet floor.

He acknowledges with practised poise. Ambers placed table-side, he asks her to dance. Q-Tipp torques the tunes (Billy knows the song order by rote) and bright strobes flash in one-sixty time. He catches her face flushed in a white Fresnel flash. Pretends not to notice. Persistence of vision falters in the strobing maelstrom, she flashes wraithlike in the throbbing, bobbing mob. He suddenly sweats. She coyly glances aside. Dizzy. Reinforcement necessary, he extracts a capsule from an upper pocket. Cap's previous contents flushed, refilled with elixirs of his own. He opens cap, half-cap snort for each nostril. Just after the nose tingle, just before the brain melt, is that the bag lady lifting a plastic sack of trash? No, only an alpha who flings a raven in the '40s jive style.

He sees she sees his ecstasy in the flashes, her face implores wide. Deft fingers procure, proffer her a capsule. She two-beat hesitates then her limber fingers linger on his, she accepts. Flash. Cap in hand. Flash. Capsule apart. Flash nostril one, flash nostril two. Her head lolls, plain-Jane inhibitors down now and she's girl enough. Tempo slows again, she flings, clings to him in a pseudo-foxtrot. He feels her ribcage in his splayed hands playing up and down her back, under her hair. No bra detected, he smiles knowing, yes, life is very good.

Full floor circuit they're back table-side he takes her hand and his ambers. She indicates no drink so they flow Joe's way, slide to the far bar wall. Joe shows, she mouths something only Joe knows and Joe's back in minutes with her tall glass. Her onyx-liquid smells of rye. He and she clink their drinks, she guzzles, breathless, and he matches her, elixirs gone one gulp. Wordless, they watch each other and she leans his way, touches his vest, indicates her nose. He procures and proffers again and her brown eyes loll after a simultaneous half-cap each nostril. Delight. She leans on the wall, elbow slumped on bar-top, legs stretched feline-style into his lap. He caresses her gam, slips off a flat slip-on and his hand ambles on. Her other now-shoeless foot is in lap, in his other hand. She leans back, his hands slide foot to shin to gam to ankle.

He stops. Feels eruptions on her heel. Sees mouldy-brown, hairy mounds in the shadowed Fresnel-red wash of her foot's arch. He rubs his hand on his pants. Those hairy mounds slither and he blinks.

This movement is a Joe-shadow delivering more ambers and onyx. They nod Joe's way. She guzzles and she's in ecstasy and digs in her skirt pocket for Ecstasy and she offers him his and they pop theirs. She decides it's time, head-gesture bathroom way and he nods his assent. She rises, hesitates, sags into him, clings to him with head on his chest. Simultaneously shadows drift through Q-Tipp's scarlet-come-blue flashing into stark-white-wash of the bathroom, saddlebag stretches in her black skirt which is really dark-brown, shiny, patched and many-washed. He scans her bruised legs, callused Achilles tendon, the scummy tiles and the florescent white-bright stabs his eyes to his brain stem. But he can't turn back now as a boilermaker wave washes over him and she drags him into a stall.

She says she's clean and safe, safe she says please, please don't worry about that, but he's too practised and procures prevention from a vest pocket and they spiral in ecstasy's cascading inevitability. Her blouse is open and he sees two c-section scars. Scalpel-cut pain slices scalp and he hastily strives, thrusts in time to the knives in his eyes and sighs because it's finally over. She quivers and slumps and asks where he's going while he cleans up with a towelette.

He wants away from this tangled web, her eyes weep pustule-like, it seems. He's shivery-cold and she's on her raw-red knees, head pressed to his groin, pleads their baby would bind them soul-to-soul, is that not what he wants because what else is there? He heaves extraction on open stall door but she's cloying, clinging, his legs bound not-quite-nightmare style. She bares her arms, red-angry parallel scabs from wrist to elbow-crook, she swears she'll do it again. Legs free he leaps, she splays bare-chested on the grimy floor.

He bolts past quizzical monkey stares of bathroom males, staggers into Q-Tipp's cacophony of dark light. Head reels, stumbles past white-shirted simians writhing in strobing simulacrum of humanity. He divines under their white shirts red eruptions of steroid indulgences, the alphas' arms extend to their knees, drag on the floor. They grope ringletted curls in their meaty paws, drag the bleach-blondes and raven-hairs to the bar's cavernous corners where girls grovel near leering Neanderthals but don't cower when clubs strike and penetrate.

While Q-Tipp's skeletal effigy strobes, reels and aches and pounds in relentless time, he searches for gilded-elixirs and finds only apple cores and retreats from that digital oblivion. Falling through lightning haze he stumbles onto the bottom landing of the twelve steps and stars fill his head. He climbs, staggers through the back door, collapses on the black-globulated asphalt beside the disposal-bin, rolls onto his back. Staring skyward he sees stars faintly through the wash of *Electronica's* neon sign.

Head spins, he raises his knees, tries to push — somewhere.

Then, hairy chin, tweed stretch-mark scars lean over him, inhibit his progress. He tries, "Help-me." She straightens, looks around. Leans down again, his vest mauled. "Wait, don't you remember me?" He gropes at stained, torn dark-brown stockings while wallet, vest pockets are emptied by grubby fingers with blackened, broken nails, and even the condoms are stashed in her shopping cart. She retreats into alley shadows.

THORN-FIELD

Inert, he feels Q-Tipp's thumping deep-bass through his back. *Electronica's* neon flickers, one hand grasps at a weed in a crack, the other splays on an asphalt globule, he feels its eruption under his palm. The breeze cools and he shivers on cold pavement. Faint stars leer down from the heavens.

Blue

HOW LONG CAN IT GO ON? Strains of "The Lord Is my God" float through my open bedroom window. I haven't had a proper Sunday morning sleep since May when that church moved in across the alley. I liked it when it was an abandoned warehouse. At least the crack-addicts and prostitutes who hid behind the building had the decency to stay away until past two in the afternoon, around the time I usually get out of bed. They also had the courtesy to get lost by 3:00or 4:00 AM — my bedtime. Being able to sleep until mid-afternoon only six days a week is taking a toll on my sanity. If I close the window, the room becomes stuffy and smells of mould. I'm not sure what I'll do when winter comes but I guess I'll worry about that later.

A warm, late September breeze billows my beige vinyl curtains, letting in sunlight. I have to close my eyes against the brightness. Why did the church people move in anyway? I'm in the church — screaming at them to shut up, smashing instruments. Kick over the drum set. The congregation scatters. My curtains drop back in place and the singing fades away, the tempo slowing, and "Amazing Grace" mellows in.

The singing finally done, a distant clamour of voices follows, then the bass rumblings of the pastor's voice, "Praise the Lord. Let me hear you." The congregation echoes His praise. Maybe I'll set fire to the place. Naw. Too much effort. I'm wide awake and really have to urinate. Bathroom bound across the matted, burnt-orange shag carpet, I brush one hand against the wall to prevent weaving too much and the bright spots pulsate on the periphery of my vision, whoa, and force me to sit down to empty my bladder.

I flop back into bed while the *praising* continues. I'll never get back to sleep. May as well get up. Let me close my eyes and rest just a couple minutes more — until the dizziness is completely gone.

The smell of a barbecue wafts through the window. Is the sermon over already? My heart flutters. I've been losing time more and more. It's not that I sleep. It's more like an absolute absence of the notice of time passing. I won't mention this symptom to the doctor. I'll hold it in reserve in case my health insurance carrier comes up with a back-to-work plan. In the meantime, I'll simply hope it doesn't get worse.

Are those children's sing-songy voices right in my backyard? I stretch, swing my legs out of bed and stand up, wavering. I shut my eyes to part the curtains with both hands and slowly open my eyes to let them adjust to the sunlight. Two barbecues on the asphalt walkway right against the building billow smoke. It seems that this outdoor barbecue worship-fest is a monthly event. The former warehouse now church, a two-storey cindercrete building with barred windows on both the main and second floors, always reminds me of the storage bunkers at the mine.

Children play soccer in the dirt lot. There's milling and laughter. A large group of people with heads hung pray in a circle. The pastor's voice booms but I can't quite hear what he's saying. He has an arm across another man's shoulders.

That pastor showed up at my front door in May with an invitation to the church's grand opening — all neighbourhood residents welcome. I was just heading out for a supply of Orange Crush so couldn't avoid talking to him.

"Good afternoon," he said, "I'm Pastor Roy from The Faith Nondenominational Church just behind your house here." He extended his hand.

I grabbed it and said, "I'm Matthew Brewster. Nice to meet you."

He pumped my hand twice, handed me one of his invitations, and said, "I'm just canvassing the neighbourhood here, spreading the word of the Lord and inviting you to join us in worship."

Stocky as a linebacker, with grey receding hair, he wore a white dress shirt that stretched over his barrel-shaped torso, and black, old-fashioned pleated cords. What kind of a pastor wears clothing like that?

"Thank you but I really have to get going."

He said, "I do hope we'll see you this coming Sunday."

"Sure thing," I replied without turning around and fled down the sidewalk.

And I've been wondering ever since about that oddball pastor and his new church behind my house, just outside my window. I could call the cops on them for disturbing the peace, my peace, but what good would that do? It would be as much use as calling in a complaint about the Friday and Saturday night stereo wars. I don't talk to cops anyway — what am I thinking? They skulk around enough, in their black, Nazi-esque uniforms or ill-fitting, plainclothes polyester suits investigating fights, knifings, occasional shootings and when they're not, they're randomly carding and bullying the neighbours — not that I care about the neighbours — I just don't want them doing that to me. My house is a 700 square foot, run-down rental with no basement, bare dirt and thistle and weeds front and back. The neighbours don't care about my abode or me either.

The prayer circle disperses — and there she is.

She hovers alone on the periphery of the worshippers; not nearly as gaunt as she was when I first saw her.

When I moved here in February, she and her co-workers hung around the street corner by the laundromat. I literally had to walk right through them, regardless of my determination to avoid the local denizens at all costs. I ran into her a couple of days after the church had its Sunday grand opening in May.

∾∾∾∾

I woke up early, a bit past noon, and couldn't find any clean socks. The street was clear since the girls normally didn't start their stroll until past two in the afternoon. I figured I could get to the laundromat and back before the day's business started. I wouldn't even have to walk by them if I timed it right. I whipped a pair of sandals on my bare feet and loaded my wicker laundry basket to overflowing with jeans, T-shirts, underwear, and the desperately needed socks. I beelined it for the laundromat. With head down, holding the basket with both hands against my left hip and only a slight spasm in my lower back and tingle in my spine, I looked up from my scan of the scaling cement sidewalk, cracks sporting a luxuriant growth of squat weeds, and she was standing directly in my path.

We made eye contact. She had hazel eyes with mesmerizing green flecks, surrounded by purplish rings and crows-feet. Her cheeks were deeply pocked and sunken, suggesting a woman in her forties.

One corner of her mouth turned up in a smile. "Hey."

I managed to mumble, "How you doing?"

"Okay." Her stringy brown hair hung to her shoulders. Densely packed freckles covered her nose and cheekbones. She wore a low-slung, blue denim mini-skirt, open jean jacket and cornflower-blue tube top. Even though she was skeletal, she had a slight roll of belly skin that hung over the front of her skirt. Stretch marks suggested a one time healthier, heavier body. Her hands were smooth and wrinkle free, and she had pert, bra-less breasts telling me she was only in her twenties.

"You got the time?" she said.

"I don't have a watch."

She made a soft nasal sound, shook her head, and said, "Oh-kaaay."

I manoeuvred around her, crossed the street, and dashed into the laundromat, up to a washer, flung my clothes inside and slammed the door shut. The palm of my hand stung when I pounded the coin in the slot. I tossed my basket on one of the scarred folding tables and stood a discreet distance from the window to watch her. She'd pace in one direction, turn, walk back round the corner, stop, glance around, and then return. She kicked at the weeds with her white sneakers. She crouched down to pluck a purple thistle flower. She smelled the flower and then tossed it. She watched crows taking flight into a partially overcast sky. Thumbs hooked into the belt-loops of her skirt, unsmiling, she looked bored, even when an occasional vehicle slowly drove past.

I wondered if, for civility's sake, I should make an effort to talk to her while my clothes washed. Maybe we could chat while she waited . . . wait, what the hell would I say? What the hell was I thinking, anyway?

I settled back in a hard plastic chair and picked at my fingernails. I was about to go grab an Orange Crush from Joe's, the small convenience store next door, but other girls were wandering to their posts. Why was everybody up so early? My wash finished and, after loading the dryer, I moved my chair to a cramped space between the end of the row of dryers and the laundromat's bathroom wall. I leaned my head against the machine beside me and scratched at my fingernails some more and listened to the hum of my dryer. The distant vibration was soothing. My eyes went heavy and my head bobbed.

The dryer was silent. A woman moaned in accompaniment to a rhythmic thumping. Both sounds increased in tempo; the noise came from the bathroom. Ah, hell. My clothes were already cool and I quickly tossed them into my basket without sorting or folding. I had no idea how much time I had lost. I dashed outside before the bathroom business was finished — I simply did not want to get involved. I was relieved to see the denim-clad girl was the only person on the street. I bolted across the intersection, cast a quick, sideways glance; she was watching me motor past. When I didn't acknowledge her, she hung her head and turned away.

I crashed through my front door, breathless. I had to swallow four ibuprofen with Orange Crush and lie down to calm myself.

The next afternoon, I decided to start my vigil. I positioned my recliner-rocker against the wall beside the front window and cracked my drapes so I could watch the street without craning my neck. There was a clear view of the intersection, the laundromat, Joe's convenience store, and anyone loitering in that vicinity.

I settled in the chair with a heaping bowl of corn flakes mixed with a couple of globs of peanut butter. I have a lactose intolerance and I can't stand dry cereal. The dull light of an overcast day marginally brightened the room. Motes of dust plumed from the faded drapes, which hadn't been opened for a couple of weeks.

Two of the regular girls were strolling in front of the laundromat.

My girl was on her corner, dressed in the same tube top and denim outfit. I decided to call her Blue. She slouched with another regular, a stocky, dark-skinned girl who wore a clingy white dress. Blue and White-Dress I decided. The two laundromat girls and White-Dress were picked up two or three times over the course of the afternoon. Blue always hung back. Even when she was by herself, she never really looked directly at any passing car. Late afternoon, a dark green Mercedes Kompressor pulled up and some dude with white slicked-back hair stuck his head out of the sunroof. He talked to Blue and White-Dress for a moment. The girls spoke to each other and Blue stepped back, shook her head and gestured for her co-worker to go ahead. The passenger door on the Kompressor swung open. White-Dress shook her head more vigorously, grabbed Blue by her shoulder, pushed her into the car. She waved when the sleek little Mercedes took off. I wondered where they would go, what would happen . . . but then I felt absolutely fatigued. I had to lean my head back and close my eyes, just for a moment.

I came back later to see Blue back on station. She was not picked up again and a heavy downpour drove the girls off the street around evening news time. I pulled my drapes shut, and then fumbled in the dark for the table lamp. I turned on the TV, having had enough reality for one day, and skipped from the news to the Turner Classic Movies channel. I couldn't concentrate on Errol Flynn's swashbuckler antics though. Listening to the downpour, I wondered what Blue was doing at that moment. What the hell did I care about some scrawny prostitute? Get a grip for Christ's sake.

I had a spasm in my lower back and felt that tingle in my spine, like thorns reaming the cord's central canal, and realized that I hadn't taken my medication the whole day. I chugged a full can of Orange Crush and swallowed four ibuprofen and waited for the pain to subside. Was Blue watching TV? Stop it — focus on the diminishing pain. I stared at the TV, lost in fictional black and white lives, until I climbed into bed around 4:00 AM after more ibuprofen. The rain continued outside, perhaps soaking Blue's hair, plastering it to her freckled face.

The next day was clear and bright and I resumed my vigil at the window over another bowl of corn flakes and peanut butter. Business carried on much the same as the day before. Blue only managed one client again: a brown Saturn SL1 trolled the block four or five times before the driver had the gall to park right in front of my house. A fat, fiftyish guy, with only a rim of hair bordering his sweaty chrome dome oozed out of the car, looked furtively around, and then slowly moved toward her corner, constantly looking over his shoulder. He was wearing a white dress shirt and no tie. His collar was loose and he had enough back hair creeping up his neck that it joined seamlessly with the dilapidated growth on his scalp. His wrinkled grey dress pants matched the wrinkled blazer he flung over his shoulder. He waddled over to her. Talk about pork-belly, butt-ugly. And the nerve — leaving his car in front of my house. I wished I had the energy to do something about it. My eyes began to feel heavy.

Pork-Belly walked up to Blue and talked to her. The whole time he glanced around, looking directly at my house at one point. I could see the sweat glistening on his bald head.

Blue, arms crossed, stood rigid.

Pork-Belly touched her arm and White-Dress, lounging in the shade of Joe's store, yelled something. Pork-Belly opened his wallet and pulled out a wad of bills. Blue snatched the bills and shoved them in her skirt pocket, then strode across the street to the laundromat with the wide-assed waddler in tow.

She looked so bored. Was she experiencing the same excruciating tedium I went through every day? With my Journalism and Communications Degree in hand it had started immediately—ten years of churning out corporate newsletters, reports, and articles for the Liverwood Potash Corporation's Information Department. Everything was irrelevant. The company. Life. Where did my words go? What purpose did they serve? I felt like Oblio, banished to my own version of the Pointless Forest. Except I had no heroic purpose. My spine had been tingling for years and I had to keep shifting in my office chair every five or ten minutes to head off the pain. I hated the meaningless reams of words. When boxes containing the thick annual report, two informational brochures, plus thousands of envelopes for a mass mailing showed up, I hefted them all myself, with the full knowledge of the possibly dire consequences.

The next day, I couldn't get out of bed and had to call an ambulance. I had a compressed spine and the muscles in my lower back were badly inflamed. I learned to keep the condition constant by twisting suddenly and by ignoring the physiotherapist's recommended stretching and strengthening exercises. With prescription pain medication and ibuprofen, I could keep the resulting discomfort at a bearable level and I was able to score long-term disability.

I spent my slightly less tedious days reading; *Stranger in a Strange Land, Bend Sinister, Catch 22.*

Now I wondered when that fucker was going to move his car from in front my house? My back hurt. I closed the drapes, took four ibuprofen and turned on the TV, flipped stations. I didn't feel like reading. I tried napping. But all I could think of was the sprinkling of freckles on Blue's cheeks, those intriguing green flecks in those hazel eyes. If it wasn't for the pocking all over her face, she could have passed for a teenager. Maybe she was a teenager. I'd heard tell that crack-addiction tears a person's face to shreds. I tried to imagine her as a young girl. A child. I closed my eyes and tried to remember the sound of her voice.

The VCR clock said 10:35 PM. I peeked through the curtains and saw that the Saturn was gone, the inter-section deserted. In the laundromat, the machines were idle sentinels, except for one dryer with its door hanging open. I was goddamned if the pastor wasn't in there folding his laundry. At that hour? He stopped for a moment and looked toward the street. He must live in the neighbourhood.

Did Blue live nearby too? Did she use the same washing machines I did? I imagined her tube tops and denim skirts tumbling around in the dryer I used.

A sudden back-spasm stabbed and my spine burned. I gritted my teeth. Switching on the table lamp, I found my ibuprofen bottle and gave it a little shake. The pill count was dangerously low. I needed more ibuprofen, and groceries. I had to venture out. Maybe tomorrow. I took the last six of my pills and drifted off to sleep in the recliner. What did Blue eat from day to day? Did she have enough money to survive?

The bus trip to Superstore was uneventful and tediously long. It was an overcast, drizzly day so I wore my over-sized, fleece-lined windbreaker, which was appropriate for the weather, but also necessary to augment my ibuprofen stock. I had slit open a pocket's seam so I could slip extra medicine neatly to the bottom of the inner lining. Over-the-counter medication was not covered by my health plan, therefore I had the right to obtain what I thought necessary to live by any means.

Once at the store, I grabbed a couple of boxes of generic corn flakes, a litre tub of peanut butter, a six-pack of Orange Crush and wandered over to the pharmacy and asked a zit-faced, teenage runt stock-clerk new to the store to help me find my pills. Pretending to be stupid as well as half-blind, I asked him to grab me two bottles. He reached down and the split-second before he closed his hand on one, I said, "Oh, I see them now," darted out my hand and hit his arm to knock stock off the shelf. With a broad sweep of my arm, I flung a cascade of stock to the floor and apologized profusely. While the frustrated clerk crouched to pick things up, I passed him some stock from the floor and managed to slip four bottles of ibuprofen through the slit in the pocket of my windbreaker.

Rising, the clerk said he would be more than happy to carry my purchases for me. I smiled at him, picked up four more bottles of ibuprofen and followed meekly.

I didn't get back home until past 6:00 PM and then flew into a rage. I was good-goddamned if that Saturn wasn't parked in front of my house again. That pork-bellied jerk's plastic-wrapped rattle trap would draw unnecessary interest from the cops. I dumped my purchases on the kitchen table and sat down, staring at the car through my living room window. How would the vinyl body shatter if it was hit with a hammer?

Pork-Belly came out of the laundromat with a smug look on his face, and hoisted his pants up to his fat gut before he waddled to his car. He then had the gall to sit there and talk on his cell phone. Before I realized, I was standing directly in front of the window in time to see Blue, hands in her skirt pockets, head down, her hair covering those freckles, wander out of the laundromat. I moved back. Pork-Belly switched the cell phone from his right to his left hand and reached for something in the back seat. I caught the flash of a gigantic stone on his ring finger.

When he took off I plopped down in my recliner without bothering to close the curtains. I looked around the confines of my dusty living room and took stock. The heavy wall-to-wall drapes and hide-a-bed in lieu of a couch. The laminated coffee table. My lamp and pressboard shelves on cindercrete blocks. My TV. My overstuffed recliner-rocker. I had walked away from our condo and Barbara, my partner for twelve years, a few months after going on disability.

I had been reading *Catch-22* when she appeared in front of me in her black silk housecoat to say, "I can't live with your belligerent silence. What do you want to do?"

It took a minute to register that she was actually speaking to me. "Do about what?"

"What do you think?"

I shrugged.

"I can't keep doing this. Whenever we had a fight before we'd fuck our brains out afterward. Now all you do is read. You don't even touch me anymore. Am I that hideous?"

She was six foot two, a couple of inches taller than me, and slender with a sexy belly that stretched her housecoat. Large breasts prevented the silky housecoat from ever completely covering her cleavage. Her wet, jet-black hair framed her face in that sweaty, pouty perfume-ad kind of way.

"I wouldn't say you're hideous."

"You bastard." She clenched her fists. "What the hell has happened to you?"

What had happened indeed? I couldn't concentrate. I was tired all the time and only wanted to read or sleep.

"Say something." Her lower lip quivered. "You were always there for me. And now you're not. Now you're not anything. Matthew, I'm asking once more: what are you going to do?"

I opened my mouth a couple of times and then looked at the book splayed on my lap just to avoid her glare.

Her pitch rose slightly. "Talk to me."

"Uh, I'm working on it?"

"Work harder. I'm not going to let you drag me down with you."

I had no response. So I picked up the book. Her eyes were moist, red, and she shook slightly, fists still clenched and held tightly at her sides. I had to admire her. She did not cry.

"Have it your way," was the last thing she said to me.

Barbara handled it. When I returned to our condo from a CAT-scan, to verify my long-term disability eligibility, my key didn't work. Inside an envelope taped to the door was a key, a yellow sticky with an address, and cab fare all neatly folded inside a note. It said she'd found me a furnished rental house through a friend at a property management company. He and his buddies had moved my chair and personal stuff. The first month's rent and damage deposit were on her. She'd added the landlord's and property manager's contact information. I walked over to the Golden Mile shopping centre and called a cab.

Recalling all this made me just want to sleep. My head was bobbing. I took some ibuprofen. The outside light didn't seem much different from when Pork-Belly had taken off. So help me, if he parked in front of my place once more I would take action. Blue and White-Dress exited Joe's with bottles of pop. They leaned against the front window of the store and drank. I saw a flash of orange in Blue's hand. She drank Orange Crush.

I needed one too. But a cold bottle, not the warm can on my kitchen table. I stood. My stomach twisted and my mouth went dry. I sat. Then bolted toward the front door. Grabbed the knob — stopped. Who really wants a bottle? Me, damnit. Out the front door, I headed diagonally across the street, straight for Joe's, deep-breathing to counter my racing heart, trying to keep my eyes steady on the store. White-Dress poked Blue with her elbow and then sauntered away. I slowed down when I reached the sidewalk. Blue set her bottle down on the brick sill of the window. She pressed herself flat against the glass, stretched her arms up over her head and arched. Her denim jacket pulled up exposing a substantial amount of midriff. Pink stretch marks glared angrily at me.

"Hey." She dropped her arms and stood straight. "No laundry today?"

I swallowed hard. She remembered me. "Uh, yeah." I hung my head and darted past her, stumbled, panting, into the store.

"Hiya, Joe."

Joe was sixtyish, short and pudgy, balding, with two double chins. He greeted me with his typical grunt in some European accent without looking up from his *Guns and Ammo* magazine. I stood in a fog checking his four shelving units. Condoms, jellies, and creams, more brands than I ever knew existed; chocolate bars, licorice, and gummies; chips, potato and taco; dips and salsas; countless two-litre bottles of pop; behind the counter, cupboards of tobacco products, and probably controlled substances. I turned to the two old-style coolers, with top sliding lids, under the storefront window.

Through the bars I could see Blue's hair pressed flat against the glass. I grabbed a six-pack of Orange Crush, slammed the cooler lid shut, went to the counter. Joe set his magazine down and wiped his hands on his smock.

"How's business, Joe?" I said.

"Same as last time you ask. Girls buy many rubbers. Hardly no time to keep up. Those kids then. Always buy chips. Buy cheesies. Never enough time for me to smoke *mad-icinal* cigarettes."

"Yeah, life's tough all over."

"You still on pogey?"

"Disability."

"Whatever. You buy more from Joe's. I stay in business then for you to buy your orange drink."

"You bet. Keep the change."

Joe grunted and picked up his magazine.

I hesitated at the door and took a deep breath. The conversation with Joe had momentarily soothed me but I had to push on. I stepped outside.

Blue pushed herself away from the window. "Hey, again."

I didn't say anything, just nodded, avoiding eye contact, but at least I had the courage not to run away. I stood remarkably steady and examined the freckles on her face; I wanted to reach out and touch each one; like counting candies in a jar.

"Orange Crush, eh?" She waved her bottle at me.

"Yeah." I lifted the pack and gave it a little shake. "Uh, I only started drinking it to settle my stomach."

"Gut problems, eh?" Her voice had an Alanna Myles scratch to it.

"Just for medicinal purposes for an ailment I have."

"Uh, sure." Blue ran her fingers through her hair, fluffing it.

"Yeah, the meds make my guts burn bad. This juice settles it up good. You want another one?"

"I guess." She twirled her hair in her fingers. "Sure."

I passed her a pop.

She pressed her empty into my hand. "Don't wanna rip off your deposit."

"Thanks." I squeezed the empty into my pocket.

Crows cawed distantly in the silence. A Bic lighter peeked out from under the flap of her jacket pocket. I thought of Pork-Belly parking in front of my house and wondered what it would feel like to slide my 14-inch flat screwdriver into his gullet. My face felt hot, my teeth clenched hard.

"Fifty bucks 'cause you live around here."

"Pardon?"

"You heard me."

My face turned hotter and I could feel sweat under my arms. I was not Pork-Belly. That was not my game. What the hell was she thinking? I said, "Uh, no offence, but we're like, neighbours, aren't we? I'm here because

I — just want to talk to you." I had trouble believing those words had actually oozed from my mouth. I couldn't tell if Blue thought I was simple or just nervous, but at least her face softened. "Besides, I don't drive a brown Saturn."

She said, "That guy a friend of yours?"

"That fat-fuck who always parks in front of my house? I'll gut him for bacon if he doesn't stop doing it."

I could clearly see the green flecks in Blue's wide eyes. She took a step back. "Sure."

"I mean . . . I hate it when he parks in front of my house."

She took another slow step back. "Whatever. But, hey, I gotta blast. Thanks for the drink."

My head throbbed and I wanted to lounge in my recliner. I chastised myself for stupidly getting involved with the locals. What the hell was I thinking? I managed to stumble home, popped some pills and flopped in the recliner. The conversation with Blue replayed in my mind. I'd showed her I was just another testosterone-laden, tongue-tied jerk. How could I prove that wasn't the real me? But what the hell for and what did it matter? But it did matter and what could I do? The debate rolled on and on until past dark.

Then I was really good-goddamned. Blue was inside the laundromat talking with the pastor. She stood erect and rigid, arms crossed, on one side of the folding table while he stood on the other. As they talked, she dropped her arms, threw her head back in laughter, and then slowly moved to his side. The pastor put his hands on her shoulders and they both hung their heads, praying.

After a few moments, the pastor stepped back, pulled out his wallet and extracted what could have been a business card and wrote something on it with a pen from his shirt pocket. He pulled bills out of the wallet and passed them to Blue along with the card.

They left the laundromat together and walked past Joe's, away from the church, him with his laundry basket under one arm and his other hand on Blue's lower back. Now what the hell was a pastor doing with a prostitute at that hour of the night? He towered over the scrawny girl.

How was I supposed to redeem myself? The damn thought popped into my head.

The mailman clunking my mailbox lid woke me up about 11:00 the next day. The thought still there: how was I supposed to redeem myself? My disability cheque was in the box. My pain medication prescription renewal coincided with the arrival of the cheque so I had to head out.

No one was out when I walked the two blocks over to Albert Street, stopped at the Credit Union to cash the cheque, pay my utility bills, and make a small deposit just to keep my bank account solvent. I headed to the pharmacy and renewed my prescription. I had over fifty dollars to spare. Sitting on a bus stop bench watching traffic whiz by, I couldn't decide what to do with my extra funds. I wasn't hungry and even the thought of corn flakes and peanut butter made me nauseous. The Credit Union sign gleaming up the street seemed to beckon so I headed back there.

A young plump teller with frizzy hair and a fuzzy pink sweater gave me a cursory glance when I asked for a new fifty-dollar bill. "It's for a gift," I told her. She returned from the cash machine and handed me the bill.

"Thanks. My daughter will appreciate it." I folded the bill and stuffed it into my front jeans pocket. The girl raised her eyebrows then looked over my shoulder at the next customer in line.

Back at home, I plopped down in my recliner and fondled the fifty in my pocket. Then I went to sleep for a while and came back just as Pork-Belly pulled up outside. Blue was out and rolled her eyes and slumped her shoulders at his approach. He paid, took her hand, and dragged her over to the laundromat. Blue's arm was fully extended as he beetled along at flank speed. White-Dress shook her head as they disappeared into the laundromat. I retrieved my screwdriver from the front hall closet and the whetstone from a kitchen drawer. I stroked the tip of the screwdriver with the stone.

Eventually, he wandered back to his car with his smug, horn-dog rooster strut, and then he had the gall to have another cell phone conversation. All the while I stroked the screwdriver tip with the stone. Stroked and stroked some more.

It seems all I did from that time to the following Saturday night, just past dusk, was hone the edge of the screwdriver. Blue wasn't around but I'd be damned if that Saturn wasn't trolling the streets all day. I fondled my screwdriver while I watched and waited for him to park in front of my house. I pondered the possibilities until I saw Blue walk into Joe's.

Pork-Belly must have spotted her too because he was parked in front of my house within moments and waddling toward Joe's. I had about twenty minutes.

It must have been the ibuprofen. I felt miles from myself. I would not be one of Kafka's hapless heroes bogged by bureaucracy. I headed outside with my screw-driver. The stereo wars had yet to fire a volley and the streets were deserted that moonless and cool, early August night. At the pay phone outside the laundromat I called 9-1-1.

When the operator answered, I said, "Some fat guy with a brown Saturn SL1 just dragged a young girl into the laundromat next to Joe's. I think she's in trouble." I gave the laundromat's address, a description of Pork-Belly's car, and my own address for the vehicle's location.

When the operator asked who I was, I replied, "I'm really worried about that girl," and hung up.

I had only punctured two tires on the passenger side of Pork-Belly's car before I began to worry. The cops never used their sirens in this neighbourhood and they might show up any second, so I darted inside my house and peeked out between the curtains. Pork-Belly must have been late for a function with his wife. Already he was speeding from the laundromat with his obnoxiously light step as a police cruiser, its roof-bar lights inactive, pulled up behind a beat-up Chevy van across the street from my house. Another cruiser pulled up a little way down from Joe's. Blue lurked in the doorway of the laundromat.

Pork-Belly obliviously headed for his car. As he reached for his door handle, there was a blaze of flashing blue, red, and white lights, and four cops had him across the hood, arms cuffed behind his back.

Blue turned will-o'-the-wisp and disappeared.

The next hour-and-a-half was anti-climactic. Cop cars came and went. Pork-Belly sulked in the back seat of the laundromat cruiser. Neighbourhood denizens came, gawked, and left. A cop knocked on my front door with his flashlight and then shone the light around, right across the front window, then wandered off. Pork-Belly was driven away and his car was dragged onto the back of a flatbed tow-truck. My spine burned and my lower back screamed at me but I stayed stock-still. I continued to watch until only the cruiser across the street remained. The dome light was on inside and I could see the cops writing on their clipboards and entering data into their on-board computer. They were just getting ready to head out when Blue wandered up to the car from behind. She stopped at the cruiser and leaned in the passenger side window. She and the cops chatted. The driver laughed and then the cruiser peeled away, with both cops waving out their windows. Blue gave them a quick wave back.

Then she turned toward my house and looked directly at my front window. Blue looked right at me. Then she crammed her hands into her skirt pockets and shuffled off, head down. I couldn't get to my ibuprofen fast enough.

Pork-Belly never came back. For the next few days Blue's step seemed lighter and she didn't look nearly as bored. Business dropped off with the increase in police cruiser drive-bys. I was mildly concerned about the possible financial hardship the girls may have to face. But at least Pork-Belly's vinyl-wrapped crap car wasn't contaminating my street anymore.

I felt bad for Blue as she wandered pointlessly from day to day. I needed to help her out somehow. But why should I? I fondled the fifty-dollar bill constantly in my front pocket. White-Dress and Blue lounged in the shade in front of Joe's. Not my business. What did I care? I didn't care. When White-Dress wandered away from Joe's, Blue looked so forlorn, all alone, leaning against the window of the store, feet and bare legs stretched out in front her. Not my concern.

I crossed the intersection on a diagonal.

Blue stood up straight when she saw me. She took one step forward with the slightest smile on her face. Then she became nonchalant and slouched her shoulder against the window.

What the hell was I doing? I neared the curb. Felt the fifty. I hesitated, considered turning back and stepped up. My toes slipped off the curb and I stumbled forward, just catching myself before I did a face plant.

"You okay?"

My face burned. "You're too cool, Brewster," I mumbled.

Blue said, "Huh?"

"If I was any more clumsy, I'd be, like, a quadriplegic."

Blue laughed. She threw her head back and let out three chortling gasps in her gravelly voice. She said, "Yeah, I wondered how you'd make out in this neighbourhood."

I liked the way her hair fell over her face and seemed to meld with her freckles. I said, "Well, I don't get out much and I don't talk to strangers."

"You're talking to me."

"You're no stranger."

Blue sniggered. "Yeah, I know. You watch me through your window."

"No way," I said in a high-pitched squeak. My face was in flames.

She pointed at my house. "I watched you move in. Think I can't see you?"

I didn't believe it. But when I looked over, the west sun was streaming directly into my living room, the walls were lit up and my recliner was in plain view even though it was pushed back from the window.

"I'll be goddamned," I muttered.

Blue seemed to shrink. She took a deep breath. "So why'd you watch me? I'm nothing. Nobody looks at me." When I didn't answer, she continued, "What do you want, anyways?"

I wanted to sleep. I wanted to go to the place of missing time — no matter how much of it was lost. But I was afraid of walking away, not finishing whatever the hell I had set out to do.

So I simply plopped down on the sidewalk and leaned my back against Joe's. I sat right beside Blue — almost touching her bare leg. The rough brick of the storefront jabbed into my back, kind of a soothing tingle. I crossed my arms round my upraised knees, leaned forward and closed my eyes. My mind was a complete blank.

Blue shifted and I could feel heat from her leg against my bare arm. I kept my eyes closed. After a long, long silence where I could have sworn I'd gone to sleep, Blue said, "You know what I am, don't you?"

"I know what you do." I hesitated. "So how much time does fifty bucks get me?"

I could sense her slump before she mechanically listed a few available options for that price.

"No." My aggressive tone caused her to move slightly away. I noticed the immediate lack of warmth and I didn't like it. I looked up at her and said softly, "No. How much *time*? I'm not interested in that other stuff. Anyway — I can't. With the medication and all. How much time?"

I could see she was tensing to maybe run for it. I was way too strange for her. This wasn't the straightforward demands of the men she was used to dealing with. I pulled the fifty out of my pocket and waved it at her. "How long?"

She hesitated. Then snatched the bill. "What do you want for it?"

"I don't care. Maybe an Orange Crush. Buy us a couple. Keep the change."

I leaned my head against my crossed arms again. Then I sensed she was gone — for good, probably.

But she actually came back with the pop. She sat down on the pavement beside me and opened them. She handed me a bottle. I held it against my forehead, feeling its coolness.

Blue said, "Do you really wanna just sit here?"

"Sure. Easy money."

"You're a nut case, hey?" She didn't just up and leave. She didn't slap my face or stab me dead. She simply said, "You wanna talk or something?"

I set my bottle down. "Sure. Talk. Start with your name."

"Lydia." She finished her drink while she gave me a summary of her life. I only half listened, numbly, thinking only about ibuprofen, while she recounted her story. Broken home, physical and sexual abuse, drug addiction, life on the street, search for a way out, inability to act. It sounded too pat and I wasn't sure how much of it was true. But I didn't really care. We all have our problems. I didn't say so out loud.

"I'm pathetic, hey?"

I slowly turned my head and reached out to take her hand. She recoiled, shifting her whole body away.

I said, "We all wallow in our inaction. We don't have to, if we really don't want to, but we do."

She blinked at me, her face blank, and shook her head slightly.

I said, "You are not pathetic." I must have got the emphasis right that time because she tentatively took my hand. It felt nice.

I stood and then helped her up. "There is something I want after all."

Blue, or Lydia, if that was her real name, shrugged and said, "You paid."

I hugged her. At first, she stood rigidly, then relaxed as I splayed my hands out over her back, under her jacket but outside the tube-top. She put her arms around my waist and leaned her face into my chest. I held her for a minute and felt the ridges on her spine protruding like the backbone of a starved old cat. Nothing but bone on her scrawny body.

I stepped back, ran my fingertips across the freckles on her left cheekbone, turned, and walked away. I needed my medicine. Lots of it.

She said, "You know we don't hug our tricks."

"Maybe see you around," I said without looking back.

At home, I ignored a goldenrod church notice sticking out of my mailbox and descended into an ibuprofen stupor which lasted for a day and a half.

Blue disappeared.

I kept watching the street, not caring if I could be seen or not. There was a delirium of panic. Ibuprofen. More panic. More ibuprofen and lots of missing time. Did I cause her disappearance? Ask White-Dress? No. More ibuprofen fixed that idiotic notion. The ibuprofen ran out and I could not manage an extended bus journey so I took the last of my money and headed to Joe's.

I stumbled through Joe's front door. He kept his various medicines behind the counter with his tobaccos. I ripped open the package the instant he handed it to me, fumbled with the bottle top and safety seal, and popped some pills. Then I paid his extortion prices. Joe just went back to his *Guns and Ammo*, and I left.

I almost crashed into the pastor dude. He caught me by my shoulders. Blue was with him. Euphoria — she was all right!

The pastor let me go. "Could we talk to you, please? Only if you have a moment, of course."

I glanced back and forth between them. "Why?"

He said, "This is a remarkable coincidence, if you choose to word it that way. Lydia is here to confront her past. Interesting timing, your presence at this very moment, you think?"

"Uh, if you say so."

"Your previous act of kindness. She told me. Kindness from a stranger is one of a number of things that have happened to Lydia to guide her away from life on the street to embark on her walk with the Lord."

I held my hand toward Blue — or Lydia, assuming she wouldn't lie to a pastor about her real name. "Well, I hope it works out for you."

She grabbed my hand and gave it a gentle squeeze. Eyes downcast, she said, "I need to thank you."

"For what?"

She could only look at my chest and shake her head.

The pastor said, "More than you realize. You have been mentioned numerous times over the past week."

"My role in whatever's happened, I'm sure, is overrated." I looked at Lydia's freckles and said to her, "That's great — you getting out of your situation."

"She didn't do it alone," the pastor said. "And you didn't act on your own either. You both had guidance from a higher power. I'd like you to give that some consideration."

"Sure thing, Father." The pastor didn't correct me. "Look after her, will you." I walked away at a fast clip. I needed my recliner because the pills were kicking in.

I was half way across the intersection when Lydia called, "I'll be at the church on Sunday."

And here she is. She's been at the church every Sunday since. She lingers after the other members of the prayer circle head toward the barbecues. The pastor always strolls up to her and puts his hand on her shoulder; she always watches my bedroom window. In a minute they will turn away. I'm pretty sure she doesn't see me. After all, the sun's shining into the front of the house by this time of the day.

Iliana's Daily Reminders

EVERY MORNING IS THE SAME. Grey daylight oozes in through the bedroom window.

Bertram awakes with a start. The throb in both knees is immediate. The fall dampness plays hell on the joints. He sits up and feels a dull lump of something in his abdomen. The doctor doesn't know what it is and can't find anything wrong so he prescribes pills.

He has dreamt of his beloved Iliana again. She stands in a circle of light just inside the bedroom door. She holds her palms toward him and tells him, not yet. This is when he awakens. He sighs and rubs his eyes, making them water.

They were together for fifty years. Spouses, friends, lovers, life partners. He feels half his body has been torn away, and he is teetering on one leg. Ready to topple.

The diabetes ate her up; the doctors hacking away pieces of her bit by bit; medical staff repeating that she could only be made comfortable. They assured him she couldn't feel any pain.

Iliana is cradled in his arms, her cheek in his chest. He can feel the damp of her sweat through his shirt. Her

221

breathing, slow, shallow. She moans. Her head lolls back. Lids half open, her once-piercing blue eyes are faded grey orbs. The slightest smile is on her lips. She seems to know he is there.

He sees Iliana smile and hears the rattle of her breath over and over again.

His eyes have stopped watering but the pain in his abdomen creeps up into his heart. He knows what this pain is. The worst pain of them all. He no longer tells the doctor about it.

What day is it anyway?

He slips on his glasses and looks at the calendar the home-care lady left him on her very last visit. It's Wednesday. The monthly trip to the doctor. The day to buy more pills.

Well, at least that's something to do today.

First, the morning routine. Empty the colostomy bag. Check there's a new one in case of another accident. A hot bath to ease the pain in the knees. A breakfast of a poached egg and one slice of toast. One cup of coffee while he watches the world news. Only one cup. He loves his coffee but it makes his stomach hurt.

Then the multitude of pills. First, the ones he understands; a multi-vitamin, an iron pill with a B-12 supplement, and a children's ASA. Then an orange one, white one, pink one, and never forget the little yellow one, or he will feel like puking all day. A second little yellow one at bedtime and for sure the light-blue one or he can't sleep. The home-care lady made up a colour-coded chart.

She suggested he use Iliana's daily pill reminder instead of buying a new one.

He washes the breakfast dishes, slowly, to fill the morning.

The dishes are done already. No need to clean the bathroom. He does that Mondays. Tuesdays, vacuuming. He stands and stares out the window. The day is drizzly. The glass of the office building across the street reflects the barren grey of the sky as clouds swirl overhead.

Drizzle turns to rain and he goes away for a while.

∾∾∾

Around Echo Lake in the fall to see the leaves turning. Today the weather is colder; ready to rain or even snow. The crispness of the air at this time of year. Iliana sings "Echo Beach" while he manages only the small echo — *echo beach* — in the chorus. Iliana laughs and claps when he gets the pitch and tone almost right. They stand on the shore, arm in arm, watch the water and listen to the lapping of waves. Leaning together for warmth, they protect each other from the cool wet mist off the water.

∾∾∾

He snaps back.

Wasn't I just watching the damn news?

He looks out the window again. Rain has changed back to drizzle.

What day is it? Don't I have to go somewhere?

He checks the calendar. It's Wednesday. Doctor and pill day. The doctor's appointment is at 2:30 in the afternoon. It's 9:15. May as well go to the mall for a while.

He ambles to the front closet, takes his raincoat from its hanger and gives it two shakes. He examines the grey fraying material. The shiny spots on the elbows. He slips one arm in a sleeve. Then the other. He does up the buttons, slowly.

The big red SHOES! sign on the door reminds him to take off his slippers and put something suitable on his feet. The home-care lady made the sign for him.

Now why in the hell couldn't I have thought of this sign?

He wishes she would come for a visit again. He doesn't even remember what she looked like. She had the same stature and graceful demeanour as Iliana. *Doesn't matter anyway. She's not Iliana.* He used to have such a good memory.

He steps into the hallway, closes the door, and makes sure it's locked by trying the doorknob once, twice, three times.

The hallway's matted beige carpet and fading off-white walls look as decrepit as he feels. The elevator door scrapes when it slides open. Bare metal shines in a narrow strip where the white paint has long since worn away.

The ride down is quick. He exits the elevator, passes through the brown mottled marble of the lobby into the vestibule. He braces himself, holds the raincoat's collar tight to his throat, steps into the street and is pelted by a stinging drizzle.

Grey sky broils overhead, that constant prairie wind driving the clouds. Head down now, he shuffles past the parkade exit ramp, the glass storefront of the next building, and the stained white marble of an old bank building, now turned skater shop. There are no punk kids loitering outside in this weather.

He follows the black globs and scaling in the cement sidewalk. The long haul to the mall in the dampness intensifies the throbbing in his knees. Why is there no enclosed walkway? How many times has he walked alone this way since Iliana died?

At the mall's main entrance the walkway stonework has cracked and heaved and a lone thistle has taken root in one of the cracks, its scrawny stock desperately reaching skyward.

Inside, he buys a scratch bingo card from the lottery kiosk on the main floor. Then he rides the escalator up to the second-level food court. He buys a hot chocolate from the old A&W.

Other old people sit in groups. They chat and sip from disposable cups. They don't notice him and he ignores them. They are all strangers. He sits by himself at a table for two at the far end of the court.

Almost everyone he knew is dead. He and Iliana had a wide circle of friends. Iliana is gone too. This leaves only Jimmy, who lingers in the palliative care ward dying of lung cancer. Jimmy was his executive assistant and sometime drinking buddy when they were both employed at the Liverwood Potash Corporation's Head Office. Jimmy can only moan now. That's all he did during the last visit. Too much of a reminder. It led him to take the bottle of pills. He puked for two days afterward and has never felt so sick. He flushes with shame.

He just can't visit Jimmy anymore.

The food court fills with suits and skirts from office buildings attached to the mall. He scratches the bingo ticket and doesn't win. He listens to the din for a while. He finishes his hot chocolate, then stares at the silty dregs at the bottom of his cup.

The office workers looking for a place to sit are all so young. He surrenders his seat and rides the escalator back down to the main floor. Steps outside, once again gripping his collar against a now pelting rain.

ᏬᏬᏬ

Iliana hugs his arm with both of hers and presses her cheek against his shoulder. He wraps his arm around her waist and holds her against him as they stroll for miles in silence around Echo Lake. Her rain hat is pulled low and the collar of her blue plastic coat is turned up high. They pause on the shore and he gazes down into her eyes. Her round face peeks out and she smiles up at him, so bright. So alive.

ᏬᏬᏬ

"Your order's not ready yet." The girl behind the counter is in her twenties, slender and small breasted. She says, "We'll call your number." Her black hair is shaved on one side and hangs to her shoulder on the other. Iliana's light brown hair is so full, and consistently shoulder length. Her body is full too. She would never starve herself to such a gaunt state.

"You're not fat, you're pleasingly plump," he says.

"We'll call your number," the skinny girl repeats, not acknowledging his comment. She abruptly turns away.

He blinks back to reality. He wonders where the hell he is, then realizes he's ordering lunch at the KFC about two kilometers from downtown. *Did I really walk this far? No wonder the knees ache.*

He sits on one of the sterile plastic benches and feels a touch of pride for not panicking. His pants are damp against his legs. Both his knees ache. This helps him ignore the ever-present dull pain near his heart.

The skinny girl calls his number. A two-piece lunch special with fries and no gravy. Nothing to drink. Soft drinks play hell on the stomach. He takes the skin off the chicken to help mitigate more intense gut pains. But it is something different to eat.

After the meal, he takes the bus back downtown instead of walking, even though the rain has stopped. He steps out the bus's back door near the mall entrance.

I have to go somewhere today, don't I? I better get back to the apartment and find out where.

Back inside the apartment, he checks the calendar. It's Wednesday. Doctor's appointment and pill day. At 2:30. It's almost 2:00. Too late to take the bus. The doctor has moved his office to a strip mall on the outskirts of the city.

Good God, I'll have to drive. I really shouldn't anymore.

He tries to think what happened to make him late.

I was just at the mall. Where did the time go? What's going to happen when my whole day is gone? Someone will have to look after me then. That's the last thing in hell anybody needs or wants.

After making his way to the parkade via elevator, he carefully maneuvers the car out of its parking spot, down the ramps, and out of downtown. Driving eastward, he instinctively knows the way, and he's at the doctor's office just on time, but has to wait half an hour anyway. Flu season. The room is filled with sniffling, wailing kids, and complaining adults.

"Mr. Ross?"

He blinks and turns his head.

The receptionist is talking to him. She is a middle-aged woman with dark hair, obviously dyed by the way white roots shine beneath the overhead lights. She wears a pink cardigan and is pleasantly plump like Iliana. But she is not Iliana.

"The doctor will see you now," she says.

Another twenty-minute wait in the examination room. Sitting in his underwear, he shivers against the chill, which aggravates the pain in his abdomen. He stares down at his ribs poking through his skin, which is spotted with brown blotches and grey hairy patches. His breasts are sagging more and more.

Rocks-in-socks, rocks-in-socks, he sings.

The doctor bustles in. He is a balding, beanpole of a man. His white smock hanging down to his thighs elongates his body even more. His face is pale and the bags under his eyes are darker than they were last visit. "You got the flu, too, Bert?" the doctor asks.

"No, I don't have the flu. This is my monthly visit. Those new orange pills upset my stomach worse. And I'm still depressed. I'm still having bad dreams. I keep seeing the wife. My knees still hurt."

"We just changed the prescription for the setraline hcl. That's the orange pill. Let's try it for another month. We'll change your antiemetics to something a little stronger. They'll still be yellow. And we'll just renew your others." The doctor barks these instructions while he presses the cold stethoscope on Bertram's chest. He quickly checks his blood pressure and then scribbles on the chart and the prescription sheets.

Why does the doctor still use a paper chart? Why isn't he using a portable electronic device connected to the provincial health system like the hospitals and medical clinics do these days? He doesn't get a chance to ask.

"See you again in a month, Bert," the doctor says. "We don't need a blood test until two visits from now. The receptionist will telephone you a reminder when the time comes around. Don't forget to keep visiting the psychiatrist."

"I haven't seen him in six months. He said I don't have to. He said you'll refer me again, if necessary."

"Oh, that's right. Good progress, then." The doctor slaps the chart shut. "Keep looking after yourself. 'Til next time, Bert."

He slowly gets dressed and stares at the human muscle chart hanging on the examination room door.

Why do these rooms never change?

∿∿∿

He is in another examination room. They just lost their second child. A second spontaneous abortion. It is unlikely Iliana can ever bring a child to term. The medical consensus is they should stop trying.

Iliana weeps. Her body heaves. Bertram, so struck by her grief, can't find any words of comfort.

He clings to her while she sobs. *You can't control biology. You are no less a woman for this. It's not your fault.*

He holds her a long time. He has to stay strong for her. She turns her pale chubby face and presses her cheek against his chest. Her tears soak through his shirt.

∿∿∿

Bertram speaks out loud to his steering wheel. He doesn't recall what the doctor just said. He doesn't remember leaving the examination room or doctor's office or even getting into his car. In the parking lot, the engine idles. The grey drizzle persists and blurs the windshield with droplets. The wipers clear the window.

He puts the car into gear and, for something to do, he navigates onto the Ring Road instead of going back home. He traverses the length of the expressway, reversing his course at the last interchange and returns to the doctor's office parking lot.

He has to retrace his route home from here so he doesn't get lost again.

The drive fills the rest of afternoon.

He carefully parks his car in its spot and descends the parkade stairwell. His knee-joints burn on each step down. The stairwell leads to the street beside the exit ramp. He follows the same path he took in the morning to the mall's main entrance, the black globs and scaling his guide markers. He shuffles to the main floor drug store and finds his way to the pharmacy.

Another wait. The bill is over $500.00 for this new batch of pills. The pharmacist blathers on about what to take and when. It seems there's a new person behind the counter each month. This one is a middle-aged bone-rack. She is also not Iliana.

How wet his pants are below the bottom of his raincoat.
No damn wonder the knees pain me so much all the time.
The pharmacist just smiles and nods.

Back at the apartment he heats a Salisbury Steak TV dinner in the oven. He sits at the kitchen table and watches *Jeopardy*, the local news, and the world news while slowly eating his meal.

At 7:00 he switches to CNN and turns the volume down low. He gets out the new pill bottles. The old pill bottles. Iliana's coloured pill reminder. The chart. With pen and pad of paper at hand, he's ready for the pill ritual. He goes over the instruction sheets, consults his chart, and then writes down each name, colour and the daily dosages. He cross-references notes, bottles, chart, pill reminder once, twice, three times to be sure. He can't pronounce the names of the pills. He doesn't know what they do. As long as he can fathom what colour at what time of the day. This is the key to being comfortable.

Except these damn pills are no comfort. Iliana is comfort.

∾∾∾

It is 1998.

He and Jimmy are in his twelfth floor office at the round dark-oak guest table. A bottle of Chivas Regal sits on the leather tabletop. Two four-ounce glasses, each with a shot, sit untouched in front of them. They stare at their drinks. There's a view of nighttime downtown, city lights reflecting off the lake.

Jimmy suggests maybe they should head over to The Coffee Cavern across the street. Their co-workers are mourning over there.

Bertram shakes his head. He just wants to go home.

They toast the man who died at the mine site. It is the first ever death of a miner at the Liverwood Potash Corporation.

At home, Iliana cradles his head against her chest. He is soothed by her rhythmic breathing. He does not cry. But this is the first time he feels this ripping pain across his chest. This pain of loss.

Iliana reminds him that, yes, it is his role to maintain production, but only as ordered by those sitting on high. The miners do the best they can, but too much overtime leads to worker fatigue. And fatigue hunts for any opportunity to inflict pain and suffering on its prey.

"That miner's death is not your fault," she tells him. Then she says, "Listen."

He tilts his head and hears rain falling on the roof.

∾∾∾

He sits up from where he has set his head down on the table.

Now why was I thinking about that dead miner?

He feels a pang of regret for the dead man he never even met. Life insurance provided for the man's wife and daughter. The Workers' Compensation investigation determined that worker fatigue was indeed the cause of the accident, just as Iliana had predicted. The company had taken steps to correct the excessive overtime situation long before the investigation was completed.

He moves to his chair in front of the TV after putting away Iliana's daily reminders. CNN plays ongoing coverage of the West Virginia coal mine accident and fire and this must have triggered his own memories, even though there are no injuries or deaths in Virginia.

Nodding off and on while the TV babbles, he realizes that he will need some extra pain relief tonight. Maybe two of the light-blue pills and some extra strength ASA. One shot of scotch, neat, with the late news will also help. He watched his intake today, so the scotch shouldn't cause too much more stomach discomfort.

But definitely not half the bottle and all the pills like his second attempt to end it all. After three hours of puking and dry heaves, he'd had to call 9-1-1.

Damn the cops to hell. They poured the rest of the scotch down the drain. Premium Blue Label, no less. What a waste.

About midnight, he rubs some arthritis cream on his legs and goes to bed.

He drifts off to sleep.

∾∾∾∾

Sunshine brightens the whole room. He sits up in bed. There is no pain in his knees. No pain in his abdomen. No pain in his heart. Above the office building across the street there is not a single cloud in the azure sky. He swears he can see infinity.

Movement at the door. Iliana is there. She is pleasingly plump. Her body is intact and healthy. Her light brown hair is full, the greying streaks at the temples barely noticeable. Her blue eyes sparkle, their irises match the sky outside, brighter than the light in the room. His heart pounds but there is no pain.

She holds her rain hat and has her blue plastic coat draped over one arm.

The light in the room fades but a bright circle surrounds her.

No pain. It is finally over.

Iliana holds her palms toward him. "Not yet."

The Catherine Sessions

You once were my grey stone home
Timeless ageless oasis
in dusty prairie gloam
forgotten not, forgotten not . . .

— The Gryphonic Techno-Bastards

W HEN WALKER SAW CATHERINE'S PICTURE on the cover of *Modern Office Design*, he marvelled. She looked matured but not aged. The intervening decade-and-a-half had not changed her. The Go Kart Mozart CD — *Older, Balder, Fatter* — came to mind when he thought of himself. The cover photo did justice to her cool sky-blue eyes. The article said her career had progressed from interior office design to architecture and engineering. She specialized in oceanside building, preventing structures from sliding into the Pacific. He searched for her contact information on the internet, did a reverse number lookup on her telephone number, and found a man's name associated with that same number. So, she didn't live alone.

Alone like him. He wondered if she'd kept her own name so maybe he could find her one day. No, he thought, that was simply a delusion from a prairie-baked brain. Platonic. That's what their relationship had been. Yes, they had both worked for Liverwood Potash Corporation, right here at the company's downtown head office, and yes they'd liked to torque the rumour mill by hugging in the foyer of the building at quitting time.

"You're scaring me," she had said, fifteen years ago when they last spoke. She'd uttered those final, parting words, moved her drink to his side of the table, and then left. He'd stared at her empty chair until closing time. The server had been annoyed with him because he hadn't ordered anything else. He had dropped a twenty-dollar tip before he finally wandered home.

Now, he's at that same table in the restaurant side of The Coffee Cavern just across the street from the corporation building where he still works. He slouches, elbow on table, chin on palm, near the back beside the old fish tank. It was their usual spot. The place hasn't changed for the better in the intervening years. The dark hardwood floor has dulled and the subdued lighting disguises the scaling of the brownish brickwork and dry rot of the support beams and pillars. The fish tank, converted to a terrarium with a desert motif, has only a thin layer of sand at the bottom, a couple of rocks, and a bleached branch. The only life inside is two hermit crabs that have yet to move.

He orders two dark rum and cokes with lemon, which was her drink of choice. He sets one on the other side of the table and the server raises an eyebrow. She is young and chunky with cascading black hair. She wears a low-cut top and a fire tattoo leaps up her left ankle. He pays her with a twenty-dollar bill and tells her to keep the change. She gives him a broad smile. He needs to write a letter, he says. She nods and leaves him alone.

He sets the magazine beside a pad of lined yellow foolscap so he can study Catherine's photo; the brunette pageboy hairstyle, her round cheeks and full lips. She was at least six inches shorter than his six feet, but looks tall leaning against the gleaming desk, the Vancouver skyline visible through office windows in the background. Her professional, conservative, grey suit makes her look subtle, seductive.

He intends to compose some kind of a plea. He taps the ballpoint pen on the blank yellow page, writes "I," and stops. He stares at the light blue lines, which begin to waver like heat waves in the prairie distance.

"I can feel vulnerable around you," she had said one hot summer day at a nearby pedestrian mall. He bought her a single carnation. The flowers were two dollars each in support of some charity. She placed the stem between her middle and ring fingers with the flower-pod resting on her knuckles. They sat on the edge of a planter, cluttered with weeds and a lone thistle, mindless of the grey concrete walkway and buildings around them. He watched her smell the flower.

She said, "You sure know how to cheer me up."

"What are friends for?" he replied.

"Well, for one, for letting me vent all the time. How do you put up with me?"

"I don't know. You're such a horrible person. The real question is, how do you put up with yourself?"

She laughed and said he was her outcrop to lean against, providing shelter from a relentless sun. Her ex-husband — Mr. *Misogune* she had named him, a play on the word "misogynist" — kept telephoning, emailing, sending letters. The communiqués ran from toadying to pleading to threatening. He wanted her back; he begged; he would do anything. She was glad he still lived in Halifax. An impoverished and perpetual Dalhousie student forever working on a Masters Degree in Political Science, he didn't have the financial resources to come after her.

She told Walker she was glad she could talk to him freely and randomly without being judged. To talk without getting unsolicited advice, just to have someone to listen. He was totally unlike her ex-husband, she said.

He never knew exactly what the man had done to drive her away, she never talked about that and he never asked. She lent him her copy of *Men Who Hate Women and the Women Who Love Them*, and their bonds of trust grew stronger. One thing he knew for sure was that he would never treat her the way the people in the book treated each other.

He said, "So what does your current boyfriend—Marcel, is it? What does he have to say about your ex sleazing around you?"

238

"Marcel doesn't know. It's none of his business. Besides, he's not," her inflection turned nasal, "my boyfriend."

"What do you mean 'not your boyfriend'?"

"Come on. You're not naïve. We all have urges. And he satisfies a particular one. This relationship is on *my* terms."

"Well, I think you could do better. How is he for emotional support?"

Catherine sniffed and said, "I don't need a man for that. That's what I've got Phoebe for. She set me up here. Helped me through the rough patches when I thought it was all my fault. Introduced me to Marcel. It's her I can't live without. You know, soul mates."

He only nodded. A song — recognizable as a Gryphonic Techno-Bastards' number by the discordant guitars — played from a scratchy speaker outside the music store next to them. *Soul mate, I can do that*, he thought as they walked back to work. She said, "Besides, Walker, I can always rely on you to listen."

I can rely on you, I can feel vulnerable around you, sluiced around in his consciousness afterward. He forced those thoughts over the horizon and tried to feel nothing. Nothing, even when she cancelled that dinner date. She'd said, "So I told Marcel, 'I'll go with you to that funeral if you make it worth my while. Make it a holiday and I'll consider it.' But he just needs me to 'attend him,' quote, unquote. I told him to forget it. I'm not interested."

"Whatever will you do this weekend all alone?" Walker asked.

"I don't know." She wiggled her eyebrows twice. "Any ideas?"

"Maybe Saturday we can grab a bite somewhere? Check out a movie?"

She thought for a moment. "You and I always go to a restaurant. Let's see. You claim you're a cook. Why don't I come over and you can whip me up some fish. That pickerel thing you always talk about. Unless it's too much trouble."

He swallowed hard. "No trouble at all."

"Good. Say, seven-ish then? What's your address?"

For the rest of that week he focused on planning the meal. Come the Saturday he set out early in the morning to North Lakes fresh fish to pick up miniature shrimp for appetizers and fresh pickerel for linguine in curried cream sauce. He bought fresh ground coffee and picked up a French Cabernet Sauvignon and an Italian Chardonnay, and dark rum and Bailey's Irish Cream for afterward.

He assembled a fruit salad with a honey cardamom sauce for dessert and put it in the refrigerator to chill. He prepared a pepper mixture and the miniature shrimp for a Brushetta appetizer. Once the mixture was simmering, he sliced a baguette and carefully re-wrapped it in its brown paper bag. He showered and groomed before grating parmesan for the Brushetta and crumpled blue cheese for a simple stuffed mushroom appetizer. The two appetizers would be ready at 7:00 so they could nibble and chat while he finished preparing the main course.

He was carefully cleaning and de-stemming mushrooms when the phone rang. Catherine. Phoebe was having a crisis and couldn't possibly be left alone. He knew it was none of his business so he didn't ask. She said they would talk Monday and hung up.

He wandered from the kitchen to the living room stereo. Blared The Gryphonic Techno-Bastards' *Catherineberg Sessions*. He stood listening to "My Catherine" before selecting random play. He decided to go ahead with the meal, dining alone by candlelight. Except he didn't. He didn't light the candles. The singer crooned about always remembering his girl under "greyling prairie skies." He sniffed the Brushetta after removing it from the oven, then placed it and the mushrooms beside the fruit salad in the refrigerator. He poured the linguini water down the drain and left the pasta in its box. He tasted a morsel of pickerel directly from the sauce pot, while telling the Chardonnay that everything was fine, just one of those things, then froze the rest of the fish and cream sauce. When the wine bottle was empty, he meandered into the living room with the rum, turned the CD off, and played a videotape from his collection. It was a documentary on the Battle of Kursk, the largest tank battle in history, fought on the open Russian Steppe.

He didn't watch the show though. Instead, he studied the dark liquid sitting still and flat in the confines of the rum bottle on the coffee table. He saw himself exit a lone house surrounded by endless prairie and walk and walk until the sun set and the landscape became as black as the rum. Under a starless and moonless sky, he finished the bottle and wandered directionless in the pitchy blackness toward a merciful oblivion. The videocassette player powered itself off after the battle and the machine sat idle.

After the cancelled dinner date it was a relief to be in his office Monday morning, looking down at the city's tree canopy. From the tenth floor, he had enough elevation to see the prairie beyond as it fell over the edge of the horizon. With his door closed, he immersed himself in audits, variances, and reconciliations of the company's various departmental operating budgets. Plunged in weekly ledgers and columns of numbers, he strained not to think of her three floors below, down in the Facilities Department. Then he got an email from her, an invitation for lunch at the Wascana Park Marina Restaurant to make up for missing Saturday — her treat. A while later another email arrived. It simply said, "Running to a meeting, late. Meet you there at lunch."

"There" was where he waited, at a window seat overlooking the rough wooden deck and the lake itself. He watched a lone Canada goose leisurely paddle toward Spruce Island.

His cell phone rang. "Hi, sorry. Still running late. Order me the fish special. Salad instead of fries. Be right there. Toodles."

He ordered two specials and they arrived ten minutes before she did.

She sat down across from him and started eating. "Sorry I'm late. I had a meeting with Personnel on my contract renewal."

"Oh? You didn't tell me your contract was up. How did it go?"

"They don't seem to know how valuable I am. We'll see." She suddenly looked past his shoulder, her face lit up, glowing. With a squeal of delight, she called out, "Phoebe!" She said to him, "Be right back," and breezed past.

He turned to watch her stride toward Phoebe, a stringbean of a woman with shoulder length, mousy-blonde hair. They hugged and kissed each other's cheeks in European style. It appeared Phoebe had survived her weekend ordeal, judging from her grin.

After the hug and kisses they leaned toward each other and spoke intently. He could see Catherine's face and watched her lips move. If he concentrated, he could just hear her. At one point, Phoebe's head tilted questioningly in his direction and, with the slightest glance in his direction, Catherine replied, "Just some guy from work."

He turned back, poked at his fish and thought over what he had intended to say. No problem with cancelling Saturday's dinner. I understand. No, don't worry about me. I wasn't disappointed. I'm not disappointed over this aborted lunch, either.

He looked out the window at Spruce Island again. The beautiful prairie surrounding the city and this small oasis of water was becoming hostile and inhospitable. The plain would soon evaporate the lake and leave him standing in a dusty expanse of dead weeds and thorn fields under a grey sky thick with clouds, a place where he wouldn't even bother to try and get his bearings. He'd have nowhere to go.

He looked at his cell phone and pretended to answer a call. Catching Catherine's attention as he stood, he waved the phone, shrugged, and turned to leave. She nodded and mouthed the words, "I've got the bill. Go ahead."

He bolted toward the exit with only one quick glance backward. Catherine was leading her friend by the hand toward his recently vacated table.

She didn't phone or email that afternoon to ask how he was, why he'd been called away, or to apologize for missing lunch.

They stopped going to movies and restaurants; when she sent an email invitation, he always found an excuse; his responses were curt yet civil, and then he began to delete her messages without even reading them. He focused on his work; ledger lines distracting and comfortable horizons.

After a while of this, she appeared at his office one day at five o'clock.

"Hi grumpy," she said, leaning against the doorjamb. "I think it's time we went to The Cavern and I bought you that meal I owe you. I won't take 'no' for an answer." Her blue eyes were as intense as a cloudless, hot afternoon sky.

What was the point in defying her? His computer was off and he was clearly making his way out of the office. A couple of his accounting clerks were still at their desks in the common area. They didn't glance up, but they obviously were dying to see what would happen next.

He was not going to be the first to talk, so the elevator ride to the main floor and the walk across the street was in silence.

In The Cavern restaurant, she took charge, asking the server for their usual table and then ordering their dark rum and coke on the way past the bar. She plunked down in their spot by the fish tank and said, "You've certainly been in a contrary mood lately. What's going on?"

He shook his head. "Nothing's going on. It's all just business as usual."

"I don't believe that. There's obviously something wrong. You've listened to me through crisis after crisis. Now it's my turn to listen to you."

"There's nothing for you to listen to."

"Why are you behaving like this?"

Here it was again, that cloudy, endless plain, sun obscured, no particular direction to go. *Now* was the time to send up a flare for help. But what if no one saw?

Or worse yet, what if someone saw and turned away?

"Like what?" he replied after his moment's pause. "I've got nothing to say. Or is that answer not acceptable to you? Are you going to keep picking at me until you hear something you want to hear? If you want someone to toady up to you, give that Marcel dude a call."

"Ooh, that stings. I'm offering to be here for you. If you need to talk. But I don't put up with that kind of crap from anyone anymore. I've had more than enough of that type of attitude from my ex."

"I'm sorry *this* relationship isn't on *your* terms."

He watched his drink; watched the ice float in flat blackness.

So he missed whatever expression was on her face when, after what seemed like an hour's silence, she simply said, "You're scaring me." That was when she moved her drink and left. Decision made, he wandered nowhere in that empty plain. Then, there in the far distance — was that a stone house on the edge of the prairie, teetering on the very rim of the horizon? Should he check it out? Perhaps, but the walk there would be eternal and ultimately pointless.

He turns to the server hovering near him, her leg on fire.

"Sorry to interrupt your letter. Can I get you anything else?"

He waves at the two untouched glasses. "No. Thank you. Lost in thought here." He picks up one drink, has a sip. He sets the glass down over the face on the magazine cover.

She didn't even say goodbye when her contract expired. He rips the page with the single letter "I" from the pad and crumples it up. The Gryphonic Techno-Bastards' song plays in his mind and he jots the lyrics on the clean, flat page:

lost in a dust storm of despair
I can't find my way back
to my timeless stone home
you'll never see what became of me.

This Girl Next Door

THE EVENING BLAKE'S MOTHER SAID, "Don't you dare bother with those people," he waited until they'd both gone out and got his dad's extension ladder and leaned it against the neighbour's seven-foot back fence. The Castle Frankenstein rankled him. Why such a high fence? All the others in the neighbourhood were only about three feet high and were picket-style or had wide-gapped horizontal slats. Given his bony six-foot body, he could almost step over those fences. But this monster fence was impenetrable, with vertical slats butted tight together and no gaps for spying.

The only break in the rampart-like caragana hedge surrounding the front yard was a bulky trellis at the end of the front walk, with a heavy wooden gate. The gate was locked, as he had discovered one night last winter, just after his thirteenth birthday when he tried to sneak in.

His parents mostly didn't talk about the people who lived there. No one in the neighbourhood did. The only things he knew for sure was that the place had once been a farmhouse before the city's urban sprawl eventually surrounded it, and two women and a girl lived there. The house was two-storey, with garret windows on the second floor. It stood out like a citadel among the stock neighbourhood bungalows with their manicured and treeless yards.

And just what was the deal with the girl always in sunglasses, and her long black hair and swaying hips? All he knew about her was she was picked up by taxi and driven downtown to the only private school in the city.

The evening wind gusted gently and the leaves in the neighbour's trees rustled just as Blake breached the top of the fence. His first look inside the yard lasted a second or so before he ducked. Too late. That black-haired girl stood nearby, hands on her hips, looking up at him. Her raven hair, thick and wavy and hanging loosely past her shoulders, contrasted sharply with her pale face. Apparently in the shade of the backyard she didn't wear her sunglasses and was way too Wednesday Addams for his liking. Suspended in time near the top of the ladder, he was certain he'd been seeing things. No normal girl should look like that. Right?

He cautiously peered over the fence again. Well, she really was standing right beside the fence — staring up at him, hands still on her hips. He took in her long black T-shirt and black jeans; her bare feet made him think of lilies on a dark coffin lid. Her eyes were bright blue. He'd expected dark irises.

"What do you want?" she said in a gravelly voice, neither accusatory nor hostile. She sounded more like a teacher asking if he knew the square root of nine.

"I wanted to see what was behind this fence."

"What for?"

"I'm nosy? This fence is way different from everyone else's?"

"Are you satisfied or would you like to come over for a better look?"

His heart lurched, but he did not hyperventilate and his voice did not crack when he said, "Seriously?"

"No. I said it to see if your face could get any redder. Of course seriously or I wouldn't offer. I don't want you gawking down at me like I'm a reptile in a zoo. Now put that stupid ladder away and meet me by the back gate." She pointed to the middle of the fence along the back alley.

"Okay. Sure. See you in a minute."

His foot slipped off the bottom rung and he scraped his shin. He dragged the ladder back to the garage and caught his fingers between the ladder and its hanger on the garage wall. What the hell was he doing? This simple reconnoiter had turned into an actual meeting with the girl next door. He had to stop and take a breath to calm himself.

∾∾∾

It was July, summer holidays, and a scant hour before everything had been normal; he had been at the kitchen table eating supper with his parents.

He'd said, "Why is the place next door such a dump? Why doesn't the city tear it down or something?"

His mom asked, "Why the sudden interest?"

"Dunno. We always argue about Vietnam. Maybe I want to talk about something else tonight."

His mom sniffed. "We have to talk about something else only because you want to?"

"He's just trying to have a pleasant conversation, Hannah," his dad said.

"That boy doesn't just do something. What are you up to?"

"Nothing. I just want to know what the deal is. Those women. Are they gibbled or retards or what? Why don't you talk to them like you do the Joneses?"

"Because I don't talk to witches. That's what they are. Horrible, Catholic witches."

Dad rolled his eyes. "Don't exaggerate. They're just off a little, is all, Blake. They're not worth your interest or trouble. Forget about . . . "

That's when his mom said, "Now look, I know you're bored but don't go looking for trouble. Don't you dare bother with those people."

∾∾∾

The gate was open and the girl was waiting for him just inside the fence. She said, "Took you long enough."

Blake stepped into the backyard with a shrug.

The girl closed the gate and clicked the latch in place.

There were about a dozen trees in the yard, birch and the taller poplars, all providing a jungle-like canopy. The place was cool relief from the early evening heat. There was no grass. The ground was hardpacked, light brown gravel. A path of round stones led from the gate to a stone patio. A short caragana hedge was planted against the back of the house, broken only by the back door. The rustling of leaves in the breeze soothed his taut nerves.

The girl was several inches shorter than him. She looked up to say, "I'm Angel."

"Blake." He held out his hand, a conditioned reflex from years of his mom's constant etiquette nagging.

Angel hesitated and raised one eyebrow. She then took his hand and squeezed once. Her hand was soft and cool. She said, "No cracks about my name?"

He shook his head and shrugged once again.

She gave him a half-smile. "No name games then."

"I'm down with that. Is Angel short for anything?"

"Nope. Come sit down."

She led him toward the patio and a pink picnic table. He watched her buttocks sway a moment. Feeling guilty for gawking, he focused on the picnic table.

For the second time in a few short minutes, he didn't quite believe what he was seeing. Beside a black glass ashtray littered with the plastic butts of Colt Cigarillos, was a spike nailed to the middle of the tabletop. A tight white string was attached to the spike. Tied to the string's other end was a struggling cutworm.

They sat opposite each other and Blake rested his chin on the tabletop. He stared at the worm. "Did you do that?"

"'Fraid so," Angel replied and grabbed her hair with both hands and threw it behind her shoulders. Her ears were like small, delicate seashells.

"How?"

"You make a slip knot first. Then hold the worm and the knot with one hand. Pull the string with your other hand 'til it's tight on the worm. Then tie the string to the nail."

"Cool." He straightened up and watched the worm struggle in its circle. "Why?"

"Those worms eat my mom's herbs. And it upsets her. She needs those herbs. So I get them back. Stupid, I know."

"Not stupid. My mom yaps about these worms all the time. Why don't you just squish them?"

"Mostly I do. But sometimes, when mom's not happy. You know."

He looked around and said, "Uh, so, herbs? I don't see any garden back here."

Angel let out a short chortle and said, "Garden's in the front."

"What? Yards around here don't have gardens in the front."

"Ours does. The sun is mostly in front. So that's the best place for growing stuff, isn't it? Wanna see?"

"Sure."

They walked between their two houses. If that high fence had not been in the way, he would have been able to see the window of his basement bedroom.

He had never seen such a front yard. A rock garden was arranged in the perpetual shade of the hedge along the street. The herb garden itself was a disorganized mass of mostly strange plants. In the tangled growth, he recognized some sort of peppers, and the smell of sage was strong, but he did not recognize the hearty stocks and long narrow pointed leaves of the lush plants right up against the front of the house where the sunlight was strongest.

He turned to ask Angel, but she was hunching her head and shoulders and shading her eyes with both hands.

"Are you okay?"

"Just the sun. I should wear sunglasses even in the evening light. I'm not nearly as bad as Mom, though. She breaks out in hives and always has to wear sunglasses even inside."

"That sucks. What's wrong with you?" He inwardly cringed at his abrupt and pointed question.

Angel, however, seemed fine with it. "The easiest way to explain it is we have kind of a sun allergy. The doctors can't do anything about it. Because it's so bad for Mom, she smokes her own medicinal cigarettes." She pointed at the row of plants.

He said, "Let's go back then."

Again he watched Angel's buttocks sway as they retreated to the backyard. And again he felt self-conscious about staring and hung his head to watch her feet instead.

Angel said, "Do you want to see something cool?"

He nodded.

She untied the cutworm from the table and knelt beside the hedge. "Check this out."

He crouched beside her. His bent knee was close to hers but did not touch.

In the bottom leaves of the caraganas were wolf spider webs. Angel tossed the cutworm into the thick of one of the webs, near the opening to the spider's lair. He watched, fascinated, as the spider darted out, bit and paralyzed the worm, and then dragged it back inside.

He scanned the numerous webs built in the caragana leaves. "These are so neat," he said. "Mom sweeps the webs away so I never get to see the spiders in action. I used to check out the webs over by the creek but I don't go there anymore."

Angel stood and went back to the table. She sat cross-legged on the top. He followed and put one foot on the bench a good foot away from her. He leaned his elbows on his knee and tried to think of something to say but she spoke first.

"So why don't you go over to the creek anymore?"

∿∿∿

That Saturday this past spring had started typically. Blake and the usual pack of boys swarming the city playground two blocks away, some of them harassing the big-breasted supervisor and the high school girlfriends who hung around with her. The boys would tease the older girls, get them to chase them, and then let themselves get caught. The girls would pin the boys down and spit in their faces or give them "pink belly." It was all worth it because it was way easy to cop a feel of either a breast or butt — sometimes even a crotch.

That day he was just leaning with his arms crossed against the supervisor's shack and watching. The game lasted until high school boyfriends drove up and then all of the high schoolers locked themselves inside the shack, leaving the younger kids in the playground to supervise themselves.

Bored, he and the boys wandered to the creek that ran parallel to his back alley. The backs of the houses and the garret windows of the two-storey peering above the trees were all in clear view across the flood plain filled with tall prairie grasses and Canadian thistle and various other weeds. His pack joined another group of younger brothers and sisters right across from his backyard and they all massed on the creek's edge.

The older boys, led by his friend Darryl, threw rocks at a large western painted turtle sunning itself on the opposite shore. The turtle didn't move, oblivious to the danger.

Sidling up to Darryl, Blake snatched a softball-sized rock from his hand and said, "What are you doing, Hannigan?"

Darryl took a step back and gawked. "Whaddya think you're doing, Rake." His glaring white T-shirt revealed broad shoulders and a bulky chest but he was six inches shorter than Blake and had a much shorter reach. "Gimme that rock back, pecker-breath."

Blake snorted. "You're smelling your own breath. Throwing rocks at a turtle? You're one tough mother, aren't you?"

The other kids formed a circle around them.

Darryl fisted his hands. "What's it to you? Are you some kind of fag standing up for a stupid turtle?"

Blake said, "A fag's a cigarette. You're the homo, knob-gobbler."

"Take that back."

"Make me." Blake knew his reputation for strength, agility and reach at basketball was common knowledge. It would be a short fight.

Darryl's older brother Frank, and a friend of his, stepped up, one on each flank.

Blake grinned, realizing they didn't have the tactical intelligence to surround their opponent. He tossed the rock lightly up and down. "Well? Come get some."

The three boys took a tentative step forward. Blake underhanded the rock straight up. All attention was drawn to that movement and he hit Frank's chest with an open palm and the boy lurched backward onto his buttocks.

Blake deftly caught the falling rock overhand with a loud slap and grabbed Darryl's shirt with his other hand. Darryl twisted back and forth, tried a right and then a left hook but did not make contact. The chops on Blake's inner arm didn't hurt, but something in his head clicked and his only thought was to smash Darryl's face with the rock, once for every rock thrown at the turtle.

It was only when Frank, still sitting, shrieked, "Let him go, creep!" that he realized he had red rings flashing in his vision. He pulled Darryl toward him and shoved him away. Darryl stumbled but did not fall. Frank's friend however, dropped to his knees. He could smell their sweat, their reek of fear. His knuckles were white, hand still gripping the rock.

The circle of kids backed away and formed a semi-circle behind the defeated allies.

There was a moment of silence until his mom yelled, "Blake! Get out of there. Right now!"

He instantly dropped the rock.

Someone in the mob said, "That freak is just too big."

Someone else said, "Freak is right-on. Giant freak. Herman Munster, man."

Inside his house, Blake took his mom's lecture. He did not try to justify his actions and did not even utter a single, "yeah, but." She spent ten minutes lamenting on how she wouldn't be able to live down the embarrassment of having a fighter and a bully for a son. "Just wait until your father gets home."

He remained silent the rest of the afternoon. He only remembered the smell of sweat, the urge to smash Darryl, that red flashing.

"It's a good thing the Liverwood people are easy to get along with," his dad said as soon as he stepped through the door. "Between the government slogging their feet like molasses in winter and tradesmen taking coffee breaks every fifteen minutes instead of fifteen minute breaks, we're falling further and further behind schedule. It makes the corporation look bad even though . . . " He stopped mid-sentence.

He glanced from his wife to his son, opened his mouth to speak, then closed it. After a breath, he said, "Hannah, are you two fighting?"

That was the signal flare. His mom launched into an excruciatingly detailed account of the day's events, from her point of view, of course. Her main concern seemed how to survive her embarrassment.

Dad listened with pursed lips and the occasional scratch of his head. Rubbing his chin in the ensuing silence, he said, "Blake, I see you feel pretty bad about this."

Blake nodded. He hung his head and simply said, "You're both totally right."

Hannah harrumphed.

Over the following weeks, he occasionally thought he should apologize to Darryl but he also felt that he had crossed the Rubicon — a phrase used in some of his war books, meaning a point of no return. The damage was irrevocable.

Boys still hung around the flood plain behind his house, but he never went out to join them.

∾∾∾∾

Blake took his foot off the bench and stood up straight. Right then he firmly believed he didn't deserve friends and didn't deserve Angel either. How was he supposed to tell her that story without looking like some sort of freakish outsized bully? He closed his eyes and focused on the sound of the leaves in the breeze.

"Blake?" Angel said. "You cool?"

"Yeah. Sorry. Kind of faded there," he replied and opened his eyes.

Angel said, her gravelly voice soothing, "Want to talk about it?"

He plopped down on the bench, his back to the house.

He stared at the tabletop and eventually decided to expose both flanks. He told Angel the whole story, including the urge to smash and the red flashing. After he finished, he said, "I'm pretty big and probably scared the crap out of all of them. You probably think I'm a bully."

Angel said, "Sometimes you have to do things you don't want to."

Blake sighed. "Even if it's wrong?"

"Sometimes. Sometimes things happen, even when you mind your own business. But you have to be willing to take the consequences, too."

"'Take the consequences.' That's what Mom says I have to do every thirty seconds." His face went hot. He slapped his forehead with his open palm. "I mean, I'm not saying you're like my mom. I mean, oh, holy shit, do I ever have a stupid mouth."

Angel laughed, leaned forward and touched his arm. "It's okay. I know what you mean." Her hand lingered for a moment. "At least, I think so. I don't think I'm like your mom. Am I?"

"Oh, god no. Believe me. And be thankful you're not." They both laughed.

A woman's voice behind him said, "What's so funny?"

He scrambled up. He banged his knee on the underside of the table.

Two women stood on the patio near the back door. One, not much taller than Angel, stood with her hands on her wide hips. She wore sunglasses and had Angel's black hair, cut short and flipped back exposing ears which were also shell-shaped. She wore a black, sleeveless T-shirt which showed large braless breasts. He knew he'd been caught checking, even though he darted his eyes toward the other woman. She was taller than Angel's mother, with a nondescript, bone-rack of a body, lost in a loudly coloured and flowing blouse and ankle-length skirt ensemble. Her mousy-blonde hair was tied up in a bun with a bandana, also loudly coloured. To his eye, none of the components of the outfit matched.

"Who's your friend?" said the woman in the sunglasses in the same gravelly voice as her daughter's. Her tone was in no way accusatory, considering the serious faux pas he had just committed.

"This is Blake. From next door. Blake, this is my mom, Gloria, and this is Michelle." Angel gestured toward the taller woman.

Gloria extended her hand and said, "Pleased to meet you, young man."

Young man? Blake had never thought of himself that way before and thrilled at the idea. "Pleased to meet you, too, Mrs., uh?" said Blake, shaking hands with her.

"Just Gloria." She exchanged a quick glance with Michelle and said to Angel, "Sorry Kiddo, we gotta smoke."

The two women sat side by side on the opposite bench with their backs to the door and Angel shifted, looking from them to him. He continued to stand and wondered if he could be any more of a klutz.

"How polite," Gloria said to Angel, "Waiting for us to take our seats first."

He quickly sat down.

Both women took a Cigarillo from the same package and lit them with Gloria's lighter. There was a moment of silence before a general and vague discussion about the weather ensued.

Uncomfortable with the silence following the weather talk, he asked the two women where they worked. He wanted to slap his forehead yet again, this time over his perhaps too forward question.

However, the women were unfazed. Gloria answered easily for both of them while they smoked their cigarillos. Michelle worked as a paralegal at a downtown lawyer's office. Gloria was on disability but did freelance work for Michelle's firm and other law firms, proofreading or typing transcripts. She admitted that they made a comfortable living and the best part of the arrangement was that Gloria had been able to stay home during the day when Angel was small. They didn't need or want a car to pollute the environment; public transit and taxis provided adequate transportation.

Blake kept his eyes on the bridge of Gloria's sunglasses and hoped that no one detected his discomfort.

Her cigarillo finished, Michelle said in a surprisingly soft voice, "Time we went back inside." She nudged Gloria, and nodded in his and Angel's direction.

"Pleasure, again, meeting you," Gloria said as she slid off of her seat.

Blake jumped up again. "A pleasure too, to meet you, Mrs., I mean Gloria, I mean both of you ladies, uh, I mean . . . "

Gloria didn't let him squirm like that worm tied to the string. She smiled right at him and said, "It's all good. Maybe see you again."

They sauntered to the back door, Michelle slightly in the lead, with Gloria's hand on her lower back, almost guiding the taller woman.

Angel took one of the Cigarillo tips from the ashtray.

He ventured, "They seem kinda cool."

"I like them," Angel replied and picked the paper off the tip.

After a silence, Blake said, "I acted pretty lame, huh."

"You didn't." She chewed on the plastic tip. "I like the taste of these."

Blake grinned. "So do I. Dad smokes them and I scoff them from the garbage."

Angel said, "You can chew on one of ours if you want. We're not poison."

He said, "Cool, thanks," and grabbed one of the tips. It was still warm. Angel seemed far more at ease now. She smiled.

He smiled back and immediately focused on scratching at the paper. When the band was off, he raised the tip toward Angel in a mock toast. She reciprocated and more silence followed while they both glanced at everything but each other.

He wanted to reach over and touch her hair. But he didn't. He was just about to ask something about the house when a car drove down the alley and stopped. A car door thumped and his garage door opened.

"Sounds like your parents are home," Angel said.

"Uh, they don't know where I am and I didn't leave a note. Mom's gonna freak."

Angel said, "You should probably go."

He wondered if a paratrooper landing in enemy territory felt like he did at that moment. "Angel," he said, her name sighing from his lips.

"It's okay." She slid off the table and, with long strides for such a short girl, hurried toward the back fence. He followed at a jog, but when she opened the gate he hesitated. He heard his garage door shut and the muffled voices of his parents heading for the house.

Angel leaned her head on the edge of the gate and said, "Maybe see you again."

"That'd be cool," he replied and stepped into the alley. He turned to face her. "But, I'm not just sure how or when."

How could he even begin a conversation with his mom about this meeting, given her attitude toward this family of Catholic witches?

Angel said, "Mom and Michelle are making me a cake for my birthday on Saturday. Before we go to my grandma's. Come over at two o'clock. I'll unlatch the gate for you. Just give it a push."

He wanted to hug Angel. Maybe even kiss her, if she'd let him. But he didn't dare try. He extended his arm to shake hands.

She didn't hesitate.

He savoured the cool, soft feel of her hand in his.

Angel slid her index and middle fingers onto his wrist momentarily and abruptly released her grip. Quietly she said, "Bye."

He listened to her bare feet padding on the stones; her back door closed seconds later. That paratrooper was now a POW and the compound gate had just slammed in his face. He stared at that awful gate until he heard his mom call his name from their backyard. He turned immediately and sprinted down the alley and across to the floodplain and then doubled back.

His mom was at their gate when he jogged up. "Where have you been?"

"At the creek. I got bored. Sorry I forgot to leave a note."

"That's fine," she replied with a scowl. "It's like yelling at a deaf-mute from behind when I ask you to do simple things. You didn't lock the door either. If you were by the creek, make sure you check for ticks."

"I wasn't in the grass."

"Doesn't matter. Ticks are everywhere."

"Mom, it's late July. Most of the ticks are dead."

"Most," she echoed. "Some linger until late August."

"Well, I am kind of sweaty so I'm gonna go in for a bath. I'll check then."

"Throw your clothes out the bathroom door. I'll check them for you."

∼∼∼∼

Blake struggled to distract himself from obsessing over Angel.

After his bath, he hunkered down in his basement room and tried to lose himself in his *Ballantine's Illustrated History of World War II* collection but kept thinking about Angel's hair, her fingers brushing his wrist, and it wasn't until 6:00 AM that he finally drifted off, after hearing his dad get up for work. He remained in a merciful, dreamless oblivion until past noon, and waited until his mom was engrossed in her afternoon soap operas before creeping upstairs to use the bathroom and sneak some bread and cold meat from the refrigerator.

Back in his room, he broke out his old World War II Airfix 1/32-scale model soldiers and combat effects charts. He had developed his own charts with Darryl over the last couple of years. They were handwritten on sheets of loose-leaf paper, and individual soldier and squad positions, enemy target acquisition and combat resolution were determined by rolling a die. They'd played lengthy and elaborate combat scenarios, that is, until the big fight.

He managed to lose himself in battles, some of which were based on combat descriptions from *Ballantine's*, until he was called upstairs for supper. He smelled fish cooking but he definitely was not hungry.

Stomach churning, he trudged up the stairs, certain that his mother would break him the moment she saw him. In a matter of minutes she would extract intelligence about Angel's party and absolutely forbid him to go. He dragged himself up the last two steps to the kitchen like a wounded and starved POW on a forced march, and launched a pre-emptive, direct assault. He said, "I thought only Catholics had to eat fish on Fridays."

She harrumphed and banged her spatula on the frying pan. Whirling on him, she said, "They have to eat fish Fridays. We eat fish because we *choose* to."

Blake snorted. "I don't know how the United States can stay together with Catholics running one half of the country and you Lutherans running the other half. It's no wonder they had a civil war and your family moved to Canada."

Dad dropped his fork midway between his plate and open mouth. He said, "That makes absolutely no sense."

His mom said, "I'm Baptist and you know it, Blake. I moved here with your gran and gramps so he could work his ministry. And, and," she waved her spatula, "we moved here long, long before the Vietnam draft, which Daddy did not evade!"

"I never, ever said Grandpa evaded. But I wouldn't blame him for doing it. You Americans shouldn't even be in Vietnam, supporting petty dictators and multinational corporations enslaving the natives."

"Hey, now." His dad tapped his fork on the table. "What kind of talk is that? Your mom has her Canadian citizenship. What's the matter with you?"

"What's the matter with him?" his mom said. "The boy's turned Commie is what's the matter. That's Commie talk if I ever heard it, Dwight."

She turned on him. "Where do you learn such garbage?"

"It's on the news every night!"

Dad tried another unsuccessful intervention. "Don't talk to your mother with that tone."

Mom's spatula targeted her supposed ally. "And you. You, Dwight. Encouraging that boy. Indulging him with the crap on TV. Discussing it with him. Those phony pictures from the front."

"Front? What front?" said Blake. "The Americans are so unwelcome they have enemies everywhere. Even behind their own lines."

Dad thumped his palm on the table. "Take it easy. Both of you."

Mom crossed her arms, spatula tight against her shoulder. "Oh, sure. Take his side again."

"I'm not taking sides, Hannah. This one has gotten out of hand in record time."

Blake knew his attack had been without provocation and was an absolutely wrong and immoral tactic. He felt he'd jumped up, gun blazing, when his movements should have been stealthy, cautious. But he'd had to protect himself from his mother's attention; her instincts were too sharp. She could read him like a *Ballantine's* and would stop him from seeing Angel tomorrow if he gave her half a chance.

She said, "The American government knows exactly what it's doing. That is the end of this conversation."

"The end of it. Just like that?" He snapped his fingers. "Just like a typical American puppet-dictator."

"You take that back."

"Make me."

"That's enough!" Dad yelled, surprising them. "Blake! Basement. Until you shit out whatever's crawled up your ass."

Dwight rarely swore. He rarely yelled. Blake knew he'd pushed too far and immediately trundled down the stairs without another word. He heard Mom say, "I'll skin that boy alive, Lord help me."

Dad said, "You shouldn't always provoke him."

"Provoke him!? Where were you just a second ago? He started it the second he was upstairs!"

So. Tactically, a victory. He'd escaped Mom's reconnaissance for a few more hours. Strategically, a total failure. He still had no plan for Saturday and the party.

He went back to his *Ballantine's* in vague hope of inspiration and again fell asleep reading.

ოოოო

He opened his eyes to the dusky light.

Angel's hair and her fingers on his wrist immediately flooded his mind. It was Saturday, midmorning. He still didn't have a plan.

How was he going to manoeuvre his way next door for her birthday? In just a few short hours, no less. He didn't want to lie. That yard was out of bounds for him. He resigned himself to the fact that he would once again have to conduct a direct attack on his mother. If she knew the truth, she would forbid him to attend the party. He had no intention of remaining a POW. He would disobey direct orders — torpedoes be damned. There was no alternative. Then he heard the back door shut. Silence upstairs.

Could he be that lucky?

He checked his alarm clock. 11:45. Squirming into his jeans and T-shirt, he ran barefoot upstairs.

Dad was alone in the kitchen, counting the money in his wallet. He shoved the wallet in his back pocket and said, "Well, well. If it isn't the afternoon shift."

"Where's Mom?"

"Opening the garage door."

"Are you guys going out?"

"Yup. Going downtown to Simpson's to get that new Black and Decker lawnmower on sale. Then we need groceries. For some reason, your mom doesn't want to have anything to do with you today. I can't begin to figure out why."

Blake was dumbfounded. In such moments, he almost believed his grandfather's and mother's stories about an all-powerful being guiding human destiny. He just as quickly rejected the idea in the belief that no superior being would plausibly manipulate things on behalf of a non-believing freak of nature such as himself.

Regardless, he wanted to shout, jump up and down, but he restrained himself.

His dad scrutinized him before saying, "I was your age once, remember? I know how complicated things get. I don't know exactly what those things are right about now, but I get it. And I'll help you through it."

Blake said, "Thanks for covering my rear flank, Dad."

Dwight sauntered down the back steps and waved over his shoulder and stepped outside.

Ecstatic, Blake took another bath and put on clean clothes. It was only 12:15. What to do for the next couple hours? Can't just sit around and wait for this birthday party. Birthday party? He slapped his forehead.

He grabbed his house key, bolted out the back door and speed-walked to the corner confectionery. He had no idea what to get a girl. Wandering aimlessly up and down the aisles, he felt lost in a foggy no-man's land between fronts until he spied packages of gummy worms on an endcap.

Gummy worms? Is that appropriate? She'd get the reference. He did a tour of the store again, stopping at a bin of small stuffed animals and other cheap toys. Typical and lame. But gummy worms?

He rummaged through the bin and found a panda bear, posed in a sitting position. The little stuffed bear fit in his palm and was pear-shaped, its tummy sticking out. Its button-eyes were dark brown and it looked like the panda was wearing sunglasses because of a black patch across the bridge of its nose.

It was the best he could do. Mom always said it's the thought that counts.

Back at home, he scoffed a couple of green bows from the Christmas wrap stored in the basement. His plan was to get to Angel's party and back before his parents came home. But then what? Would he have to continually plan these sneaky missions until he left home? There had to be other options. But he couldn't think of a single one. Fretting more and more, with still an hour to go, he needed to distract himself.

He absently fiddled with his Airfix soldiers still strewn around his room. Bored and anxious, he studied individual faces on the moulded figures. There was a surprising amount of detail, including wrinkles in the plastic to represent facial hair.

But the expressions were all the same. The eyes all blank.

Those blank eyes reminded him of the war-weary soldiers in his *Ballantine's*. Or casualties from Vietnam on the evening news. Haggard faces in wide-eyed shock. He turned a figure over and over in his hand. He could not imagine being in combat. What an awful thing.

Then he remembered the red flashing over the helpless turtle. And what he almost did. Could he execute an act of real violence? If he let that flash overpower him? He suddenly had to urinate.

He peed, then scooped up all of his Airfix figures and tossed their storage box back in the closet. He studied his effects charts a moment. He tore them up and threw them in the kitchen garbage. Slouching against the wall on the back landing steps, he let thoughts of Angel wash over him.

∾∾∾

Two O'clock.

He grabbed his gifts, bolted out the back door, and almost forgot to lock up. He sprinted to Angel's gate and pushed. The gate was unlatched, just as she had said it would be. He stepped through the threshold and closed the gate behind him. In the coolness of the backyard, he stopped to let the soothing rustling of the leaves slow his pounding heart.

The backyard was vacant. He headed to the door and stepped onto the patio. The door was open and he waited outside the screen door, hiding the gifts behind his back.

As if she sensed him, Angel came outside.

She smiled and he smiled back.

"Come," she said and sat cross-legged on the tabletop once again. "What's behind your back?"

271

"Pick a hand."

"Left."

It was the gummy worms. *Damn.* He offered both hands. "Happy birthday."

"Thanks. You didn't have to." She examined the little bear a moment and said, "Kinda looks like Mom." He liked the way her lips curved when she smiled, the way her nose wrinkled ever so slightly. He said, "Pretty lame presents, huh?"

She ripped open the gummy worms, stuffed one in her mouth, and offered him the package. "How did you guess I liked these?"

He shook his head no and replied, "Just lucky. I guess."

"Come. Sit down."

Blake sat on the bench, facing the back door.

Angel said, "I'm glad you came."

"I didn't think I'd be able to." He could easily reach the mere few inches and put his hand on her knee. He didn't. Not without permission.

Angel touched the bear's head. "I'd have understood if you couldn't come."

"Would you be mad?"

"Disappointed. But sometimes there are things you can't do anything about." Her tone was gentle. She said, "I suppose your folks don't like us much?"

He was unable to read her. He said, "The only thing I know is they don't talk to you. They want me to do the same."

Angel's brow furrowed.

"Mom says you're Catholic witches."

Angel just laughed her rasping laugh. "We're definitely not Catholic. Do we look like witches? Because we're not. We're Wiccan. Just because mom and I dress in black doesn't mean we eat toads."

"What's Wiccan?"

She briefly described the religion and finished by saying, "Mostly we care for Mother Earth and use herbal remedies."

Just then Gloria and Michelle barged through the back door, yelling "Happy birthday."

"Welcome," Gloria said. "We weren't sure if you would be here."

"I really wanted to come."

Gloria carried a small chocolate cake with no icing. She wore an oversized black Joan Baez T-shirt. Michelle followed with plates and utensils. She wore another loud flowing skirt and blouse ensemble. Maybe the same outfit as before, but he wasn't sure. The only clear difference was that she wasn't wearing a bandana. Her straight hair cascaded over her shoulders.

Michelle and Gloria sat down together. Angel slid off of the table and sat right beside him, touching her leg against his. He looked at her hair, listened to the leaves rustle.

"It's awfully nice of you to invite a stranger," he said. "Thank you."

Gloria said, "You're not a stranger. You're our neighbour."

He just breathed. Closed his eyes a second, concentrating on the sound of the leaves.

273

Gloria touched the panda. "Very kind of you, Blake, but just for future reference, we don't believe in giving presents."

Her tone was gentle and not accusatory. He did not feel reprimanded. But why was no one else at the party? How did Angel feel about that? How would she have felt if even he hadn't shown up?

Michelle cut the cake into four equal parts and put a slice on each plate. "Happy Birthday, Angel." Then she said, in that soft voice of hers, "So, Blake. What's the deal?"

"Deal?" Blake replied, confused.

"Angel said you climbed a ladder to look in our yard. What for?"

He glanced at Gloria but couldn't tell what she might be thinking with her eyes camouflaged behind sunglasses. He turned desperately to Angel, but she had her head down.

"Well, uh, Mom said I shouldn't dare bother with you. So I wanted to find out why she would say something like that."

"And?"

"And, what? Everything's cool. I don't know what her problem is."

Michelle shrugged. Gloria, very much to his relief, shifted the conversation to the upcoming school year. Angel was going into grade ten at Luther High School, a few blocks away.

Blake said he was going into grade nine at Sheldon Williams Collegiate. Then he and Angel agreed that they were looking forward to meeting new people and making new friends.

"We're from completely different galaxies, you know, Blake," said Michelle. "I hope you appreciate the differences between your family and ours — as well as our commonalties."

A back gate slammed in his mind's eye. He didn't like this POW feeling at all. He set his fork down beside his half-eaten cake and said carefully, "Well, everybody's different, aren't they? So we should all live and let live, shouldn't we?"

Gloria nodded. "You know that Angel's father doesn't live with us, right? He and I are divorced and he's gone for good. The three of us here are a family and we're quite different from yours."

Blake blurted, "I don't have a problem with that. You two are way less uptight than my mom — "

"Is that any way to speak about your mother?" said Michelle.

"Yes," he said without hesitation.

Michelle raised her eyebrows.

"I mean," he said quickly, "we have our arguments. Some of them are my fault, sure, but she's so, you know . . . uptight. I can never get through to her."

"You don't have to explain." Gloria's voice was soft as the leaves. She said, "People living in close proximity to each other inevitably have fights. But there has to be give and take. It doesn't work when only one person does all the taking." She stood up abruptly. "I think it's time for a smoke. We'll go 'round front so you two can finish your cake in clean air." She grabbed the ashtray and one of Michelle's hands. They walked side by side and disappeared around the corner of the house.

Blake found he couldn't eat any more. He said, "What happened? Did I say something wrong?"

Angel shrugged and kept eating. She said, "They just went for a smoke."

"Can I ask you something? Tell me if you don't want to answer."

"Sure." Angel shifted to face him.

"What happened to your dad?"

Angel said her father had left when she was a baby. She barely remembered him. He used to hit her mom. One night he put her in the hospital in a fight about Michelle. Then he was gone. She did remember spending a short time living alone with Michelle when her mom was in the hospital, and concluded by saying, "And here we are, the three of us. Our little family in our old farmhouse, surrounded by brand new city."

Blake looked around at the yard. The still leaves on this rare windless day were calming in the dappled shade. He said, "Your dad sounds mean. What would stop someone like him? He could've hit you next." *What would stop a freak like me from hitting?* — that red flashed in his mind. If he got in a rage what could he do to someone as gentle as Angel? A creeping-flesh feeling rippled up his spine.

Angel's voice was edged with concern. "You cool? You're shivering."

"It's just," Blake said, "it's just I don't think I like your dad, if you don't mind me saying that."

"I don't mind. You'll never meet him anyhow. He went to America to join the army. He's probably in Vietnam. Plus he doesn't even know where we live. I don't miss him even a little."

Blake tentatively reached to touch her arm. She didn't pull back, and when he did touch her, she took his hand in hers. She said, "So can I ask you something personal?" She didn't wait for him to respond. "What do you think of my little family?"

"Your mom and Michelle are with it. They aren't dictators like my mom. They're cool."

"It doesn't bother you, two women living together? You don't think it's strange?"

"Angel, it's not odd. I like them and they really get along. I couldn't imagine two of my mom in one house. There'd be war without end on two fronts. There's no way I could have escaped two Hannah's and made it over here."

She squeezed his hand. "And you're glad you're here?"

He squeezed back and said, "Totally."

Her nose wrinkled as she blinked and tilted her head down.

When he heard Gloria and Michelle crunching the gravel between the houses he let go of Angel's hand and jumped up. She leapt up too and stood right beside him.

The women exchanged glances and Gloria asked if everyone was done with cake. Michelle cleared the table.

Gloria said, "We have to visit with Angel's grandma soon. Sorry to have to throw you out, Blake. Will we see you again?"

"Only if it's okay with you."

"If it's okay with Angel, it's okay with us." She gave Angel a quick smile. "We trust Angel's judgement."

She opened the back door for Michelle. "Come inside when you're ready, Angel. We'll call a cab then."

Michelle said over her shoulder, "Bye, bye, Blake."

The screen door closed.

Blake said, "That's so neat your mom trusts you. I wish mine would trust me too."

Angel shrugged. "She respects my opinion on lots of things."

"Like what?"

"For one, my opinion of you."

He took a step away from her. "Me? You hardly know me."

"Maybe I know you better than you think. Like, I knew most of that turtle story before you even told me. I've been watching you."

"Why?"

She took his hand again. "I saw how it all started. And how you walked away." She pointed up toward the two garrets on the second floor. Obscured behind the leaves from ground level, both garrets had a clear view of the floodplain over the trees' canopy.

"But what if I don't always walk away?"

Angel squeezed his hand again. "I think you will." With that, she put her arms around his waist and leaned into him.

The top of her head came only to his chest and he leaned his face down, pressing his cheek against her hair. He was suspended in time once more, like when he first saw her from the ladder. He closed his eyes and inhaled the hint of lemon in her shampoo. Her warmth was in his nostrils and against his body. He let out his breath in a long luxuriating exhalation.

They held hands and slowly walked to the gate.

He undid the latch. "I hope I can see you again."

"Here's a secret," she said. "Just push hard on the gate. That latch will pop open."

The gate swung wide and he stepped out.

As he left the cool soothing comfort of Angel's backyard, he felt as though he was squeezing through a dark tunnel into the blinding light of day.

Angel's voice called, "See you soon," and the gate closed and her feet padded along the paving stones to the house.

A car came down the alley and pulled up to his garage, his mom in the front passenger seat, her face dark, scowling out at him.

The battle lines formed. Both sides awaiting the signal. He thought of blank-eyed soldiers shuffling away from combat and took a long breath and held it. He counted to ten before exhaling. There would be no signal from his camp.

He stepped lightly toward his parents' car, arms held loosely at his sides, open palms toward his mother.

JAMES TRETTWER was a winner in the Saskatchewan Writers Guild's John V. Hick's Long Manuscript Award in 2016 for this short story collection. He has also won the SWG's Short Manuscript Award. He has been most recently published in *TRANSITION, Spring,* and the anthology *Wanderlust: Stories on the Move,* (Thistledown Press, 2017). James Trettwer lives in Regina, Saskatchewan.